Fighting Red

Book Three

Jana` Chantel

About Right Media Group | Detroit, MI | 2023

About Right Media Group, LLC.
http://www.aboutrightmedia.com

Fighting Red
Copyright © 2023 Jana` Chantel

Library of Congress Cataloging-in-Publication Data
Names: Chantel, Jana`, 1988—author.
Title: Fighting Red/ Jana` Chantel
Description: Detroit: About Right Media Group, LLc. 2023. | Series: Fighting Red; 3
Identifiers: LCCN 2023914600 (print) |
(ebook) | ISBN 978-1-7330788-6-3 (hardcover) | ISBN 978-1-7330788-7-0 (paperback)
Subjects: | BISAC: FICTION/ Science Fiction/Apocalyptic & Post-Apocalyptic. | FICTION/ Science Fiction/ Action & Adventure. | FICTION/African American/General.
Classification: LCC 2023914600 (print)
LC record available at https://lccn.loc.gov/2023914600

Cover design by Moe Balinger and Fred Evans
Book Design by Jana` Evans

Printed in the United States of America
10   9   8   7   6   5   4

<u>*The Surviving Red Series*</u>

Surviving Red

Razor & Helena: A Surviving Red Prequel

For Jamie and Dariyah,

Auntie loves you both very much.

~*D.C.*~

Bossman

The office that Nick impatiently sat in was a very fancy one. It was pristine. Mahogany armchairs. Hand-carved wooden desks. Large, exquisite bookcases. Rare, precious knick-knacks were displayed in different areas in the room. The President's study was fancy. It was probably the nicest place that Nick had ever been in, but he hated being there.

Frustrated, he drummed his fingers impatiently on the armchair. A speck of red on his finger made him stop. It was just below the cuticle on his index finger. Nick frowned. He could've sworn that he washed all the children's blood off him. He picked at it aggressively—all to no avail. Ironically enough, his finger began to bleed. He no longer knew where his blood began and the children's end.

Nick cursed under his breath as he kicked over the chair next to him. Images of the children's death ran through his mind. Of all the horrific things he's done, killing those innocent children was by far the worst. But what choice did he have? That was the only way to free the woman he loved—Jade. She was bound to them. And she couldn't truly be herself if they were alive.

That was how he was freed—by his son's horrific death. Before that, Nick was a weak shell of a man. He fought off his natural urges, determined to be a great father. And because of that, his son was killed. Nick vowed never to be that man again. And he wasn't. He just wanted to give the love of his life that same kind of freedom. Jade may hate him now, but she would understand his reasoning over time. Right now, he just needed to find her...

...if he ever got out of this room.

"What the hell?!" Nick shouted, looking at the door.

He had been waiting for President Dooms for almost an hour. Nick hated being summoned. He was the boss—the creator of the DC task force. He wasn't a man to be summoned. Nick did the summoning.

After a few more minutes, the study's door finally opened, and President Chase Dooms walked into the room, followed by some armed, aggressive-looking men. These men were Chase's new guards. Well, not new, per se. These men have been with him for some time now, ever since Nick choked him.

For a long time, Nick and Chase had been terrific friends. They met while working at a low-end hospital (before the new world). Nick was head of security there, and Chase was a plastic surgeon. Chase spent most of his time at the hospital doing charitable surgeries, fixing cleft lips, procedures for burn victims, and more. Both men instantly became friends. Nick viewed Chase as someone he was inspired to be. And Chase saw a lot of potential and ambition in Nick.

And after his son's death, Chase was there for Nick. Nick appreciated that and even appreciated Chase more when he accepted Nick's personality change. In fact, it seemed like Chase preferred the new version of Nick. From there, the two men grew.

Chase eventually decided to try his hand at politics. He ran for US Senator and won. Nick was brought on as part of his security detail. The two men were thick as thieves. And then the world began to end. Through the chaos, Chase somehow made his way to the presidency. They implemented the new medical law, and Nick oversaw the new task force.

It was all going so well.

Until Dr. Cole Blackwell.

The man threatened Chase's presidency and the DC task force. Blackwell was bringing hope into the new world. And courage. And compassion. It was a big problem for the men. And the situation put both men at odds.

Usually, when the two men hung out, Chase wouldn't have any security detail. He was with Nick. And he trusted that no one could get to him when he was with Nick. But he eventually found out that no one could protect him *from* Nick. After Nick choked him, Chase hired a new security detail.

After Blackwell's death, the two men's relationship has never been the same. Chase allowed Nick to run the DC task force as he saw fit. And Nick stayed out of the politics.

They granted each other a wide breadth, until now, that is.

Chase entered the room and sat behind his desk silently. Two of his guards stood behind Nick, while the other two took their place beside Chase. Nick instantly tensed up.

"You look stressed, Mr. President," he finally said after a long, strained silence.

"You haven't been making things easy for me, Nick."

"Haven't I? I've been keeping our medical resources safe."

"The officials are not happy with our system," anger laced Chase's tone.

"Who gives a fuck about them?"

"I do! And so do the people!" Chase rose to his feet. "They are looking to this Jade person to be a leader. She's gotten Razor, your number two, on her side! And she's his wife's sister!"

"Razor hasn't been on our side since he met Helena. And Jade is no leader."

"It doesn't matter! The people see her as one!"

The two men glared at each other.

"Why am I here?" Nick finally asked.

"Please tell me you didn't actually do it," Chase sighed and closed his eyes. "Please tell me you didn't kill two children and allow Jade and her group of rebels to escape. To Canada, nonetheless."

Nick didn't say anything. Instead, he looked down at his hands—his index finger was still bleeding.

"The people are rioting in the streets and attacking DC officers and government officials in the name of Jade. And the officials are appalled that you've brutally murdered two innocent children...my hands are tied here, Nick."

Nick frowned as he slowly rose to his feet. "What are you saying, Chase?"

Chase didn't say anything. Instead, he gave a brief nod, signaling his guards to move. And they quickly attacked.

The guard to his right moved in and tried to apprehend Nick. But Nick swiftly jabbed him in his throat. The guard to his left immediately wrapped his arm around Nick's neck. He applied pressure on him. Nick tried to fight him off, but the guard was much stronger. He tried to fight as best as he could but quickly got weak...

...and then darkness.

~1~

Jade

When she was seven, Jade got her first lesson about death. She was sitting outside in the backyard with her pet rabbit, Bun-bunn. It wasn't a creative name, but that was the first name that came to mind when Jade met her light brown fluffy rabbit. A three-year-old Helena was napping in the house, and their mother allowed Jade to play outside with her rabbit.

Jade watched as Bun-bunn hopped around the backyard, and she would sometimes follow behind him—mimicking his hops. Jade giggled and bounced when a hawk flew down and scooped Bun-bunn into the air. She screamed out in horror. It all happened so fast.

Before she knew it, Jade was running out of the backyard and down the street—desperately trying to follow and save Bun-bunn. Her father trailed behind her, trying to get her to stop. The hawk flew further and further out of her reach and out of her view. Bun-bunn was gone.

Devastation crushed Jade.

That night, her parents talked about the concept of death. They explained the natural selection of things. None of this comforted Jade. All she could think about was Bun-bunn's horrible death.

**

The faint skyline of the Detroit River was far off in the distance, and Jade longed to be on the other side. She sat on a log, struggling to get a good view. But her sight had always been terrible when it came to things that were far away.

A man screamed in the background.

Jade turned toward the screams. She sighed. The screams were normal to her. She glanced around the wooded area—hoping to spot the person she was waiting for. The man screamed out in pain again, and she instantly got annoyed. She wished that he would shut up.

Finally, Raina stepped into view. She looked healthy—healthier than Jade had ever seen her. Jade sighed with relief and rose to her feet.

"You're late," she said to Raina.

Raina gave her a weak smile. "Sorry, I got held up."

"Are you ready?"

The man screamed again.

Raina looked in the direction of the screams. Fear covered her face. "I don't want to do this, Jade."

"We've been through this, Raina," Jade sighed. "I *have* to make you strong," she didn't wait for Raina to respond. Jade walked toward the direction of the man's screams. Raina sighed and reluctantly followed.

An abandoned warehouse quickly came into their view. Reagan and Clay stood on the roof with rifles. Tatianna and Junior stood guard at the door. The screams got closer. Jade said nothing as she and Raina walked past Tatianna and Junior. They entered the warehouse, and Raina quickly stopped at the door.

A man was hanging upside down in the back corner. Chains wrapped around his ankles, and Razor was beating him savagely. Helena, Yoko, and Danita stood a few feet back. Keeper and Calvin sat on the other side of the warehouse next to an unconscious Jackson.

Jade noticed that Raina lingered at the door—too afraid to enter. Too scared to watch.

Tears ran down Raina's face as she shook her head. "I can't do this, Jade."

"We've been through this, Raina. This is how you survive in this world."

"It's not me."

"It's who you *have* to be," Jade walked over to her and placed her hand underneath Raina's chin. She looked into her eyes, and Jade could feel the tears coming. "I can't live in this world without you, my little munchkin."

Raina lowered her head. Jade grabbed her hand and pulled her along.

"Who do you work for?!" Razor demanded as he punched the guy in the gut.

The guy cried out in pain. "No one!"

Razor punched him again. And again. And again.

They were all paranoid and on edge.

On the night they first crossed over, the group was ambushed. Enraged, Jade basically killed them all. Razor stopped her from killing the last person. They needed information from him. Razor tortured the guy all night and well into the morning hours. They learned they were attacked by a group called the Radicals. It was basically a group that was unleashing chaos on the poor citizens. They were a group of thieves, looters, and murderers. But that was all that was left in this world.

Since they killed the group, Jade and the rest of the survivors have been hunted down by the remaining members. But whenever a small group of the Radicals came to attack, they were swiftly killed, mainly by Jade.

The man hanging upside down was just their latest victim.

Canada wasn't the promised land like everyone claimed it to be.

Jade finally let Raina's hand go when they reached Razor. He had just punched the guy in the face.

"Who do you work for?!"

"I'm a part of the Radicals," the man finally admitted. "I was sent to stake you all out."

"How did you know where we were?" Helena finally stepped forward.

"Our last scouting crew was found dead not too far from here. We knew you all were staying close to the border."

"We've only been here for a week," Razor growled. "Why are you all following us?!"

"That's how it works here!" the man wiggled in his chains. "You cross the border. You provide us with something, or you get killed."

"Who's your leader?"

The guy stayed silent. Razor resumed his beating.

Raina shut her eyes. Jade looked over at her.

"Open your eyes."

Raina shook her head as her eyes remained closed.

"Open your eyes. You have to be brave, my little munchkin."

"Jade!" Helena looked at her, terrified—and a little concerned.

Jade looked around the warehouse. Everyone was looking at her funny. Razor had even stopped torturing the captive. Fear was in his eyes. Jade glanced over at Raina, but she no longer looked healthy. Instead, a machete was sticking out of her stomach, and blood was oozing down her mouth. She stared at Jade with a horrid look on her face.

Jade jumped back and screamed in terror as Raina slowly disappeared. She looked back around the warehouse. Helena was crying as she looked at her sister with worry. Jade screamed again as she pushed Razor to the side. She removed one of her knives from her thigh strap and slit the man's throat. Jade sighed with relief as she was coated in his blood.

Finally. Freedom.

 ~2~

Jade

"What the hell were you thinking?!" Razor yelled in the background.

He sounded far away, but Jade was tuning him out. She stared blankly in the distance as she sat on the steps in the warehouse. Reality was hitting her—*again.* Raina was gone. And Levi. And David. They were killed. Killed by Bossman. That was real. It wasn't a nightmare. A nightmare that Jade was convinced she'd wake up from.

"We needed him alive, Jade!" Razor continued. "How else are we going to learn where their setup is and who their leader is?!"

Someone began to wipe her face with a wet cloth. Jade looked over to see that it was Clay. There was a faint smile on his face, but he still looked concerned. Ever since they crossed over, he had been closely watching her. Jade didn't understand why until now. She was breaking and slowly losing it. During moments like these, she was aware of just how far gone she was. Her denial was blurring the lines of reality. She was given false hope, and she knew precisely who the cause of that was...

...Jackson.

After the ambush, the group found him floating in the river. Razor, Keeper, and Junior quickly fetched him out. He was unconscious, of course, but alive. It appeared that he somehow moved his head at the last minute, so the shot wasn't fatal, at least from what Keeper could tell. Under Razor's demanding request, they looked after Jackson and carried him around. Although, the majority of the group felt he was a huge liability—even Keeper.

But seeing that someone actually made it out alive during that altercation gave Jade hope that the others could be alive too. So, Jade prepared herself mentally for what she would say and do when she saw them. First, she would teach Raina and Levi how to be strong in this world. Innocence would get you killed. They needed to be tainted. And Jade was prepared to taint them. Then she would tell David how much she loved him, but they could no longer be together. Her loving him could get him killed. And she had to protect him. No matter what.

"Are you even listening to me?" Razor stomped toward her, a frown prominent on his face, but then he stopped. He paused for a moment. And then his face looked pained.

"I'm sorry," Jade whispered. She hadn't noticed it, but tears were falling down her face. Razor was quickly at her side, wrapping her up in his arms. Jade held onto him tightly. She needed convincing that he was really there and not dead in the river somewhere. It seemed like she didn't know what was real anymore. "Are you really here?"

Razor sighed. "I'm here," he pinched her arm. Sometimes she needed that to be convinced. "And I'm sorry. All this shit is my fault."

Jade shook her head. Although there were times when she was angry at him, she never once blamed Razor for the predicament they were in. Bossman was just crazy and had a strange obsession with her, and no one was to blame for that.

"We will find Blackwell, Jade. And I promise, once we do, we will go back and kill Bossman."

Jade looked up at him. Pain and regret lingered in his eyes. He was hurting too, and she hated that fact. Because she knew that she was the cause of his pain, Jade rested her head back on his shoulder.

"I just really need you to hold it together until then. We need information about this group. And we need them alive to get that."

"I'm doing my best, Razor."

"I know...but I need you to do better."

Jade closed her eyes and nodded.

Razor kissed the top of her head and released her from his embrace. He stood. "We need to scavenge for food. Keeper, Tatianna, can you come with me?" They stepped forward and began to head out.

"Be safe out there," Helena walked over to Razor and kissed him goodbye.

Clay resumed cleaning the blood off Jade's face. She looked up at him and gave him a weak smile. It seemed like she was looking at him for the first time. He had long, curly hair that fell between his shoulder blades but always wore it in a single braid to the back. He had a thick beard, of course. With the end of the world, hair maintenance usually goes out the window. His skin was tan, and he was tall and very muscular. Jade wondered if he played sports in his past life.

"I know what you're going through," he said after a while. "My girlfriend died."

"I'm sorry."

"This was before the chaos. A drunk driver killed her."

Jade just gave him a sad look. She didn't know what to say. There were no words to heal that kind of pain.

"I blamed myself for a long time."

"Why?" Jade frowned.

"Because she was leaving from one of my lacrosse games and meeting me at an afterparty."

"I don't see how you're to blame for that."

Clay sighed and stopped wiping Jade's face. "She didn't want to go. She was tired and wanted to chill and watch TV at her place. But I was being a dick and insisted that she come," he paused and looked down at his feet. "I even implied that I would cheat on her if she weren't at the party."

"Wow...that was a dick move."

He chuckled and then sighed. "Yeah...the drunk driver was an attendee of that party."

"Did you ever stop blaming yourself?"

"No," he resumed cleaning her face. Jade began to wonder how much blood was on her.

"That's helpful," she mumbled.

"I just wanted you to know I get it," he explained. "I used to see her and talk to her too. I understand your dilemma."

"And does that ever stop?"

"Eventually. Once you come to terms with everything," Clay finally finished.

"Thank you."

"You're very welcome, Jade...I should probably join Reagan on lookout."

Jade nodded and watched him walk away. She sat on the steps wondering how she would get on with her life. She didn't know what to hold on to anymore. She was now afraid of anything that meant something to her in this world. Could Jade really live her life like that? Afraid of anything meaningful?

Helena, who had been lingering by, finally joined her sister on the steps. She took a step above Jade. Jade hadn't noticed, but Helena had a cup of water in her hand. She began to spritz the water into Jade's hair and then started to finger-detangle it.

"The bright side to rocking short hair," Helena began. "Is that you don't have to spend hours detangling it."

Tears welled up in Jade's eyes. She hated to ask it, but she had to. "Are you still here?"

Helena responded by tugging on Jade's hair.

Jade instantly sighed with relief. She would've completely lost it if Helena wasn't really there. She and Razor were the only things keeping her there. Without them, Jade was sure that she would end it all.

Helena sprinkled more water into Jade's hair and continued to finger-detangle it. Jade closed her eyes and rested against Helena's legs.

"Your hair's a mess, Jade," Helena complained.

Jade smiled a little. "Sorry, *Mom*. I haven't had the time to attend to it."

"That's why you should cut it."

"Never. It's my lion's mane."

"Lionesses don't have manes."

Jade rolled her eyes. "You know what I meant."

"Well, I'm not going to spend all my time trying to make you look decent."

"I don't care about looking decent."

"Obviously," Helena said sarcastically. Helena began to part Jade's hair and started cornrowing her hair to the back. The braids were small.

Jade winced every now and then. Her head was tender from neglect. And Helena was a little heavy-handed with the braiding.

"This should last you for a while."

"I didn't realize my hair was such a problem for you."

Helena sighed. "It's not...I miss her too," her voice cracked.

Jade turned around to see Helena quickly wiping away her tears. She didn't know what to do. How could she console her sister when Jade was grieving too?

Helena turned Jade's head back around and continued to cornrow her hair. "I used to do her hair all the time. This makes me feel closer to her."

"I guess that's something. I have nothing."

Helena remained silent for a while, and Jade could tell she was struggling to find something reassuring to say.

"I'm sorry, Jade," was all she could say.

When Razor, Keeper, and Tatianna returned, Helena was almost done with Jade's hair. Razor saw the two sisters on the steps and smiled a little. He then went to prepare the food.

It was quiet in the warehouse. Reagan and Clay were on the roof, keeping watch. Junior and Razor were in the back corner preparing dinner. Keeper was attending to Jackson, and Tatianna had joined him. Yoko and Danita were sitting with Calvin.

"Where's the prince and princess?!" he boomed. "I can't find them!"

Yoko rubbed his back and whispered to him.

Tears fell from Jade's eyes. Calvin was having a hard time accepting their deaths too. He met her eyes from across the room. He frowned with worry.

"Where are they, my Queen?"

"Sleeping, my sweet knight," that's the story they've been telling him.

"Forever?"

"Forever."

Calvin frowned again and nodded. He understood what that meant. But every day, he would look for them. And every day, he would get frustrated when he couldn't find them. On the days that the Radicals came, Calvin would take it out on them, which was very unfortunate for them. But on the days he couldn't violently release his frustration, he broke down and cried. And Jade usually cried with him.

Dinner was ready by the time Helena was done with Jade's hair.

"I'm digging the new look," Tatianna winked as she gave Jade a bowl of beans and corn.

"Thanks," Jade frowned down at the mixture. Dinner was not going to be good for their stomachs.

"It was all we could find."

"Just expect a lot of bathroom breaks tomorrow."

Tatianna laughed. "We're prepared for that."

Jade ate her food in silence on the steps. Helena had gone over and sat with Razor. She was consoling him. That was all Helena did these days—consoling Jade and Razor. Jade felt bad. Who was comforting her sister?

When she was done, Jade went to her sleeping area and lay down. It wasn't anything special, just a pallet of old clothing and blankets. But it was better than sleeping on the concrete floor. A few hours passed before Jade finally got up. She walked across the warehouse and stopped at the pallet near the door.

"Clay?" she whispered. It was clear that he was sleeping.

Clay woke up groggy. He rubbed his eyes. "Again?"

Jade nodded.

Clay made room for her on his pallet. Jade quickly lay down. She scooted close to him. Clay wrapped his arms around her.

"Like this?" he asked.

"A little tighter, please."

Clay adjusted, and Jade sighed with relief. "Is this how he held you?"

"Just like it," Jade confirmed.

"Goodnight, Jade."

"Clay..."

"I'm really here."

"Goodnight," she sighed as she closed her eyes.

As soon as she was unconscious, he was there waiting for her. David smiled brightly at her. His green eyes sparkled like stars. He held his arms open for her. Jade leaped into them. David laughed at her eagerness. He looked healthy. And happy. Why has Jade never seen him that way?

"I miss you," she said.

"Miss me? Jade, I never left."

Suddenly, they were in a bed. David held her tightly as Jade's head rested on his chest.

"Wait," she frowned at his statement and looked up at him. Surely, this was just a dream. Right? "Are you really here?"

David looked at her. His green eyes bore into her soul. He kissed her forehead and then tenderly on her lips. It felt so real, and it was just like how she remembered.

"I'm here," he finally said.

~3~

Razor

When it came to the Willer sisters, Razor seemed to have a knack for making them lose themselves. He started to lose Helena back in the prison as she desperately tried to save female prisoners from being raped. And now he was losing Jade, as she was determined to save the whole world. But he loved that about them. Despite everything going on, the two sisters had a thing about putting others before themselves. They were the selfless type.

But Razor was losing Jade.

He leaned against the staircase and watched as she slept in Clay's arms. They had been growing closer over the week, and Razor wasn't sure how he felt about that. It appeared that Clay just wanted to help Jade get through this difficult time. Razor overheard him mention that he had an ex who was killed too. But Razor couldn't shake the sense of loyalty he felt toward David.

Razor fought off the memory of their last conversation. He had lied to Jade. The night after Nick attacked their camp, David came to him. It was David's first time seeing Jade interact with Nick, and he came to the same conclusion that Razor did, they would never leave each other alone—unless one of them were dead.

"You have to let me free her," David had said. "She won't be the same if she keeps going at it like this." David wanted to know where he could find Bossman so he could try to ambush him.

"David," Razor sighed. "You're likely to die before you even get close."

"I have to try!" David paced back and forth. He was fighting back the tears. "I'm already losing her...you see it, don't you?"

"Jade's a fighter," Razor crossed his arms. He knew what David was getting at, and Razor didn't like it.

Helena was right when she said Jade was a passionate, strong, fearless woman—the moment he met Jade, Razor instantly loved her. Finally, he had a sibling he could relate to. Jade had rage, but she wasn't as out of control as he was. Yes, lately, her anger was getting a little out of hand, but who could blame her? With everything that's been going on, how could she not be? Razor hated being judged for his rage, and he certainly wouldn't allow someone else to judge his sister for it.

"She's not a killer, Razor."

"And your hands are blood free?"

David sighed.

"There's nothing wrong with her being a fighter, David. In this world, you have to be. If you don't understand that, then walk away. The last thing she needs is to be judged by someone who claims to love her."

David stopped pacing and looked at Razor, appalled. "I love her more than you could imagine, and that's why I'm doing this."

"And you think she'd be happy with you trying to go on a suicide mission? Please think of how devastated she'll be. If you think you're losing her now, imagine how she'll be if you're killed."

David frowned at his words. It was clear that he had never thought about that. But after a few seconds, David shook his head—determined not to be persuaded otherwise.

Razor sighed in frustration. "I'm not sure where Bossman will be," he finally admitted. "He's been way too unpredictable. But I have a small hunch that he might be at the Detroit River."

"How can you be so sure?"

"I think we might have a mole within our midst," Razor said through clenched teeth. It was a nagging suspicion that he's had for a while now.

How did Nick know precisely where their camp was? Their lookout patrol was flawless. So, how did he know exactly where to hit without someone feeding him information?

"What?" David asked, alarmed. "Do you think they survived the attack?"

Razor shrugged. "I'm not sure, but we'll know if Nick shows up."

David began pacing again—anxious with this new piece of information.

"Either way, you'll get your shot, Loverboy."

"You can't tell Jade about this."

"I know," Razor sighed. "But if something happens to you, I have no choice."

"Just tell her that I love her."

"Tell her yourself, Loverboy."

Without thinking, Razor punched the railing of the staircase. The wood cracked a bit. He quickly looked around. No one seemed to hear it. Razor looked back over at Jade. She was still sleeping. But even in her sleep, he could see she was a shell of her former self. How was he going to tell her this? She was already losing it. This piece of information was likely to send her over the edge.

Razor sighed in frustration. Another time. He would tell Jade the truth at another time. Right now, he had more pressing matters to attend to...

...the mole.

Who was it?

Razor was convinced that the mole survived the attack at the camp, and Nick being at the Detroit River was proof enough. Plus, the fact that David and the rest of the group were captured so quickly was another confirmation that someone in the group was feeding information to Nick. Razor was sure that the mole crossed over with them. It was so chaotic, and at that point, he was certain that Nick wasn't thinking about outing that person once Jade was in his midst.

Over the days, Razor narrowed down his list to one person: Junior.

Out of all the people there, he was the only person Razor couldn't place.

Most of the people there, Razor recalled from the prison. Tatianna, of course. Clay and Reagan. Razor was the one who made sure that Reagan always had her brother with her. He had encounters with Danita before. Of course, he knew Keeper. And he did a thorough background check on Yoko and Calvin (he hacked the DC database), and it was confirmed that Calvin was a debtor and Yoko was a provider (a person who got someone else medical treatment under their name).

None of them would've been working with Nick.

Razor wanted to be sure that he was thorough before he made this claim, so he even thought about those they lost on the River. Lang was a debtor and was in his prison. And so was Rosalind. And Sarah. Jackson and Beverly were ruled out for obvious reasons. And David and the children were never even considered because the whole notion was ridiculous.

In the end, it had to be Junior.

Razor didn't recall seeing him in prison, yet he was with the prisoners at the Black Deficit headquarters. He even tried to do a background search on him, but nothing came up. There was only one reason for that; he wasn't a debtor or a provider. But he was at his prison. There could've been only one reason for that: he was a newly hired bounty hunter.

That fact was a little unsettling, but Razor saw no other way around it.

So, lately, Razor's been keeping Junior close to him. He's been watching his movements—waiting for him to slip up. Of course, Razor knew that Junior could not communicate with Nick at the moment. But it was only a matter of time. And Razor was patiently waiting.

For the time being, Razor kept this information to himself. He didn't want any more discourse in the group. They all had been through enough already.

"Can't sleep?" Helena asked as she wrapped her arms around his waist and rested her head on his back.

Razor was still watching Jade sleep. "Haven't tried."

"Keeper and Tatianna are keeping watch for the rest of the night."

Razor nodded.

Helena looked over at Jade and Clay. "Well, that's an unexpected sight."

"She can't sleep without him."

"Clay?"

"David. She's been having Clay hold her like David used to."

Helena was silent. Razor turned around to see a frown on her face. He turned his attention back to Jade and sighed.

"We're losing her."

"She'll make her way back to us. It's a lot of shit she has to wade through."

"David would still be alive if I had stuck to the plan."

"Stop it, Razor. You can't keep beating yourself up over this. This is Bossman we're talking about here."

"Still, my thirst for revenge got everybody killed."

"There's nothing I can say to make this feeling go away?"

Razor shook his head.

"Then, should you be helping her seek revenge?"

Razor turned back around toward Helena. She looked up at him with those beautiful brown eyes of hers.

"If your quest for revenge left you feeling this way, then should you be helping her do the same thing?"

"What was done to her was ten times worse than what was done to me, which deserves vengeance."

"But you said it yourself. We're losing her. So, is this a really good idea? Jade might not come back from this."

"I love her, Helena. I won't let her go too far in the deep end," Razor turned back toward Jade. "I at least owe her that much."

Helena walked in front of him, blocking his view of Jade. She looked up at him and smiled. She stood on her tippy toes and kissed him deeply. Razor recognized the look in her eyes when she pulled away, and she quickly grabbed his hand.

"Come on," she pulled him away from the staircase. "Come keep me company."

Razor knew what she meant by that. Ever since they got there, Helena had been overly affectionate. He knew that David's death really frightened her, and she wanted to have as many moments like this as she possibly could.

If he was being completely honest with himself, Razor wanted it too. So, he never once denied it to Helena—even though he wasn't sure if he *really* could. And it was just what he needed. Sex with Helena always melted his stress and worries away. She was his drug. And right now, he desperately needed a hit.

He would worry about Jade and the mole in the morning.

But for now, Razor would enjoy the pleasures of being with his wife.

~4~

Jade

The sun was bright when Jade woke up the next day. At another time, she probably would've taken that as a good sign, but right now, she frowned. Her interaction with David left her confused. Surely, it was all a dream. But he told her he was there, and everything felt real. Maybe it was a sign. Maybe David was alive and just washed up on a different side of the river. Jade just needed to find him.

The arms that were wrapped around her moved a little. Jade turned around to see Clay. He was already awake, and he was fighting off a smile.

"Morning."

"Hey," Jade didn't understand why he was so cheerful.

"Did you have a nice dream about David?"

Jade instantly felt horrified as other parts of her dream came to mind.

Clay laughed. "You know, I've never laid with a girl who called out another guy's name all night. It takes a hit to the ole self-esteem there."

"Oh my God, Clay," Jade groaned in embarrassment. She put her hands over her face, trying to hide from him. "I'm so sorry. I swear, I won't have you do this again."

"It's all right, Jade, seriously," he chuckled. He removed Jade's hands away from her face so she could look at him. "I'm just poking fun at you. Honestly, I'm glad you had a nice dream about him."

"Thank you," Jade sighed. "But I swear, this is the last time."

"I don't mind helping you out. You have to sleep, you know."

Jade just sighed again. She hated feeling like she was using people. Clay was very kind and understanding. She didn't want to take advantage of him. She just needed to figure out a way to sleep without someone holding her. If she could do that, she would be on the road to recovery...if that's what she really wanted.

Clay stretched and sat up. Jade followed. As she stood, Helena came from the back of the warehouse with a big smile. Jade groaned again as Clay chuckled. They both knew what that expression meant.

"Looks like both Willer sisters had a good night," he mumbled.

Helena stopped in front of them. Apparently, she didn't hear Clay's remark. "Morning, you two."

"Morning," they both greeted.

"Jade, I'm going on watch in a little bit. May I borrow one of your knives?"

"Sure thing," Jade began to walk over to her sleeping area but paused to look at Clay. "Thanks again, Clay. You've been really helpful."

"You're welcome, Jade," he smiled.

Jade made her way to her sleeping area, and Helena followed. When she was there, Jade began looking through her bags for a knife that Helena could have. The one bright side about being attacked by the Radicals so often was that Jade managed to obtain an excellent knife collection.

"So, Clay has been overly helpful," Helena said. She was fiddling with the bottom of her shirt.

"He knows what I'm going through."

Helena nodded and bit her bottom lip. She did that whenever she was uneasy.

Jade sighed. "Just say what you want to say, Helena."

"I just hope he's not trying to take advantage of you," she mumbled.

"I'm the one who went to his pallet last night, and I'm the one who asked him to hold me. Trust me. He's not taking advantage."

"Just be careful. That's all I'm saying. You're very vulnerable right now."

"Well aware of that, Helena," Jade finally found two knives suitable for Helena, and she began to search for a thigh strap. "And while we're on the subject of guys, you and Razor seem to be doing it *a lot*."

"He's my husband," Helena sounded offended.

"Still, I never pegged you the type to be having sex in public places," Jade looked up to see a pained look on Helena's face. She instantly regretted her statement. She handed the knives and thigh strap to Helena. "I'm sorry."

"Don't be," Helena took the weapons and turned to walk away but stopped. She turned back to Jade. "I got freaked out by his death, ok. To see David die like that... terrified me. And the thought that Razor could die like that too...I need to take my mind off it. I need to create moments that I can remember forever."

"I get it," Jade sighed and looked away, ashamed. "I just think a small part of me is jealous."

Helena quickly went over and wrapped her arms around her sister. Jade held onto her tightly. After a while, Jade began to fight with her emotions. Was this real?

"Helena?"

Helena responded by yanking really hard on one of Jade's braids.

"Oww!!" Jade's screams echoed around the warehouse. Everyone turned toward them, alarmed.

Razor ran over to them, looking confused.

Helena smirked as she pulled away. "Now you're forgiven."

"What's going on?" Razor demanded.

"Your wife is being a jerk!" Jade rubbed her head; it was really sore.

"Because you were a jerk first!"

"Seriously," Razor looked back and forth between them in disbelief. "Do I need to separate you two?"

"No, *Dad*," Jade laughed.

"Eww, gross," Helena scrunched up her face.

That only made Jade laugh even harder. Laughing felt foreign to her. After a few seconds, tears began to hit her cheeks.

Helena rolled her eyes. "Ok, *crazy*, let's go get something to eat," she took Jade's hand and pulled her along. Razor followed them, looking stressed.

Jade continued crying-laughing all the way to the back corner of the warehouse. Tatianna, Danita, and Junior were back there, and they all looked at her with concern.

"Ignore her," Helena sighed. She made a plate of rice and shoved it into Jade's hands. "Go sit with Keeper, my little crazy girl."

"Yes, *Mom*," Jade said in between laughs. She was making her way to Keeper when she noticed Razor cautiously walking behind her, and she immediately stopped. "Oh, for God's sake, Razor! I'm perfectly sane enough to walk across the warehouse!"

Razor didn't say anything. He continued to follow. Nothing Jade could say that would make him walk away. So, she ignored him. Yoko and Calvin were sitting with Keeper. Jackson was still lying unconscious on his makeshift gurney. Jade sat on the floor next to Calvin. She rested her head on his shoulder. She began to eat her rice.

"Good day, my Queen."

"Good day, my sweet knight. Did you eat already?"

"I did."

"That's good. I need my knight to be fed and strong."

Yoko looked over at her and smiled. "Hey, Jade."

"Hey."

"What was all of that earlier?" Keeper asked.

Jade ate some more of her rice. "Helena thought it was a great idea to verify that she was real by pulling on my braids."

Keeper chuckled.

"Ouch," Yoko rubbed her head sympathetically.

"Exactly," Jade frowned down at her plate. "How's Jackson?"

"The same," Keeper sighed. "I'm honestly not sure if I'm doing him any justice. All of this is way over my head."

Jade nodded.

"How was it out there?" Yoko asked Keeper.

"Quiet for the most part."

"Good," she sighed. "Let's hope it stays that way."

"Whose Helena keeping watch with?" Jade asked as she finished off her food.

"Me and Calvin. We're just waiting for her to eat. Reagan's on the roof looking out for now."

"Oh, Jade, I've finally fixed ya mask," he reached over and grabbed it.

He handed it to her.

Jade sighed with relief. *Finally*. She had been wearing her scarf this whole time. Surprisingly, her asthma has been under control. But still, it was nice to have extra protection.

"Thank you."

"Sorry, it took so long."

"Keeper, you're amazing. I could never utter a complaint against you."

"Thanks, Jade," he paused and looked down at his hands for a second. "I have something else for ya too."

Jade frowned at his hesitation.

Keeper finally handed her an old watch—David's watch. Her heart raced as she took it in her hands.

"I found it when we discovered Jackson," he explained. "It took me some time to fix it up, but I thought ya would want it."

"He needs this," Jade mumbled. "He needs this to survive."

Yoko looked uneasy. "Come on, Calvin. Let's see if Lena is ready yet."

Jade clutched David's watch to her chest as Calvin stood. Yoko quickly rose to her feet and shot a concerned look at Keeper.

Keeper frowned. "What ya mean, Jade?"

"He can't survive without his watch, Keeper."

"Jade, he's gone."

She shook her head. "No, he's here. I need to find him, Keeper. He doesn't have that much time left if he doesn't have his watch."

"Jade..."

"I'm not crazy! He told me that he's here!"

Keeper didn't say anything. Yoko and Calvin slowly walked away. Jade put David's watch on her wrist for safekeeping. She needed to look for him. If his watch washed up, then so could he. She needed to be there for him. To save him.

"Jade?"

She looked up. Helena was standing by the entrance of the warehouse. Yoko and Calvin had made it to her. Helena was prepared to take watch but looked at her sister with concern.

Then a fiery orange blast sent Helena flying back.

Jade screamed out in horror...

...then blacked out.

**

"Drop it, Jade!" Razor demanded as Jade came to. His hands were up, and she could see the fear in his eyes. Helena stood a few feet behind him. She was alive but a bit scraped up and bruised.

Jade was slowly piecing together what had happened. A small group from the Radicals came to attack them, and they had thrown a grenade in the entryway. Luckily, Reagan was able to intercede, and it missed its mark, causing it to do minimal harm to Helena, Calvin, and Yoko. Enraged by her sister's near-death experience, Jade blacked out.

But her hands were drenched in blood, and she held someone hostage at knifepoint. The girl was shaking as Jade pressed the knife against her throat.

"She's the last of their group," Razor explained slowly. "We need her alive."

Jade pressed the knife harder against her captive's throat. The girl cried out in pain. As Jade looked at Helena, she recalled that this girl had cut Helena a few times.

"She hurt my sister," Jade gritted as she applied more pressure.

"I know...I know, Jade," she could see the anger in Razor's eyes when she mentioned that. He slowly took a few steps forward. Instinctively,

Jade and her hostage took a few steps back. "And I promise you. She *will* pay for that. But not until she gives us what we need."

Jade shook her head. No. This girl was going to pay *now*. She came here to kill. And she came here with the intent to hurt Helena. Jade couldn't allow that. Helena was the only family she had left. She would kill and die trying to protect her. Jade moved in for the kill.

"Jade," Clay was right behind her. She quickly turned to face him—dragging her hostage along. His eyes were calm and gentle. He had his hands up like Razor. "Now is not the time."

She glared at him. Jade needed to kill this girl. She *wanted* to so badly. Jade longed for that freedom.

"Look at what you've already done," Clay gestured to all the dead bodies surrounding them.

"I...I...did all this," Jade frowned in disbelief. Seven dead bodies were lying in front of the warehouse.

"You protected us all, Jade," Clay smiled as he took a few steps forward. "You did a phenomenal job, but you can't kill her just yet."

"But I really want to, Clay."

He took another cautious step forward. "I know, but you want to protect us, right?"

Jade nodded.

"Keeping her alive will do that. We can get more information out of her, and we can find out where the Radicals live. And then we can go to them. And you can finish protecting us, Jade."

"You promise, once you get what you need, that I get to kill her."

"I promise you can kill her once we're done."

Jade stared into his eyes. She struggled to determine if he was telling her the truth or not. But Clay has been patient and understanding with her. The least she could do was trust him. She nodded and slowly removed the knife from the girl's throat.

Reagan quickly stepped in and removed the girl away from her. Razor swiftly had his arms around her. Jade leaned into him. She knew he was only holding her so she wouldn't suddenly attack the girl. But Jade was struggling with her emotions. It felt like she was losing it. She was afraid—terrified. What was happening to her? It seemed like she was losing herself and her grip on reality daily. Jade sighed. She was thankful that Razor's arms provided her comfort.

"I volunteer to do the *interrogating*," Tatianna yelled from afar.

Razor sighed and rolled his eyes. "Fine, Tatianna. Get her strung up."

She yelled with glee.

"You all right?" he asked with concern.

"I'm sorry," Jade whispered. Clay, Reagan, and Helena came over to them.

Razor kissed the top of her head. "You did good."

"Maybe me and Jade should make the rounds and keep an eye out," Reagan suggested.

"That's a good idea," Razor agreed.

"Are you sure about that?" Helena frowned as she looked at Jade.

"They'll be fine," Clay assured her. "And I'll keep watch at the main entrance."

"Perfect," Razor released Jade from his hold. "I'll go get your bow and arrows."

Helena quickly linked her arm to Jade's. She looked at her with worried eyes. Jade frowned once she noticed all the scrapes and bruises on her sister. It was way more than she thought. Rage filled her as she regretted not killing that girl.

"I'm ok, Jade. I promise."

Jade nodded and looked at Clay. "Thank you."

"There's no need to thank me."

Razor came out with her weapons. He quickly handed them to her. "Don't give Reagan a hard time."

"She's not a child," Reagan sighed in annoyance. "Jade will be perfectly fine."

The two women promptly walked off, leaving the others to deal with the "interrogation." As they walked silently through the wooded streets, Jade was amazed at how quickly nature reclaimed the land. Windsor was once a major city area, but you couldn't see that now. Even the buildings were covered with vines, branches, and grass. The city was hidden underneath a coverage of forestry.

When she was paired up with Reagan, Jade was immediately grateful. Reagan wasn't a big talker. And she didn't look at Jade like she was crazy. She was tired of that look and having a break from that was nice.

They had just reached the heavily wooded area on their patrol when Jade spotted him. He stood in a thicket of bushes. His head was full of curls. And his cheeks rosier than she's ever seen. Jade smiled as she looked at Levi. He was waiting patiently for her.

Jade pulled out an arrow and placed it on her bow as she reached him. "Are you ready?"

Levi nodded.

"Ok, you know the drill. Keep an eye out for any animals."

They both started walking quietly. Levi looked around intently, but Jade could tell that he was afraid. After a few minutes, he slowed down.

"I don't want to do this, Jade," he looked up at her with watery eyes. "I don't want to kill any animals."

"You have to, my little munchkin. You need to be strong now. It's the only way you'll survive in this world."

Levi frowned and then nodded. He started to walk again but paused.

He looked up at her with a strange look. "Will being that way protect me from the big, bad, scary man?"

"Yes, my little munchkin," Jade was relieved he was catching on. Raina was always so resistant to her. "It will protect you."

Levi sighed with relief and resumed walking. He sped up a little. Jade could see his determination as he scanned the area for prey. At that moment, she felt proud. Finally, someone was going to allow her to taint them. Levi froze and turned toward Jade. He pointed to a bush nearby. Jade spotted a small white rabbit hiding underneath the leaves. She reacted quickly. She fired off an arrow and hit her mark. Jade smiled proudly. She turned to look at Levi, but he was no longer there.

Panicked, Jade looked around the woods. She turned to see Reagan standing behind her. Then reality sat in. Levi wasn't there. The sadness and pain crept through her, and tears instantly fell. Jade glanced around again. She noticed that they were far off from the patrol trail.

"Why didn't you say anything?"

Reagan shrugged as she approached the rabbit Jade had just killed. "Just letting you go through your process."

"You think I'm crazy, don't you?"

Reagan silently examined the rabbit for a moment. It was much fatter than Jade thought. "No," she finally said. She walked back to Jade with the rabbit in her hand. "I think you're grieving."

"Thanks for understanding," Jade sighed.

"Don't sweat it. I used to see my brother do all kinds of weird shit."

Jade remained silent as she followed Reagan back toward the trail. She had never noticed it before, but Reagan was beautiful. Like her brother, she was tan and had long, curly hair. But she always had her hair up in a messy bun. Unlike Jade, Reagan found the time to detangle her hair every now and then. She was about an inch or two taller than Jade and had a slender build.

"He must've really loved her," she finally said. "For him to be grieving so badly."

Reagan scoffed. "I don't think my brother actually loved her. I think it was the guilt that made him grieve the way that he did."

Jade slowed down from walking. She was stunned by that news. "Oh."

"He used to be a huge dick to his girlfriends. The whole, I'm a jock, I can have anyone I want, whole ordeal."

"That's very hard to imagine," Jade frowned, trying to envision Clay that way.

"Well, her death changed him."

"I guess some deaths can change a person for the better."

"It can," she looked over at Jade with a smirk. "I see Helena got around to doing your hair."

Jade sighed. "Was it that bad?"

For the first time, Jade heard Reagan laugh. "You should've heard how much she complained about it. Keeping watch with her was awful. She really wants you to cut it."

Jade frowned.

"She just really misses her."

"I know."

"It'll get better, Jade. Just go through your process," Reagan paused. They had arrived at the trail. "But don't stay there."

Jade nodded as she spotted Levi waiting for her on the trail. She sped up to meet him. Reagan lingered behind.

"Are you proud that I helped you kill the bunny?" he asked, hopeful when she reached him.

"I am, my little munchkin," she ran her fingers through his curls. "You did a great job."

Levi smiled brightly at her. He placed his hands in hers as they continued to walk the trail. Then Jade felt him slow down. She looked at him and saw a frown on his face.

"Jade," he looked up at her, afraid. "How did the big, bad, scary man know that we were going to the river? How did he know we'd be there?"

Jade stopped abruptly. It felt like she was just punched in the gut. *How did he know?*

Reagan caught up to her and then looked concerned when Jade didn't resume walking.

"Reagan..."

"I'm here, Jade."

She shook her head. "How...how did he know we'd be there?"

~5~

Nick

Although the room was dark, Nick instantly knew where he was when he came to. He had to laugh at the irony of the situation. He had often been in the same room, but the only difference now was that he was on the other side of it. Oh, how the tables quickly turned.

Nick never imagined his downfall, but this all seemed appropriate. His number two betrayed him. The woman he loved was a rebellious debtor. And his long-time friend now had him chained to a chair in the torture room. It all appeared to be coming to an end. He knew that this was coming for a while. But Nick knew his fate was sealed when he shoved those machetes into those children.

He glanced around the room again, and then he saw him. He was cowering in the corner—fear clear in his eyes. Nick sighed. It was uncanny how much his son resembled the boy Levi. They were around the same age; his son Aiden was two years older than Levi. And they both had a head full of tight curls. Only Aiden's hair was more of a reddish-brown color. But their big brown eyes and chubby, dimpled cheeks were the same—it was all too much for Nick.

"What do you want, son?" Nick sighed.

Aiden slowly walked out of the corner. "Did you really do it, Dad?"

He looked away from him. "I don't know what you're talking about."

"Did you kill two kids? Are you like the monster who killed me?"

"It wasn't something I wanted to do," Nick avoided looking at him. "But it was necessary."

"It was *necessary* to kill two children that way," tears fell from Aiden's eyes. "It was necessary to be that cruel?"

"It's the way of the world, my boy."

"No, it's the way of *your* world."

"If I'm not mistaken, it wasn't *my* world that got you killed."

"No," Aiden looked him straight in the eyes. "But it was your job to protect me."

Nick was instantly filled with rage. He glared at his son. "Go away."

Aiden smirked. All signs of the boy he used to know were gone. "What's wrong, *father*? Did I hit a nerve?"

"Go away!"

"I guess you're not that tough after all."

"Fuck you, Aiden."

"Sticks and stones may break my bones, but words will never hurt me."

Nick sighed. "Of course not, because you're dead! You're not real! And you're not here!"

"And who's fault is that?"

"Go away, Aiden."

"Make me."

"This isn't you talking," Nick shut his eyes. "This is your grandmother. This isn't my son...this isn't my son."

"Why didn't you protect me, Dad?"

"I was trying to be good. I was trying to be a good man for you, son."

"Is that why you killed those kids? Because you were trying to be different."

"I wanted *her* to be different."

"But Jade loved them like how you loved me. And look at what my death did to you. She failed to protect them, Dad. Imagine what that's doing to her."

Nick opened his eyes and looked at his son. Aiden looked like his usual self, but Aiden's words hit him hard.

"You didn't free her, Dad. You just drove her into madness."

Tears fell from Nick's eyes. This was the first time he cried since Aiden's death. "Go away, son."

"I thought you knew this by now, Dad. I can never go away."

**

A 19-year-old Nick sat on his living room couch and played with 3-year-old Aiden. Nick was dressed for work already and was waiting on his wife, Amelia, to come home from her classes at the community college.

Amelia was Nick's high school sweetheart. They had Aiden when they were 16, and Nick proposed to her once they graduated from high school. The ceremony was small and quick. Neither of their parents approved of the marriage (or the relationship, for that matter). But Nick loved Amelia. And he wanted to make an honest woman out of her.

After high school, Nick took a security job at a hospital, and Amelia took classes at a local community college. Nick ensured he got the night shift so he could watch Aiden during the day while Amelia was at school. Neither of them had a good relationship with their parents. And they couldn't afford daycare or a sitter. Nick was already paying for Amelia's schoolbooks. That, and the cost of rent and other expenses, put a financial strain on the young couple.

But for the most part, the newly married couple was doing well and was a happy little family. Sadly, that only lasted for a little while.

Just a few months after their first anniversary, Amelia began to act differently. She started coming home late from her classes and received strange phone calls at odd times. And she insisted on going out to socialize by herself more often. Nick tried to be patient and understanding with her, but it was beginning to wear thin.

Nick dangled a toy in front of Aiden. Aiden desperately tried to grab it. Nick smiled as he tried not to look at the clock. He should've left out for work ten minutes ago. At this rate, he would be late for his shift—again. This would be the third time in two weeks. His supervisor was not going to be happy about that. Nick tried to fight off his frustration. The job at the hospital was a good one. He got great pay and benefits, and the scheduling worked perfectly for them. Nick was the only one who worked, so if he lost this job, they would be screwed.

Aiden finally caught the stuffed animal Nick was dangling in front of him. A young Aiden screamed with delight as he buried his face into the toy. Nick laughed at his son's joy. Unable to stop himself, he glanced at the clock.

"Shit," he whispered. Now he was definitely going to be late.

Nick took out his phone and called his job. He explained the situation to them. Thankfully, his supervisor wasn't too upset with him. Nick began to pack a bag for Aiden. Then he and his son left out the apartment.

It took two buses for Nick to get to his mother's house. He dreaded it, but he had no other choice. He couldn't miss his shift. They desperately needed the money. And although he didn't get along with his mother, she loved and adored Aiden. That was something that Nick thought he'd never see.

Mary Sturman was a cold, heartless woman. She had never been the same since his father's death. Nick didn't remember his father. He died when Nick was very young. But those who knew Mary before his father's death agreed she was a different woman. Nick only got the sense of that when she interacted with Aiden.

Nick knocked once before Mary came to the door.

"Nick," she glared.

"Mary."

"What do you want?"

"I need you to watch Aiden for me," Aiden had fallen asleep during the bus ride.

"Where's his mother?"

"Not sure, but I'm late for my shift."

"You don't know where your wife is?"

"It's Friday night," Nick brushed past her and walked into the house. "She probably went out with some of her classmates."

"Without running it past you first," Mary followed him to the den. "Well, now I see who wears the pants in this relationship."

"Will you watch him or not?"

She looked at a sleeping Aiden lying on her couch. "Well, since you already made him comfortable, I guess I will."

Nick sat his overnight bag on the floor. "Thanks."

"But you need to get a handle on that little wife of yours!" she shouted as Nick walked out of the house.

Nick was grateful that his shift at the hospital went by smoothly. The only annoyance he had was when he tried texting and calling Amelia. It was clear that she was ignoring him. She had sent him to voicemail numerous times. The last time she sent him to voicemail, Nick made it clear that she was never getting the car again. From now on, she would be getting dropped off and picked up if this was how she would handle things.

When he went to pick up Aiden, his mother answered the door silently. It was early in the morning, so Aiden was asleep.

"Where's your car?" she asked.

"Amelia still has it."

"Let me get my keys," Mary sighed.

"That's all right," Nick picked Aiden up. "We'll just take the bus."

"My grandson is not going to ride on a filthy bus. I'll take you home."

"He doesn't have his car seat."

"I have one in my car!" she snapped. Aiden jumped in his sleep. "Stop fighting me on this," she whispered.

"Fine," he sighed.

It didn't take long for them to get settled into Mary's car. And she indeed had a car seat for Aiden. They rode silently for a moment. And then Mary looked over at him.

"Did you ever find out where she was?"

"No," Nick began to bite his nails.

"She does this often?"

He didn't say anything.

"The little whore is probably out cheating," she spat. She glanced over at Nick and slapped his hand. "Stop that! That's a nasty habit."

Nick sighed as he stopped.

"Did you hear what I said?"

"Yes, Mary."

"And no response, huh? I guess you like the idea of your little whore wife going out to cheat on you. And it's probably with a college guy too. Or maybe a professor."

"Stop the car."

"What?"

"Stop the car! I don't need to listen to this shit."

"I didn't realize I raised such a sensitive son."

"I don't have to sit here and listen to you disrespect my wife."

"You think *I'm* being disrespectful? That little *wife* of yours is out here cheating on you and your son, and you think I'm being disrespectful?"

Nick ground his teeth in annoyance. Mary had him there.

"You're just lucky that my grandson is here. Otherwise, I would pull this car right over."

"Lucky me," he mumbled.

"All I'm saying, Nick, is get your house in order. If she doesn't want to do right, kick her out."

Nick closed his eyes. He wanted this conversation with his mother to be over with. They soon arrived at his apartment complex, and Nick was overly grateful. He quickly got Aiden and his bag out of the car.

"Thanks," he said coldly.

"Yeah, whatever."

Nick watched as Mary drove away.

When he got inside, it appeared that Amelia hadn't arrived home. He placed Aiden in his bed, then Nick lay on the couch, waiting for his wife to come home.

A few hours went by before Amelia finally walked through the door. Nick had dosed off but was quickly awakened by the keys jingling at the door. He rose to his feet as she walked in.

"Give me my fucking car keys."

Amelia looked him up and down. "Well, hello to you too."

"My keys, now."

She rolled her eyes as she tossed them to him.

"Your car privileges have been revoked."

"What am I, a child?" she went to the kitchen, and Nick followed her.

"Obviously!" he looked her up and down. She had on a tight, short dress. Her cleavage was pushed up and almost spilling out the top. It wasn't the outfit she left out with yesterday. "Where the hell you've been?"

"Out."

"Out where?"

"With friends."

"What kind of friends?"

"People from my school. You don't know them."

"And you went out looking like that. And without telling me first. I almost missed my shift, Amelia."

"But you worked something out, just like I knew you would," she opened the refrigerator and looked inside.

Nick stared at her in disbelief. This was not the girl he knew in high school. The girl he knew was head over heels for him. Whenever she looked at him, there was longing in her eyes. This woman now despised him. There was a sense of resentment there.

"You don't care if I lost my job?"

She sighed. "I don't care about your little job, Nick."

"Well, that 'little job' pays for everything around here. It pays for your books! It paid for that little slutty dress you're wearing!"

"So you keep telling me!" she slammed the refrigerator's door.

"And which one of these 'friends' are you fucking?"

"Oh my God!" she stormed out of the kitchen and went to the living room. Nick was right behind her. "I'm not about to deal with your little insecurities right now!"

"It's not insecurities. It's a fucking fact!" Nick gestured to her outfit. "I'm not stupid."

"And what if I was fucking someone else? What are you going to do about it?"

"Don't...test...me...Amelia," Nick's fists were balled tightly.

"Whatever, Nick," she rolled her eyes.

Nick took deep breaths and slowly counted to ten. He kept all thoughts of reacting violently at bay. But the ideas were very tempting. Amelia was pushing his buttons, and he wanted so badly to give in to his urges. But Aiden was lying asleep in his room. And Nick needed to set a good example for his son. So, he swallowed his anger.

"What you're doing," he began slowly. "Doesn't just affect me. It affects Aiden too. And that's not fair to him."

"I didn't ask for any of this," her eyes got watery.

Nick looked at her in disbelief. "And you think I did?"

"I wasn't ready to have a family, Nick."

"*No* was always an option. I never forced anything on you."

"Imagine how that'll look? A girl who says no to the father of her child. A guy who wants to marry her!"

"Who gives a fuck about them?!" Nick shook his head. "And you think cheating on him will make you look any better?"

"Fuck you, Nick," she spat.

Once again, he needed to count to ten. When he was done, he sat on the couch. He leaned forward and rested his elbows on his legs.

"I get that you're going through a difficult time," he spoke calmly. "But we need to work through this together, at least, for Aiden's sake. He didn't ask to be here. And he didn't ask to be put in this position. But he deserves the best. And he deserves to have a mother who is present. Can you at least do that?"

Amelia glared at him. She didn't say anything. She stomped past him, entered their bedroom, and slammed the door shut.

Things hadn't improved for the young, married couple as time passed. Amelia continued to go out, even without the car, and she became less discrete with her cheating. In fact, she was all but throwing it in Nick's face. Of course, he found out who the guy was. He sat outside Amelia's school one day and followed them. It was some guy in her creative writing class. It took enormous strength for him not to go inside the guy's place and beat him and Amelia. Aiden would have been left without a father if he'd done that. And Nick couldn't do that to his son.

Unfortunately, Nick had to take Aiden to his mother's house. Mary was no fool. She knew exactly what was happening and ridiculed Nick whenever he dropped Aiden off.

"What kind of example are you setting for your son?" she demanded. "You're teaching him to be a pushover."

"I'm providing my son with a two-parent household."

"You're showing your son how to love a *whore*," she spat. "You're going to make him weak. Weak, just like you!"

Nick turned and walked away before giving in to his urge to hit his mother repeatedly. He slammed the front door behind him.

A few weeks later, Nick came home with Aiden to find Amelia at the kitchen table. There were bags packed by the front door. Nick sent Aiden to his room as he joined Amelia in the kitchen. He sat down across from her. She kept her eyes on the table.

"I can't do this anymore," she admitted. "I want a divorce."

"Off to live with Peter?"

She looked up at him, alarmed. It was clear that she didn't expect him to know his name. She didn't say anything. She only nodded.

"Fine, go. I won't force you to stay somewhere you don't want to be."

"Aiden's coming with me."

"Like hell he is," he growled. He was so close to hitting her.

"He's my son."

"And I've been the only one raising him!" Nick rose to his feet. The chair fell back as he stood. Amelia looked up at him with tears in her eyes. "*You* can go. But Aiden is staying."

Amelia slowly got to her feet. "I'm his mother."

"You touch my son, and it'll be the last thing you do."

"Then I guess I'll see you in court."

"I guess you will."

The custody battle for Aiden was a brutal one. Nick was granted temporary custody of Aiden since Amelia didn't have her own place. She refused to return home since she and her parents never got along. Her relationship with them was a volatile one.

The battle for Aiden went on for a year. In the end, Nick won full custody while Amelia received visitation rights. She got custody of Aiden every other weekend. Nick could tell that the judge despised him. However, she had no choice but to grant Nick full custody since Amelia hopped from one boyfriend's house to the next and couldn't hold a stable job. It was a bonus that Aiden went on the record stating that he preferred to be with his dad instead of his mother.

Nick could tell that Amelia held a lot of anger and resentment toward him. But he was able to make peace with her for Aiden's sake. So, the next year and a half went by smoothly. It wasn't until a few months after Aiden's 6th birthday that things started to go array.

First, Aiden became fearful whenever it was time for him to go with his mother. She had a new boyfriend, and she'd been with this one much longer than the others. Nick hadn't bothered to know his name because they never lasted. But when he saw his son's reaction, he asked him about it.

"He's very mean, Dad."

"Who?"

"Theo."

"Your mom's new boyfriend?"

Aiden nodded.

"Why do you think he's mean?"

"He hits on her. And yells at her."

"He does this in front of you?"

Tears fell on his face as Aiden nodded.

When it was time for Aiden to go with his mother, Nick lied to her and told her that Aiden was sick. He even had Chase forge a note for him. Then he immediately took her back to court to get her parental rights taken away. Unfortunately, his request was denied. There was no proof of abuse going on. And the judge wouldn't consider what Aiden said as evidence since he was a kid. But Nick knew it was because she didn't like him.

"Mr. Sturman," she said, glaring at him. "If you come back with these petty allegations, I will put Aiden into the system until we get this sorted out. Do I make myself clear?"

Nick bit his tongue as he nodded.

After that, he struggled to stop going to Theo's house and beating him, which would surely worsen the situation. And he couldn't give Amelia any leverage that could result in her getting custody of Aiden.

So, with reluctance, Nick had no choice but to follow the court order and allow Aiden to go over to Theo's house with his mother.

"You're such a fucking coward," Mary spat at her son once Aiden was gone for the weekend. "You know something is going on. Go over there and do something about it!"

"He's only hitting *her*. Not Aiden."

"How long do you think it will take until he sets his sights on him?!"

"I'll kill him."

"You'll do *nothing* but sit there and take it."

Nick left out for work. If he sat with his mother any longer, he was sure he would kill her.

His shift went on as usual. It wasn't until he was leaving out that things got weird. Chase immediately stopped him from leaving out by blocking the door. A strained look was on his face.

"You should give it a minute, Nick," he rushed. "It's really chaotic out there."

Nick frowned at him. He could hear the medical staff yelling and calling out different codes. None of this was new to him. "I'll be fine."

"Nick Sturman, please report to the Trauma Unit," someone over the P.A. called. "Nick Sturman, please report to the Trauma Unit."

The staff knew that he was off the clock, so he didn't understand why they were calling for him. Also, this wasn't the code for security.

All the blood immediately drained out of Chase's face. "It's Aiden."

Nick ran past him, knocking Chase against the wall. He ran through the hospital and got to the Trauma Unit quickly. It felt like he would pass out when he saw Aiden lying on the gurney, blood pouring out of the many stab wounds on his body. Amelia lay dead on a gurney near him and had similar stab wounds.

It took the whole security staff and some medical staff to get Nick under control. Aiden was dying. They couldn't slow down the bleeding that was coming out of his abdomen, his neck, and his leg. Aiden was slipping away. And there was nothing Nick could do to save his son.

"Take my blood!" he cried desperately. "Take my blood and save him!"

Nick fought off the people who were holding him back. He rushed over to Aiden. His eyes were glassy. Aiden was gone. That was confirmed as the heart monitor flat-lined. The doctors tried to no avail to revive him. Nick passed out the moment the doctor called for a time of death.

Murder-suicide.

That's what happened to Amelia and Aiden that night.

Theo was angry that Aiden told Nick that he was abusing his mother. He was pissed that they went to court about it. And although no evidence showed that Theo was abusive, he was upset that it was even discussed. According to friends, Theo warned Amelia that he didn't want Aiden around if he told his father things, but Amelia ignored him.

So, when Theo came home from work to see that Aiden was there, he was pissed. He confronted Amelia about undermining him in his home. And then he confronted Aiden about telling his father things that went on in his house. Theo tried to hit Aiden, but Amelia stepped in. A fight broke out between them, in which Amelia grabbed a knife. In return, Theo got it away from her and began stabbing her. Aiden tried to help his mother, and Theo turned the knife on him. Theo realized he would die in prison or at Nick's hands when everything ended. Wanting to spare himself from that fate, he took his own life.

The days that followed Aiden's death were a blurry haze. At one point, Nick noticed he had cuts and bruises. When he inquired about them, Chase told him that Mary had beaten him. She was so distraught over her grandson's death that she took it out on him.

"You don't remember it?" Chase asked, puzzled.

Nick shook his head.

"That doesn't seem like something you could forget."

When the time came for the funeral, Nick couldn't bring himself to look in the casket. He couldn't see Aiden that way and didn't want to remember him like that. He wanted the last memory of his son to be when he kissed and hugged him before he left with his mother. Aiden was so bright and lively at that moment. That was the moment Nick wanted to keep forever.

Nick shook with rage when he spotted the judge who presided over his custody case. She walked over to him with sympathetic eyes.

"Mr. Sturman, I'm so sorry for your loss," she dabbed her eyes as tears fell. "I can't help but partially blame myself for this tragic incident. I should've taken your claim more seriously."

"Get out of here before I snap your neck," he said through a clenched jaw. "And take your sorry-ass apology with you."

She cried harder as she walked away. Nick watched her leave out.

Nick reluctantly took his mother home when the funeral and the repass ended. She had gotten drunk during the event and could not drive. To his surprise, she was quiet during the whole ride and even quiet when he escorted her inside and upstairs to her room. It wasn't until he turned to leave that she finally spoke.

"You're a sad piece of shit, you know that?" she slurred. She struggled to sit upright on her bed. "How could you fail him like that? How could you allow that to happen to my grandson?!"

"I did everything by the book," he whispered.

"That's your fucking problem! You're just *weak*! *A weak, pathetic man*! How are you my son?!"

"Goodbye, Mary."

"No!" she stood up and swayed a little. She wobbled toward him. "You're not fit to be in this world! You're not fit to be a father!"

Nick turned toward her and glared. "Shut it!"

"A father is supposed to protect his child! And what did you do? You fed him to the wolves! You're a failure. A pathetic, weak—"

When Nick came to, his mother was lying still at the bottom of the stairs. His hands shook with rage. He couldn't remember what had happened. But even from the top of the stairs, Nick could tell Mary was dead. How long had she been that way? He didn't know. It was nighttime when he dropped her off. Now, the sun was rising. That was much time he lost.

Nick sighed as he pulled out his phone and dialed 911. At that point, he no longer cared. His life was already over anyway.

An accident.

That's what the police ruled it. And the coroner confirmed it as well. Nick didn't go out of his way to contradict them. In all honesty, he didn't *think* he killed his mother. But he wasn't going to put the possibility out there either.

As time went on, Nick became more and more unlike himself. He gave in to his violent urges. And whenever he tried to resist it, his mother's nagging voice entered his head, ridiculing him again. So, Nick spent years ensuring he never heard that voice again.

**

Nick glanced around the torture room again. He spotted Aiden standing back in the corner. This time Levi and Raina stood there with him. After seeing her, Nick finally understood why Jade killed one of his officers. Raina really did look like a kid version of Helena. It was remarkable. The girl even had the same pixie haircut. His eyes met Raina's.

"She'll never love you."

"She will eventually."

"Jade loved us more than anything in the world," Levi said. "She could never love someone who killed us so brutally."

"Jade isn't the same person you once knew," Nick sighed. He closed his eyes. He couldn't take looking at them for too long. "This new version of Jade could definitely love someone like me."

"How can you be so sure, Dad?"

Just then, the door to the torture room flew open. Nick quickly opened his eyes to see Chase and his guards walking in. The children instantly huddled up together in the corner—fear present on their faces.

Nick chuckled as one of the men stopped in front of him. "Mr. President, is the torture finally going to begin?"

One of the guards responded by punching him hard in the face. Nick laughed as he spat out blood. Enraged by his reaction, the guard hit him again. And again. And again. And again.

As Nick took his beating, he noticed how scared the children looked in the corner. This was no place for them. Aiden looked at him with pleading eyes. They begged him to do something. To take action. Anger ran through him. Nick needed to get them out of here.

~6~

Razor

The sounds of torture and beatings filled the air. Razor sighed as his back rested against the wall. It had been a while since he's heard this original soundtrack. Since he teamed up with Jade, the "interrogations" had briefly stopped. Razor never thought he'd feel so free when he wasn't allowing his hands to do damage. Of course, he killed people during that time, but it was mostly out of self-defense and to protect those he loved. It was regrettable that he was back to doing this again.

But at the moment, *he* wasn't actually doing the beating. It was Tatianna. Since they crossed the river, Tatianna took a special interest in how Razor conducted his interrogations. Of course, he had no problem with teaching her. He'd known Tatianna for years and even killed a few guards to protect her. She was Helena's best friend. But as he sat back and watched her beat the female captive, he couldn't help but feel sick to his stomach.

What was happening to all of them?

Jade was running around talking to dead people, and that's when she wasn't trying to kill every person she'd come across.

Helena was becoming a sex addict.

Clay couldn't stop watching Jade.

Junior was walking around looking sneaky and suspicious.

Tatianna, the girl who was once a provider and used to hide and cower in her prison cell, eagerly volunteered to torture and beat people.

And the rest of the group looked exhausted, defeated, and paranoid.

They were all slowly losing it. They were losing themselves.

Razor sighed again. He couldn't help but put some of the blame on himself. It was apparent that, at this point, he was unnecessarily hard on himself, but he couldn't shake the feeling. They should've been over here finding Blackwell months ago. But instead, Razor was off going rogue with his new plan. Now, dealing with this group, the Radicals, Razor wasn't sure if Blackwell was even alive.

"Who do you work for?" Tatianna asked the captive after she'd punched her in the face.

The girl, whose eye was swollen shut, looked at Tatianna and spat at her feet. Tatianna responded by smacking her. Razor glanced out the window. He was getting antsy. The hostage wasn't giving them anything, and Reagan and Jade would be back any minute. They couldn't keep Jade away for long. And if she came back, he was sure she'd kill the girl.

Razor cracked his knuckles. He hated to do it. But it appeared that he would have to torture the poor girl.

"Tatianna," Razor rose from the stool he was sitting on. She immediately stopped and backed away from the girl.

Razor looked at the captive. She glared at him in defiance. Moving fast, he backhanded her hard. So hard that she and the chair tilted over. The girl hit her head hard against the floor. Helena gasped. She and Danita were standing nearby. Yoko, Calvin, and Junior were on the roof, helping Clay with lookout. Keeper was watching over Jackson.

Razor avoided eye contact with Helena. "Get her up," he told Tatianna and Danita.

They both quickly did what they were told. They hadn't even gotten the girl up when Razor struck her again. And again, she fell over. Razor did this two more times before the girl began to cry and beg hysterically. He turned his back to her and cracked his knuckles again. He was frustrated. And beyond annoyed. They were going to get what they needed today. He was tired of being sitting ducks. They needed to find Blackwell and get out of there.

"I'm going to ask you this once," his back was still to her. "Who—"

"I'm a part of the Radical group," she quickly said. Tatianna smirked with satisfaction.

"Who's your leader?"

The girl fell silent. Razor turned around and made his way toward her. "No, no, no, wait!"

Razor ignored her cries and punched her hard in the gut. She hunched over in pain. The captive coughed for air. After a moment, she spat up blood. Helena gasped again and rushed to her side. She quickly removed a cloth from her back pocket and started wiping the blood from the girl's mouth.

"Get Helena away from her," Razor demanded as he looked at Tatianna. Tatianna froze, unclear on what she should do. Razor sighed and rolled his eyes. He marched over to Helena and grabbed her by her elbow. She looked up at him, alarmed. He gently pushed her to the side. "Please don't interfere with my interrogations."

Helena looked shocked. Her mouth hung open, words unable to come out.

Razor ignored her and punched the girl square in the face. She fell back, and this time, the back of her head hit the ground. There was a loud thud echoing throughout the warehouse.

"Get her up!" he yelled when Tatianna and Danita had yet to retrieve the girl. They quickly did. The girl looked like she was going to pass out at any moment.

"Razor?" Jade stood in the entryway of the warehouse. She was unclear on whether she should step inside or not. It was hard for him to decipher her facial expression. Reagan was right behind her. "Are you ok?"

He turned back to the girl. "I'm fine," he backhanded her again. The girl slumped over. She was awfully close to passing out now.

"Umm," Jade slowly walked into the warehouse but stayed close to the door. "How about Reagan and me help out? I can even hand over all my weapons," she added when Razor shot her a look.

"That sounds like a good idea," Reagan added. "Helena, Danita, Tatianna, go take a break."

Danita and Tatianna made their way toward them, but Helena lingered.

"Seriously, Helena," Jade assured. "Everything will be all right. Go get some fresh air."

Helena looked over at Razor. There was sadness and a hint of disappointment in her eyes. Guilt quickly ran through him. It had been a very long time since he saw that look. She finally looked back at Jade and proceeded toward her sister. Jade had surrendered her weapons to Helena before Helena left out the warehouse.

Jade slowly made her way to him. She looked at the girl and then back at him. Her eyebrow was raised, but she didn't say anything to him. Jade sat on the stool and rested her back against the wall. She folded her arms across her chest. She frowned at the ground before she looked back up at the girl.

Reagan quietly walked over to the girl and gently slapped her a few times. The captive eventually opened her eyes. Reagan got her to sit up straight.

"Hang in there, girly," she encouraged. "Now is not the time to be passing out on us."

"Who's your leader?" Jade demanded.

The girl still hesitated.

Reagan quickly pulled the girl's hair to keep her still. Reagan looked over at Razor, indicating for him to proceed. Razor made his way to her—getting ready to punch her.

"Liam!" she screamed at the top of her lungs. Razor froze in his tracks. "His name is Liam Ouellet."

"Why are you attacking us?" Jade continued.

Razor was instantly grateful that she and Reagan were there. Compared to his other partners, they were less emotional. Reagan kept a tight hold on the girl's hair. The girl winced in pain.

"We thought you were with our rival group."

"There's a rival group?" Jade couldn't keep the curiosity out of her tone.

Razor frowned. "Why would you think that?"

"Because they're the only ones who attack us."

"You ambushed us as soon as we hit your shores!" he fought to keep his rage at bay. "How did you expect us to respond?!"

"We just demand supplies," the girl explained hastily. It was clear that she was very frightened by his anger.

"Yeah, we know that already," Reagan said casually.

"But we also ask for those to join us. You all attacked and killed our group. We assumed that you were a part of our rival group. But I can tell you're not!" she added as Razor approached her.

Frustrated, he smacked her anyway. He was glad that Reagan still had a hold on her. Otherwise, she would've fallen to the ground again.

"What's the name of this rival group?" he growled.

"They called themselves the Black Coats," she cried.

Razor froze. *The Black Coats.* Could it be?

"Do you know who their leader is?"

"No one knows his name. Everyone refers to him as *the doc.* But you can tell who he is because his left hand is missing, and he usually wears a prosthetic hand that's all black."

"Blackwell," Razor mumbled. So, he was alive. And he managed to gather another group. Well, that was just fantastic. "Where are their headquarters?"

"I don't know...I swear!" she screamed as Razor raised his hand to hit her. "But we know that most of them are in Toronto! We think that's where the doc might live."

Razor backed away from her, and the girl immediately sighed with relief. Even though Reagan still had her by her hair.

"You think it's him?" Jade asked.

"It seems like it. I did cut off his left hand."

"Yeah, that's too big of a coincidence for it *not* to be him."

"Please," the girl begged. "I've given you what you wanted. Please, let me go."

"Any other time, I would," he walked over to her. She tried to move but was unable to since Reagan had her hair. He signaled for Reagan to release her when he was in front of her. Reagan did. "But you tried to kill my wife. And I just can't let that fly."

Very swiftly, Razor snapped the girl's neck. Her body immediately slumped down the chair. He looked over at Reagan. Her face was expressionless. He turned toward Jade. She was sitting up on the stool, glaring at him.

"I was promised that I'd get to do that!"

"Yeah, but I wasn't the one who promised you that. So, get over it."

She frowned at him. "Well, someone's very grumpy today."

Razor looked out the window and saw Helena standing nearby. Her back was to him. "Well, seeing my wife almost blown to smithereens would do that to you."

Jade followed his gaze. "Touché."

Reagan threw the girl's body over her shoulder. "I'll put her with the others," she proceeded out of the warehouse.

"If she asks, I'll tell Helena that I was the one who killed her."

Razor looked over at Jade. It was apparent that she noticed the look that Helena had given him. He looked back out the window. "No, Helena knows what my mission is, and she knows what lengths I'll go to uphold that."

"All right," Jade sighed. She stood. "Well, I'll go fetch my weapons then."

Razor watched as Jade left out the warehouse. Once he was alone, he looked down at his hands. They were bloody and shaking. It was from all the adrenaline and rage. It had been a while since he had seen them do that, and he wasn't sure how he felt about it.

That night, he filled the group in on what they'd learned. Keeper was excited to hear the news about Blackwell. He made it clear that they should try to find him soon. Jackson would have a better shot at surviving under his father's supervision. Razor agreed with him.

"We head for Toronto tomorrow afternoon."

Razor stared at the ceiling as he and Helena lay on their pallet, frowning. Helena had her back to him. And was eerily silent. In fact, she hadn't spoken a word to him since the interrogation.

"I'm sorry if my behavior upset you," he said.

Helena turned to face him. "Is this how you keep Jade from falling into the deep end? By jumping in yourself?"

Razor frowned at her. "Helena, I just saw you nearly killed by a bomb earlier today. If Jade hadn't beaten me to them, I would've killed everyone in that group myself. I'm not going to apologize for killing that girl. But I am sorry if I upset you."

"I'm just so tired of everyone losing their shit!" she roughly turned to lay on her back. "I just don't want to lose you, too, Razor."

"You're not losing me," he turned on his side to face her. He gently grabbed her chin and made her look at him. He stared into her brown eyes for a moment. "But you've seemed to have forgotten what my true mission is. And what I'll do to defend it."

"I love you too," she leaned over and kissed him.

Relief ran through him. It never failed. Whenever Razor lost control of his anger, he always feared that Helena would wise up one day and leave him. He was relieved every time she proved him wrong.

When he pulled away, he began to caress her cheek. "Just hang in there a little longer. We're close to finding Blackwell."

Helena closed her eyes and nodded.

Razor couldn't help but reflect on their relationship. It seemed like most of the time, he was asking her to hang in there. He frowned at that.

"Do you ever regret it?" he asked. "Deciding to come with me that day?"

A slow smile spread across her face. "Never," she placed her hand on his cheek. "Even now, I've never felt safer."

Razor kissed her again. He honestly didn't deserve to have this woman by his side.

~7~

Jade

You *can do this. You can fall asleep by yourself.* Jade thought to herself.

She lay on her pallet and stared at the ceiling. Tonight, she was going to fall asleep on her own. She would not need Clay's help. Jade sighed, closed her eyes, and imagined sheep jumping over a fence. Usually, this exercise always helped her sleep before. She was positive, with a little determination, Jade would be able to do it again.

One...two...three...

...once she counted up to sheep 105, Jade finally gave up on the whole exercise. She sighed with frustration and rolled over to her side. She curled herself up into a ball and held herself tightly. Jade tried to apply the same amount of pressure David used to, but she failed. So, she rocked herself back and forth and resumed her counting. Jade did all of this to no avail. She still was unable to fall asleep.

Frustrated, she rolled onto her back and glared at the ceiling again. She hated feeling like a failure. But that's precisely what she was at the moment. A complete and utter failure. It shouldn't be this hard to fall asleep. This should be a task that came naturally to her. How did she become so dependent on others to help her fall asleep?

"Don't go over to him. Don't go over to him," Jade whispered.

But the anxiety she was feeling was threatening to crush her. So, Jade walked over to Clay's sleeping area after a few minutes.

As she approached, Jade noticed that Clay was up. He was lying on his back, his hands behind his head, staring at the ceiling. It seemed like he was deep in thought about something. Jade hesitated before going any closer. But Clay noticed her lingering nearby. He smiled at her and made room for her on his pallet. Jade walked over and lay down next to him. Clay kept his eyes on the ceiling as she lay on her side, facing him.

Jade couldn't stop herself from staring at him. But it seemed like Clay didn't mind having her gaze on him. Apparently, he was too wrapped up in his thoughts to be bothered by being stared at. Jade noticed how muscular his arms were. Clay was wearing a t-shirt, but it had a snug fit. Even though he was relaxed, his biceps were bulging out of the short sleeves of his shirt. There were quite a few scars on his arms, though. Jade frowned at that. She wondered how he got all those cuts. It was a lot. And the majority of them were pretty nasty looking.

"They're souvenirs," Clay answered her unasked question. He was looking over at her with a smirk. "From when Reagan and I were out saving debtors."

"Souvenirs from DC officers," Jade kept her eyes on his arms.

"And a few bounty hunters here and there."

"You're very brave."

Clay shrugged and looked back up at the ceiling. "Just trying to do the right thing for once."

"Do you ever regret getting involved? I mean, you and Reagan came from a rich family. The both of you could be at home relaxing in comfy beds instead of laying on concrete floors with me," she teased. But she was very curious about what his answer would be.

Clay looked back over at her. This time, it was his turn to stare. And he stared deeply into Jade's eyes. She couldn't help but notice how light his brown eyes were. Getting a little uncomfortable, Jade diverted her gaze to the blankets they were lying on.

"No," he finally said. He went back to looking at the ceiling. "I like being here, fighting the good fight with you."

Jade thought about the conversation she'd had with Reagan earlier that day. She remembered how Reagan said she didn't believe Clay was in love with his ex. Only that he regretted her death. Jade wondered if that was true.

"Did you love your girlfriend? You know, the one who died?"

"No," he admitted. "Not until she was gone."

"It must've been tough to get over her death then. Being in love with her when she was no longer there."

"Somedays, I'm not sure I ever got over her."

"You haven't been with anyone since?"

"No. I couldn't find it in myself to love or be with someone else...then the world went to shit."

"Wow...I'm sorry."

"That's the way life goes sometimes."

Jade frowned. Clay still had his eyes on the ceiling. Her dream about David came to mind.

"So, umm, in my dream last night," she started. "When David and I were talking…"

"It seemed like it was more than talking going on there," Clay smirked.

Jade looked down and blushed. "It felt like he was really there," she was determined not to be sidetracked. "So, I asked if this was real, and he said he was really there." Jade looked up to read Clay's facial expression.

His face gave nothing away. Clearly, Jade had more to say, so he waited patiently for her to continue.

"Do you think he could be out there alive somewhere?"

Clay frowned and looked back up at the ceiling. "It's tough to imagine that David could've survived something like that."

Even though Jade knew the probability was low, she couldn't stop the tears from falling.

Clay glanced over at her. "I'm sorry."

Jade shook her head. "No," she quickly wiped away her tears. "Thank you for being honest with me. I just needed to know if that was real or not. It's so hard for me to tell nowadays, and that dream felt so real."

"I completely understand. Why wouldn't you want something like that to be real."

Jade nodded. She wanted so badly for that to be real. But that seemed to be too good to be true. And Jade was no longer sure if she deserved something that good. She thought about how badly she wanted to kill that girl earlier. The urge was so hard to fight off. It was a miracle that Clay was able to talk her down.

"I feel like I'm turning into a monster," she admitted.

"Nah, you can never be a monster, Jade. You're just dealing with something very unfamiliar to you. You'll find yourself eventually."

Jade smiled at him. She moved closer to him and rested her head on his chest. Clay wrapped his arms around her. She sighed. This was the feeling she longed for.

"Thanks, Clay."

"Anytime."

And almost instantly, Jade drifted off to sleep.

**

As they started their journey to Toronto the next day, Jade couldn't keep her eyes off Clay's back. They both had drawn Jackson duty, and for most of their trip, Jade admired how the sun shone on Clay's back. He was carrying the front half of Jackson's gurney while Jade took the rear. He wore a sleeveless shirt, and every now and then, Jade caught a glimpse of his back. It was nice the way the sun bounced off his tan skin. Jade couldn't stop herself from staring.

The way his braid swung back and forth while he walked also caught Jade's eyes. She recalled running her fingers through his silky, curly hair earlier that day. It was just before they left the warehouse. They all were packing their things, and she noticed him struggling to get his braid just right. Jade insisted on helping him. Clay had been so helpful to her lately; it was the least she could do. Jade admired how good his hair felt between her fingers as he sat between her legs.

The group entered an unfamiliar wooded area. Razor and Helena were leading the group. Junior and Danita were close behind them. Reagan, Keeper, and Tatianna were just ahead of Clay. And Yoko and Calvin flanked behind Jade. Calvin was counting his steps. He was the only one filling the silence.

David was waiting for her a bit ahead. He waited until she was close before he walked beside her. He smiled at her. Jade tried to keep her eyes away from him.

"57,58,59,60," Calvin counted. He only counted to 100 before he started over again, and this was his fifth time counting to 100. At least, from what Jade could remember.

She and David walked silently, side by side with each other. She tried not to think about those green eyes piercing into her soul. Jade kept her sight on the end of Clay's braid. Eventually, David followed her gaze.

"You two seem to be getting closer," he smiled.

Jade continued to avoid eye contact with him. She shrugged.

David sighed and shrugged too. "I guess you need someone to lean on, so why not Clay?"

Jade remained silent.

"I'm sorry that I lied to you," he continued. "I really want to be here with you. I hate that I left you in this hell hole all alone...but it's peaceful here. I wish you could experience it with me."

Jade watched as Clay's braid swung in between his shoulder blades.

"When are you going to tell Razor about the spy?"

Jade frowned. She didn't want to think about that right now.

"There's no way Bossman should've known we'd go to the river. And there's no way he should've known that we'd be splitting up...there *has* to be a spy here."

She hated to think that there was a potential spy among them. It would be a devastating blow. Who could betray them like that? The best-case scenario was that the spy died on the river. Besides, she wasn't sure how Razor would react to the news. Jade was already unstable. They didn't need another dangerous person in the group. And Jade was positive that Razor might lash out and start killing everybody. But one thing was sure: she knew the spy wasn't Clay...or Reagan. Her gut confirmed that. And Jade was more than relieved by that fact.

"Not now," she finally said. "We need to focus on finding Blackwell first."

David sighed and glanced around. "You're right."

"97,98,99,100...1..."

And that's when Jade heard it—a snap of a twig. She looked around, and David quickly vanished.

"Intruders!" she yelled out.

A group of people ran out from behind nearby trees and bushes. A fight quickly ensued.

"We need to put him down," Clay instructed. Yoko and Calvin were their gatekeepers, but that would only last so long. He and Jade gently placed Jackson and his gurney down on the ground.

Jade immediately took out two knives from her thigh straps as she stood guard over Jackson. She looked over to see Clay doing the same. There didn't appear to be many in the attacking group, but Jade stood firm. A girl came charging toward her. Jade waited patiently for her to get closer. Once she was an arm's length away, Jade struck. A quick slash to the gut. A fatal cut to the throat. The girl hit the ground. Blood seeped between her fingers as she desperately tried to stop the bleeding.

A few more people tried their luck with Jade, but she swiftly fought them off. Her last fight with a guy caused her to move a few feet away from Jackson's gurney. Jade saw Clay fighting when she turned to get back into her position. It was with a guy. The guy was lean and quick and managed to slice at Clay's back. Blood quickly seeped out the wound and flowed down Clay's back.

Jade screamed out in terror.

She charged at the guy and plunged her knife into his chest. The guy screamed and fell to the ground. Jade was still on him. She screamed as she took the knife out and plunged it again into the guy. And again. And again. And again. And again.

Jade could feel the blood covering her face and hands. But she kept going. It was clear that the guy was dead. But she kept going, and she kept stabbing until she blacked out.

"It's ok," Clay whispered to her. He had her wrapped in his arms.

Jade had finally come out of her volatile haze. Everyone in the group had survived. And they were all looking at her with fear and worry. She glanced over at the dead guy. His shirt was drenched in blood, and she could see the many stab wounds she'd given him. Jade looked around again. Keeper was attending to Clay's back. She noticed Clay winced a little as Keeper stitched him up. Jade squirmed in Clay's arm. He instantly tightened his hold on her. Jade could barely move.

"I'm ok," he reassured her. "I'm ok. You saved me."

Jade's breathing increased as she thought about the possibility of him dying. She needed to make sure he was all right. She needed to make sure they were all right. Jade struggled to get out of Clay's hold again but failed. His hold was firm. This only caused her to panic some more. To her surprise, Clay kissed the top of her head. It was a little shocking how that single act calmed her.

"I'm ok, Jade," he said again.

Jade finally stopped resisting and sank into him. She closed her eyes and rested her head against his chest. She could hear his heart beating. Jade sighed with relief. His heart was pounding. Clay was alive. He was really there. She couldn't take him not being there. She couldn't take any of them not being there. Jade kept her focus on his heartbeat.

The beating heart gave her a little strength. But she couldn't find it in herself to feel hopeful. At the rate they were going, their heartbeats were limited. And Jade couldn't help but feel somewhat weak and hopeless.

~8~

Jade

The bow and arrow rested gently against Jade's leg as she sat on a tree log. It was dark. And the group stopped in a wooded area to get some rest. Jade volunteered to keep watch as the others slept. Their first day on the road to Toronto was a rocky one. She began to wonder if the Radicals would ever stop attacking them. The group was relentless. Not even the DCs struck as much as the Radicals did.

Jade couldn't understand the group's agenda. Stealing supplies was one thing. But at some point, you must realize that certain supplies aren't worth the trouble. What Jade and the group had was nothing special. So, she couldn't understand why the leader, Liam, kept sending people after them. That's just more people he lost. Were their supplies really worth all that?

However, their last captive did mention how the Radicals thought they were a part of their rival group, the Black Coats, so there was that. Jade was very curious about the Black Coats and wondered what they did. If the Radicals brought chaos to the citizens, then the Black Coats had to bring peace...right? Jade was ready to get to Blackwell. She wanted all of this figured out so they could make it back across the border and deal with Bossman. The Radicals were a pest, but Bossman and the DCs were the real agenda. And they would always be the real agenda.

Someone stirred nearby. Jade looked over to see that Clay had turned over to his side. Due to the cut on his back, he received earlier; he avoided lying on it. His back was toward Jade—the back of his shirt stained with blood. Anger rose within her. Yes, the Radicals were a pest, but seeing the damage they did to those she cared about made Jade want to kill them all. She didn't want to leave without slicing their throats first. She sighed as she glanced around the woods again. Were some of them lurking nearby?

Someone else in the group stirred. This time it was Calvin. He sat up and looked around. He spotted Jade sitting on the log. He got up with his sword and walked over to her. Calvin took a seat next to her. He sighed as he rested his sword in between them.

"Can you not sleep, my knight?" Jade asked quietly.

"No, my Queen," Calvin responded in a low voice.

Jade looked over at him and smiled. "Well, I'm glad you are here by my side."

Calvin was silent for a moment. He frowned as he looked at the others sleeping. His frown deepened as he glanced around the woods. Calvin was looking for something. And Jade had a hunch about what it was. She braced herself for the question and Calvin's response to her answer. After a few seconds, Calvin looked at her. Tears were in his eyes.

"Where are the prince and princess?" he cried. He was getting frustrated again.

The thought of waking Yoko and Razor crossed Jade's mind, but she pushed it aside. She could handle Calvin on her own. She sighed and then took a deep breath. She was about to answer him when Raina and Levi appeared before her. They were smiling at her, and they looked happy and healthy. Jade couldn't help but smile back at them.

"Where have you been?" she asked them.

"Sorry," Raina answered. "We got held up somewhere else."

Jade looked over at Calvin. He was watching her with anxious eyes. "They're right here, Calvin."

"In front of the Queen?"

Jade nodded.

Calvin looked at the space in front of Jade and smiled. His eyes brightened with delight. "Can the Queen speak with them?"

Jade nodded again.

"We miss him," Raina looked at Calvin and smiled.

"I miss him calling me his prince," Levi whined.

"They miss you, Calvin."

"The knight misses protecting his prince and princess," tears fell from Calvin's eyes.

Jade brushed away a few tears that escaped her. She quickly stood and looked down at Calvin. "Come, my sweet knight. We must go and make our prince and princess strong."

Calvin quickly got to his feet and took his sword. Jade caught Clay looking at her just as they were about to walk off. He sat up and smiled.

"Go ahead. I'll keep watch until you get back."

Jade nodded, and she and Calvin walked off. Raina and Levi followed behind. Jade slowed down until they caught up to her.

"Look out for animals or people," Jade told the three of them.

"Yes, my Queen."

"People?" there was worry in Levi's voice.

"I don't want to hunt people, Jade," Raina looked alarmed.

"We're looking out for people who want to *hunt* us," Jade clarified.

Raina shook her head. "But either way, you plan to kill these people."

"I plan to defend us *against* these people."

"I won't do it, Jade. It's not me."

"Yeah," Levi chimed in. "It's not who we are."

"It's who you have to be, my little munchkins."

"Being that way makes us just as bad as the people you're trying to fight against," Raina said.

"No, being that way makes you strong. And I must make you strong."

Raina and Levi remained silent. After a few seconds, Levi began looking around for animals. Raina stared at Jade in defiance. She refused to do what Jade instructed. Jade felt herself getting annoyed. She hated the way Raina was fighting against her. Couldn't she understand that Jade just wanted to protect her? This was how she did that.

"I don't want to be strong," Raina crossed her arms and glared at Jade. "I want to be myself."

"You're doing this whether you want to or not," Jade said sternly.

To her surprise, Raina started crying hysterically. Levi quickly rushed to her side and began consoling her. He whispered to her that everything was going to be ok. And that Raina didn't have to do anything she didn't want to do.

Jade stood there fuming. Why couldn't they understand? Why didn't they grasp the severity of the situation?

"Enough already!" Jade shouted. Raina, Levi, and Calvin jumped at her sudden anger. "Don't you get it?! You have to be strong to survive in this world! And I *need* you to survive!"

Levi cowered behind Raina. Raina glared at Jade through her tears.

"You're not the same person, Jade!" she shouted. "You're mean, and I hate this new version of you! *Our* Jade would never talk to us this way! *Our* Jade would want us to be the same! She would never want to taint us! *I hate you!*"

Jade stood there, stunned by Raina's comments. She didn't think she was being mean, but how Levi cowered, and Raina looked at her told her differently. All Jade wanted was to make them stronger. If they were stronger, they could survive in this world. And that's all she wanted—was for them to have a shot.

Jade opened her mouth to say something but heard a noise from a nearby bush. A man rushed out and came charging at her. Jade quickly responded by firing off an arrow. She hit the guy in the gut, and he dropped to his knees and groaned.

More people rushed out and charged at her and Calvin.

"Shit," Jade mumbled. She had left the rest of her arrows behind. She pulled out two of her knives. "Calvin, protect the Queen!"

Calvin screamed as he swung his sword and slashed at those close to him. Jade did the same with her knives. They killed quite a few people, but more was coming at them. Jade realized that they were getting backed into a corner. But both she and Calvin kept fighting relentlessly. Calvin stayed in front of Jade—determined to protect her.

Then someone stabbed him in the shoulder, and he yelled out in pain.

"Calvin!" Jade screamed at the top of her lungs. She jumped on the girl who stabbed him, and Jade quickly stabbed her in the throat.

Someone tackled her to the ground. She coughed for air as she landed hard on her stomach. Jade attempted to push herself up, but the person placed a knee on her back. Someone else pried her knives out of her hands. Jade looked over to see about five people dogpiling Calvin.

"Get off him!" she screamed.

Someone pulled on her braids. "Shut it, bitch! You're done for."

The person on top of Jade immediately fell off her. The other person who took her knives tried to run off, but Jade grabbed his ankle and caused him to fall. Once he hit the ground, she was swiftly on him. She managed to get one of her knives from him and stabbed him repeatedly. It wasn't until she got to her feet that she realized an arrow had killed the guy who was on her back.

Jade rushed over to help Calvin. She stabbed the people who were on him, and then she immediately applied pressure to his stab wound.

"It's ok, Calvin," she assured. "You're going to be ok, my brave knight."

Jade glanced around and saw the group of Radicals being chased off by people in black coats and jackets. This had to be the rival group she had heard about, and Jade was instantly relieved.

Once the last Radical member was gone, the rival group turned their attention to her.

"Are you all right?" a girl asked.

"Please, someone help him," Jade pleaded. "He's hurt."

The girl nodded as she glanced at Calvin's shoulder. "We need the doc."

"You're needed, doc!" someone shouted.

People began to part as someone walked forward. And there he was—Blackwell. He was a tall, lean man, and his head was bald, and he had a salt-and-pepper beard. He looked at Jade and Calvin and smiled. Jade glanced down at his left hand, and a black prosthetic hand was present.

"You're safe now," he kneeled beside Jade. "I'm Dr. Cole Blackwell, leader of the Black Coats, and I'm here to help you."

"I'm Jade."

He smiled even wider. "I know who you are, Jade. I've heard so much about you. Tell me, are my old friends Razor and Helena nearby?"

Jade's eyes widen in shock. How much did Blackwell actually know?

~9~

Razor

It *can't be her. It can't be her. It can't be her.* That's all Razor thought as he, Helena, Clay, Yoko, and Reagan ran toward the screams. The screams were far apart. The first scream was a male's voice. It had awakened Razor. At first, he thought he was dreaming, but then he heard another scream. This time it was a female's voice, and he could've sworn it sounded like Jade.

Razor's heart dropped when he got up and didn't see Jade sitting on the log. She was sitting there when he fell asleep, but Clay was there now. And Clay was standing up, glaring in a direction that led further into the woods. Razor immediately marched over to him.

"Where is she?"

"She and Calvin went for a walk a few minutes ago," Clay shifted back and forth uneasily.

"Are the screams coming from that direction?" Razor demanded. He was trying hard not to panic, but Clay's antsiness and Jade's absence weren't comforting.

Clay nodded.

Razor quickly woke everyone up and told them what was going on. Helena, Yoko, Clay, and Reagan volunteered to go with him while the others stayed back and stayed on alert.

They began walking in the direction Jade and Calvin walked off in when they heard another scream. Razor took off running, and the others swiftly followed suit. Helena was right on his tail, followed by Clay.

"There!" Helena pointed. There was a group dressed in all black just ahead. She swiftly pulled out her knives—ready for battle.

Razor slowed down a little. "Pull back, Helena," the group was large in numbers and looked like they could put up a good fight.

Helena slowed down but shot him a look. Razor's instincts were right. The group immediately turned toward them, armed and ready to fight. Razor and the others came to a halt. He spotted Jade sitting on the ground in the center of the group. So did Clay. He quickly pushed his way through and got to her.

"Jade," he was quickly by her side. He looked her over, making sure she wasn't hurt. Then he hugged her and kissed her forehead.

"I'm ok," but sadness dripped through her voice.

Razor frowned at their interaction. It seemed like Clay was getting closer and closer to Jade, and he wasn't sure how he felt about that.

"My old friends," a familiar voice greeted from the group's center. "Step aside and let them through."

"Cole!" Helena rushed to the center to hug him.

"Beautiful Helena, it's so nice to see you again."

Razor watched as they greeted each other. Blackwell still looked the same, even after all these years. The only difference was the black prosthetic hand.

Once they were done hugging, Blackwell looked over at Razor and smiled. "You look stressed, my old friend."

"You have no idea, but I'm glad to see you finally," Razor looked around again. This time he noticed Calvin lying on the ground, Jade sitting beside him, and it appeared that he was stabbed in the shoulder.

"Calvin!" Yoko rushed to his side, crying. "What happened?!"

"We were ambushed," Jade spoke in a low tone. Her eyes were blank, and she looked drained. "There were a lot of them this time. We got cornered, and Calvin was determined to protect me, and he got stabbed for it. They had us pinned down before Cole came."

Razor was furious at how close he lost Jade. The Radicals and their leader needed to be dealt with.

"He's fine," Cole reassured. "I just finished patching him up."

"It's all my fault," Jade suddenly cried. "I saw Raina and Levi, and I had Calvin follow me. I nearly got him killed because I can't keep my *shit* together...he can't be left alone with me. I'm too unstable."

Helena rushed to her sister's side. She hugged her tightly.

"It's not your fault, Jade," Yoko said. "It's these damn Radicals."

"Thank you, but I still don't think he should be alone with me."

"Agreed, Jade," Razor looked over at Blackwell and the group with him. "Sorry, I couldn't get here sooner. But it looks like you've been busy."

"That's all right...and of course, I had to do something about the Radicals."

Razor nodded. He looked down at the ground as he prepared to unleash the bad news on the doc. Razor took a deep breath.

"I need to apologize to you, Cole," he looked up to see Cole looking at him, confused. "I went rogue on the mission. I tried to oppose Nick myself and ended up getting many people hurt and killed...your children included."

Cole frowned. There were two different looks on his face, pain and disappointment. "I know about that."

Razor looked utterly shocked. "How?"

"I have spies out there," Cole smiled weakly. "Mostly in Michigan, New York, and D.C."

Razor raised an eyebrow.

"I had to know what was going on."

"I truly am sorry, Cole."

Blackwell sighed. "I don't blame you for what happened, Razor. I knew that could be their fate long ago, and I've made peace with that."

"Still, I promised to look after them and failed to do it properly."

"You have a lot on your plate. It's foolish to think you can save everyone."

"Well, it appears that Jackson has survived the encounter. He's unconscious but alive."

Blackwell looked at Razor with wide eyes. He could see the tears threatening to fall from Cole's eyes. "Are you serious?"

Razor nodded.

"Take me to him."

Razor looked at everyone in his group. Jade, Helena, and Clay stood from the ground. Yoko and Clay helped Calvin to his feet. Reagan took the lead and began guiding everyone back to their camping grounds. Jade held onto Clay's arm as they walked back. Razor could see how tight her grip was. He could tell she was struggling to determine if they were all there. Yoko had her arm wrapped around Calvin. Seeing someone as big as Calvin leaning against someone as small as Yoko was odd. But Yoko had always been a mother figure to Calvin, despite the apparent age difference. Helena kept pace with him and Cole.

"So, this Radical group," Razor began in a hushed tone. "How long have they been around?"

"Since the beginning, my friend," Cole sighed.

"They're relentless."

"You have no idea."

"Have you met this Liam person?"

"A few times when I tried to broker a peace treaty between everyone."

"I guess it didn't work out."

"Liam isn't the type to play well with those who won't join him."

"Well, we need to do something about him. We can't keep going on like this."

"In due time, my friend."

The campsite quickly appeared. Razor heard Reagan warn the others that they had guests. When everyone got into view, he saw that Tatianna, Danita, and Junior were keeping watch while Keeper was watching over Jackson. Keeper dabbed Jackson's forehead with a wet cloth when he finally looked up. He froze when he saw Blackwell.

"Cole?" he said in disbelief.

Razor knew that a part of Keeper still didn't believe that Blackwell was alive, even though Razor had assured him plenty of times. But Razor couldn't blame him. The rumor had been very convincing.

Cole ran over to him and embraced him tightly. "Keeper! I'm so happy to see you!"

"Ya really are alive."

"I am," Cole released him. "Thanks to Razor and Helena."

"I'm glad they've kept ya that way," Keeper looked down at Jackson. "Because I think ya the only one who can help him."

A look of sadness covered Cole's face as he kneeled next to his son.

Keeper kneeled beside him.

"I've done everything I could," Keeper explained. "But I don't think that's enough. I'm not sure if there's anything internally wrong or what. I've just been keeping him at a stable level."

"You've done great, Keeper," Cole lightly touched Jackson's forehead. "No fever, that's good...how long has he been out?"

"Eight days."

"Any motor skills?"

"Every now and then. A twitch of a hand, finger, or leg."

Cole nodded and looked around at everyone in the camp. His eyes fell on Razor.

"Where was he hit?"

Razor was hoping he didn't ask that. He didn't think giving the doc the grueling details of his children's death would be a good idea.

"Execution style," Razor reluctantly admitted.

"But we think Jackson moved his head in time that the shot wasn't fatal," Keeper added.

Cole nodded and rose to his feet. Keeper followed. Cole motioned for two members to lift Jackson's gurney. Two of them quickly obeyed.

"We'll learn more once we get him back to headquarters," he looked at Razor. "I suggest you all pack your things now. Liam will be sending another group out to this location. You've all stirred quite a ruckus since you've been here, my friend."

"How? They started it," Jade complained.

Cole smiled at her. "I'll explain all of it along the way, but we need to move out right now."

Razor glanced around at them all. "You've heard the man. Let's move out."

The group began to gather up all their things. Razor watched how

Junior eyed Cole. He was surprised that the doc was alive, and Razor knew he'd be moving to alert Nick soon. He really needed to keep a tighter watch on Junior from here on out.

Cole walked over to Razor. "Now is the time for war, my friend."

"Yeah," Razor looked at Cole's newly assembled group. The man had a knack for building a following. "But which of our enemies should we attack first?"

"That, my friend, is the million-dollar question."

~10~

Nick

You're *not drowning. You're not drowning.* Nick repeated over and over in his head. But no matter how often he said it, his brain told the rest of his body that he was, and it reacted instinctively. Although he could feel the wet cloth on his face, Nick's body was convinced it was drowning. It frustrated and angered him that his body was behaving so weakly. He didn't want to give Chase and his guards the satisfaction of knowing they were getting to him. But mentally, they weren't. Nick's body wasn't showing that.

"Enough," Chase sighed.

One of the guards stopped pouring water on the cloth covering Nick's face, and Nick inhaled deeply and immediately coughed up the water he mistakenly breathed in. The guard removed the material from his face while the other guards released their hold on his arms and legs. Nick leaned to his side and spat up water. A few of the guards laughed at him. But Nick laughed too.

"Is that all you pussies got?" Nick spat on the floor.

"I would watch how you talk to me," Chase glared.

"Why? I'm a dead man already, aren't I?"

Chase folded his arms and continued to glare at Nick.

Nick laughed again. "I would've thought you'd be a little more creative, but torturing was never your forte...remind me again, what exactly are you trying to torture out of me, Mr. President?"

Chase frowned at him but remained silent.

"That's what I thought. You have no clue what you're doing."

"I want you to know who's in charge here!" Chase snapped.

Nick smirked. "Really? And who might that be, Mr. President?" he was getting under Chase's skin. Nick could see it, and he found it amusing.

Chase looked over at one of his guards, and they immediately punched Nick in the face. Nick laughed as he spat blood in the guard's face. Another guard responded by trying to hit him, but Nick ducked and jumped on him. Nick pried his thumbs into the guard's eyes. The guard screamed and squirmed in pain. The squishiness of the guard's eyes brought comfort to Nick. And the warmness of his blood gave Nick a relief of satisfaction.

"Restrain him!" Chase shouted.

Nick laughed as the guards pulled him off their comrade. The man's screams stopped. Nick knew he was dead.

"Again! Torture him again!" Chase was desperately trying to regain control. The guards slammed Nick back on the torture table, and they held onto his arms and legs tightly.

"Who's in control here, Mr. President?" he taunted as the cloth was replaced on his face. Water was immediately poured on it. Nick laughed and coughed up water until he passed out.

**

When he came to, he was back in the chair. His hands were handcuffed behind his back. Nick laughed as his head hung low. It was no telling how long he'd been there in the torture room, but he could tell he was wearing Chase down. He didn't get the point of all this. Why not just kill him? That was the most straightforward solution here. Why keep him alive? Chase was well aware of what kind of man he was. There was no way Nick was going down without a fight. Chase had the rare chance of having the upper hand on Nick. He needed to take advantage of it while he could.

Nick glanced around the dark room. He sighed once he spotted them still huddled up in the corner. He thought they would've been gone by now. He prayed that they would. This was no place for them. And it certainly wasn't something they should be seeing.

"What are you still doing here?" he demanded.

"You're still here," Raina said as if it was obvious.

"We can't leave you here, Dad."

"Go. I'm completely fine here on my own."

"You don't look fine," Levi contradicted.

Nick could feel his mouth bleeding. He smiled. "Hazards of the job, my boy."

"You have to get out of here, Dad."

"No."

Raina stepped up a little. "Do you want to die?"

Nick avoided looking at her. It was so hard to look at any of them. They truly were innocent. And for some reason, innocence scared him.

Aiden looked at him in disgust. "That's such a cowardly thing to do."

"You have to live with what you did to us."

Nick briefly glanced at Levi. "I can't," he sighed.

"Too bad, Dad."

"I thought you said you loved Jade," Raina frowned at him.

"I do."

"Then why are you planning to die here today?"

"I never said I was planning to die!"

"Then why are you still here, Nick? We all know you could've escaped by now."

Nick sighed. Raina wouldn't let up, although he couldn't blame her. He deserved everything she was giving him after what he did to her. But still. He just wasn't in the mood for them.

"Go away."

Levi laughed. "Never."

"You should know that we'll never go away," Raina smirked at him. "We're here to haunt you forever."

"Now get your lazy ass up and get us out of here, Dad!"

Nick sighed. These children were exhausting. He just wanted to be left alone, but his past sins refused to let him do that.

"Find me something to pick these handcuffs with."

The children finally left the corner and began looking around the room. Raina looked over the table for something while the boys examined the floor. Raina picked something off the table, and Aiden found something on the floor.

"How's this, Dad?" he held it before Nick's face. It was a prong from a belt buckle.

"It's too big."

"What about this?" Raina held up a nail. It looked like a thin wire nail.

"That might work," Nick said. "Put it in my hand."

Raina dropped the nail in his hand. She backed away and joined the boys. Of course, Nick knew Raina didn't give him the nail. He had swiped it from the table a long time ago. Nick just went along with his hallucinations. It was easier that way.

The children huddled together and watched Nick expectantly. He instantly got annoyed. Why were they so impatient? Didn't they understand that these things take time? He fiddled with the nail a bit. He needed to bend it a little to pick the lock. That was easier said than done. The nail was much sturdier than a bobby pin or a paper clip.

Nick pressed down on the nail as hard as he could. The handcuffs were tight on him. It hurt to move his wrist. He continued to press on the nail. It was giving way, but just a little. The tip of his thumb started to bleed, along with his wrist. The more he moved his hands, the more the cuffs dug into his skin. But he ignored all of that. He focused on the scared, worried look on the children's faces. That was his motivation. That was the only way he would escape since they refused to leave him.

Raina turned her head to the door in a panic. She looked at the others.

"You have to hurry, Dad," Aiden whispered.

"I'm going as fast as I can," Nick sighed. "And stop whispering. No one can hear you but me."

"Hurry, Nick," Levi pleaded. "You might not survive this round."

Nick chuckled. "Trust me, my boy. It doesn't matter what they do. I'll survive it."

"Every man bleeds, Nick," Raina warned. "And every heart stops beating."

"Enough with the guru bullshit. Unless one of you can uncuff me, please, shut the hell up."

"There's no need to be mean, Dad."

"Yeah, you've proven that when you killed us," Levi chimed in.

Nick immediately stopped working on the handcuffs. Levi's words hit him hard for some reason. Just then, the door to the torture room opened. Chase and his guards reentered the room. This time the children didn't huddle up in the corner. Instead, they remained in front of him. Nick stared into their big, innocent eyes. It felt like he was punched hard in the gut. How could he do that to them?

"I'm so sorry," he cried unexpectedly. "I shouldn't have killed you the way I did."

Chase froze in his tracks—surprised by what Nick said. One of the guards laughed.

"Finally losing it, Nicky?"

"No one gives a shit about your sorry-ass apology," another guard spat. They were clearly still angry about Nick killing one of them.

"You children deserved a more peaceful death," Nick cried, ignoring those around them.

"Then why didn't you give us that?" Raina asked. "I was already dying anyway. You could've just let my disease take me."

Nick looked away. She looked too much like Helena, who, in turn, looked like Jade. And he wasn't sure if he could face her anymore.

"I needed to free her," he whispered. But now he wasn't so sure.

"But I told you, Dad," Aiden frowned at him. "You didn't free her. You drove her into madness."

"I know, my son," Nick admitted. How could Jade not be driven into madness? Nick was after Aiden's death. He's been talking to his dead son for years. How could she not be doing the same?

"Nick?" Chase was alarmed.

Nick looked up at him and smiled. "Is another round of torture about to begin, Mr. President?"

"Who are you talking to, Nick?"

"Why, you, of course," he frowned.

"I'm not your son."

"I didn't call you my son. I never even said Aiden's name."

Chase frowned at him. A look of worry covered his face. Nick very stealthily kept trying to pick the lock.

"He's finally breaking, Mr. President," one of the guards said.

Chase raised an eyebrow. "So it seems."

"What do you want us to do next?" the guard asked.

Chase paused. It looked like he was deciding on what he wanted to do. Nick chuckled under his breath. He knew that Chase didn't have a plan. All of this was just a show. A stroke of his ego. He had to prove to Nick that he was in charge. But it was all bull. Chase wouldn't have sought out Nick's counsel throughout his career if he were really in charge.

The new medical law would be nothing if Nick didn't encourage to form a task force to help enforce it. Medical care would be nonexistent if it weren't for him. And the government officials would have never approved the DC task force if Nick didn't persuade them otherwise. Chase would be nothing without him. And if he got rid of Nick, then Chase would be getting rid of himself.

"Do you need some suggestions, Mr. President?" Nick teased.

"Fuck you, Nick."

Nick laughed. No one noticed him picking the lock. Blood from his wrist was dripping down his hands. No one seemed to notice that either. The lock from his right hand clicked. Nick smiled in satisfaction. He gripped the nail tightly, contemplating whom he'd stab first with it.

Then the room door opened again. One of Chase's aides rushed in. He looked worried and afraid. The aide rushed to Chase's side and whispered in his ear. Nick noticed how the aide glanced his way. Could he tell that he picked his handcuff? Then Chase's face turned beet red as he nodded vigorously at whatever the aide told him. Now was the time for Nick to make his move. He was just about to stab the guard closest to him when Chase glared at him.

"Blackwell is still alive!" he shouted.

Nick paused and then roared with laughter. This wasn't news to him. He knew Razor didn't kill Blackwell when he showed them the chopped-off hand. It was so obvious. But, wherever he was, Blackwell had been lying low that Nick wasn't concerned about him. Blackwell was a threat to Chase, not him. Honestly, he was surprised that Chase believed Razor's bullshit story.

Bright side, Nick was grateful that his spy was still working for him. That was the only reason they were made aware of this news. His spy had traveled over to Canada with Jade and the others. He wondered if the spy would still risk their neck for him. Apparently, they were. This was a good parting gift for him. Now he knew where to look for Blackwell. That was whom he needed to take Chase down.

It was very satisfying knowing that his end would also be Chase's end. It was fitting. The two men rose together. So, why not fall together too?

Nick finally composed himself and immediately went for the guard closest to him. He jammed the nail into his neck, twisted it, and pulled it out. Blood squirted out everywhere as the guard choked on his blood. The aide screamed out in horror and ran for the exit. Nick went for the next guard. He stabbed his hand and took the baton from the guard's belt. Nick swung the baton hard across the man's skull. He heard a crack as he hit the floor.

The children quickly cowered in the corner.

Chase immediately sought refuge behind another guard. "Kill him! Kill him now!"

Nick swiftly retrieved a knife from one of the dead guards as another charged at him. He had just gotten to his feet when he plunged it into the guard's gut. Blood oozed down his hand. He always found the warmth of it oddly satisfying. There was only one guard left, and he stood guarding Chase. Nick smiled at him as he pulled out the knife.

The aide had finally got the door open when Nick threw the knife and struck him in the back. The aide dropped to the floor.

"Get me out of here!" Chase demanded.

The guard glared at Nick. "Leave now, Mr. President. I'll deal with this sad sac-of-shit."

Chase rushed to the door. Nick let him leave. Now wasn't the time for him. Besides, Chase was now guardless. It wouldn't take much to kill him now.

The two men charged at each other. The guard went for Nick's waist. But Nick kneed him in the gut and elbowed him in the back. The guard dropped to the floor, and Nick was immediately on his back. He wrapped his arm around the guard's neck and applied as much pressure as possible. The guard thrashed around as he struggled for air, but Nick stayed on him. After a while, he slammed the guard's head against the floor. Nick didn't stop until he heard a crack and felt blood on his hands. Confident that the guard was no longer breathing, Nick rose breathlessly to his feet.

"Is it safe to open our eyes now?" Levi asked.

Nick sighed as he retrieved the dead guards' weapons. "They shouldn't have been closed in the first place."

"Jade always made us close our eyes," Raina defended. It was amazing how she acted like a big sister to *both* him and Aiden.

"Well, she should've made you both look."

"Would that have saved us?" Levi asked curiously.

"Probably not," he reluctantly admitted.

"Then what was the harm in closing them, Dad?"

Nick sighed again as he looked at them. They were never going away. "Come, children. I'm going to show you how to survive in this world."

"How?" Raina demanded.

Nick briefly looked into her eyes. "By finding Blackwell."

~11~

Jade

They were traveling all through the night. The sun was just about to rise, and Jade could see the faint pink-orange color across the sky. The group had traveled silently, with nothing but Calvin's counting. Jade was relieved and thankful that he was still being himself. She felt so guilty about what happened. But Calvin didn't seem to mind his injury. He was protecting his Queen. At the end of the day, he was doing his knightly duties.

Jade saw the need to stick by him through their travel. Yoko had her arm linked to his, so Jade knew he was perfectly safe and fine. But she needed to be near him. Clay held onto her hand during their journey. She was very thankful for that. She found herself squeezing it every now and then when she wasn't so sure what was real. He always sent her confirmation by squeezing her hand back.

Helena and Razor stayed close to Cole. They were talking amongst each other in hushed tones. Jade was utterly shocked that he knew about her. That he knew everything that was going on with them. When Razor first announced that Cole was alive, Jade was furious. They could've had his help a long time ago. And with Cole running around, maybe Bossman wouldn't have been so obsessed with her. And maybe, just maybe, Raina, Levi, and David would be alive. But who could've really known? Perhaps nothing would've changed at all. But still, Jade couldn't help but wonder.

She watched the way Helena interacted with him. Cole seemed to really respect her. For some reason, Jade felt odd. She had never seen her sister in such an authoritative position. Of course, she knew that Helena had to have some power as a DC officer. But it was still strange to see. Even after the numerous fights she'd seen Helena in, Jade still viewed her sister as a meek, innocent little being. It was hard to shake.

One of Cole's members brushed past her. Jade looked over at him. He smiled apologetically at her. Jade glanced around at the other members of the Black Coats. Cole seemed to have a habit of accumulating followers wherever he went. She wondered how he managed to stay off Bossman's radar for so long. But he appeared to be a good leader. How his followers looked at him when he spoke immediately told her that. And they were hell-bent on protecting him even though it was clear he didn't need any help.

Cole suddenly stopped walking and looked at the sky. "I have a safe house coming up. We should stop and rest there for the day."

"Day?" Jade asked. "Shouldn't we be in a hurry to get Jackson back to your headquarters?"

"Yes, *safely*," Cole said. "We're too big of a group to travel during the day. It leaves us vulnerable. We should only travel during the night.”

“He has a point,” Razor confirmed.

“How far is your safe house from here?” Helena asked.

“We just passed the Windsor airport, so 1.9 km…or a little over a mile,” Cole smiled at their blank faces.

“All right, let’s get there,” Razor said anxiously.

Everyone resumed their walking. Jade noticed the strange way Razor was looking at Junior. It made her very curious. She wondered if he had done something wrong. How Razor looked at Junior made her think he was ready to kill him.

Clay squeezed her hand, and Jade looked over at him.

“You ok?” he smiled.

“Yeah,” she smiled back at him. “Just getting a little tired.”

“Well, good thing we only have a mile to go before we can rest.”

Jade nodded.

They walked in silence for a moment. Jade couldn’t help but notice how awkward it suddenly got between them. She wasn’t sure why that was or what made it change. But when she looked over at Clay, he looked embarrassed. He glanced over at her, and they locked eyes. He gave her a weak smile.

“I’m sorry if I overstepped a boundary back there.”

Jade frowned at him. She was utterly confused by his sudden apology. And she had no clue what he was referring to.

“When I kissed you on your forehead back there,” he explained. “I’m sorry about that.”

Jade’s frown deepened. She hadn’t even registered that because she was so out of it. She was so distraught about Calvin’s injury that she didn’t even notice what Clay had done. She remembered him rushing over to console her, but she didn’t remember the kiss. Jade looked at him and shrugged.

"There's no need for an apology, Clay. You didn't overstep."

He nodded. "Still, I just wanted to put that out there...I was just so relieved. Hearing your screams like that frightened me."

"I'm sorry for frightening you," Jade sighed. "I swear, one of these days, I'm going to get my shit together."

"Don't worry about it. In due time, you'll be yourself once again."

Jade nodded, but once again felt nearly impossible. It felt like she was always going to be in a state of uncertainty. She looked over at him and gave him a grateful smile. He smiled back and looked away. But Jade's eyes lingered on him a bit longer. Then she noticed Clay slowing down, so instinctively, she slowed down too. She finally understood what caused the slow down when she followed his gaze. They were coming up on a huge shopping center. And from the way Cole was leading them, they were heading in.

"Umm, is this where the safe house is?" Clay asked skeptically.

Cole turned around and smiled at him. "It most certainly is, my friend."

"It doesn't seem like the best place to have a safe house," Jade looked around, feeling exposed. She noticed Razor and Helena doing the same thing.

"Trust me, Jade. This is one of the safest places for us right now."

Jade didn't say anything. She just nodded. She trusted that Cole knew what he was talking about. He wouldn't have lasted this long or managed to form a group if he didn't. Cole led them to one of the biggest stores in the shopping center. The store was called Real Canadian Superstore. It was surprising how intact the store was. Of course, there were noticeable damages, but unlike the other stores in the shopping center, it was apparent that someone was keeping the place up.

Cole stopped at the door, knocking on it in a specific rhythmic pattern.

It was a coded knock. Someone on the other side of the door responded by knocking on the door in the same way. After a few seconds, it opened, and a stunning woman appeared on the other side. She smiled brightly as she stepped aside. She glanced at everyone as they slowly walked in.

"I see you've found them, doc," she greeted.

"I did," Cole smiled and looked at the group. "Everyone, this is Zara. She's my second in command here."

Jade couldn't help but stare at her. Zara looked young, maybe in her early 20s...*maybe*. And she was beyond beautiful. She had dark chocolate skin, high cheekbones, full lips, a wide nose, and a shaved head with interesting tattoo symbols on each side. On one side, there was a symbol that looked like a dart board. Three circles were circling each other. Each circle was bigger than the last one. Then on the other side of her head were two swords that looked like boomerangs, clashing against one another. Jade remembered learning about these swords in her history class. They were commonly used in World War I. She believed they were called kukri. It was obvious that these tattoos held some meaning. Jade just wondered what it was.

"I've been with Cole since he crossed over," she smiled.

Cole walked up to her and gently touched her shoulder. "Zara, my son Jackson is alive, but we must get him to our headquarters quickly."

Zara quickly glanced at the members who were carrying in Jackson's gurney. Jackson was still unconscious.

"I can assemble a team to leave out ahead of us," she said quickly. "I can radio ahead and tell the team to be ready for his arrival."

Cole shook his head. "I don't want to leave my son again."

"But you said he needs aide quickly."

"I'm confident you'll get us there in great timing," Cole smiled.

Zara nodded her head and locked eyes with Jade. Jade didn't realize it, but her mouth hung open from staring. She immediately closed it. Zara smiled at her.

"I can show you where you'll be resting."

Jade cleared her throat. "Umm, thank you."

"Yes," Cole turned to face her. "You all should get some rest. Especially you and Calvin. There's a nice spot for you upstairs."

"I'll join you," Helena quickly chimed in. She discreetly pushed Clay aside and claimed her place next to Jade.

Zara smiled. "Great, right this way."

Jade shot Helena a look, but she just smiled at her. Jade couldn't help but laugh under her breath at Helena's overprotectiveness. She glanced around as they walked up the stairs. The store was picked clean. The supplies there were things that Cole and his group brought. But the place was clean and suitable to be lived in. Jade wondered how much fighting they had to endure to keep this place. She guessed a lot.

Zara stopped in front of a room resembling the manager's office. "Here we are," she opened the door to reveal a small room with two cots.

Jade slowly walked inside. The room had no windows. For some reason, it made her feel claustrophobic.

"It's very...cozy," Helena said as she glanced around.

"Well, it serves its use," Zara smirked. "I've got the best sleep of my life in this room."

"It'll do," Jade assured her. Although, she was confident she'd have a hard time sleeping in this room.

"Great, I'll wake you when it's feeding time."

"Thanks," Helena smiled.

Zara left out the room without saying anything else. Once the door was closed, Helena turned to her.

"I didn't think we'd find Cole this soon."

"Finally, some good luck," Jade sat on a cot and slowly untied her boots. "Did you have to be so mean to Clay?"

Helena frowned as she sat on the other cot. "I wasn't being mean," she focused on untying her boots too. "Besides, it's my job to be there for you."

"He was just being helpful, Helena," Jade sighed. She really didn't understand what Helena's problem with Clay was. Jade pulled off her jacket and took off her combat nebulizer mask.

"Still...David's only been gone a little over a week, and Clay is already making his move. It's tacky and disrespectful."

Jade paused and then frowned. "That's what you think he's doing?"

Helena shrugged. "I just don't like it," she mumbled.

"Helena," Jade sighed. "Trust me, that's not what's going on. He just knows what I'm going through. That's all."

"Just be careful."

Jade rolled her eyes. "Yes, Mother."

"Anyway," Helena pulled off her jacket. "I think you shouldn't be left alone...after this last incident."

"I think you're right," she sighed. "At least until I get my shit together...that really was a close call."

Helena nodded.

"My only request is that you have Reagan or Clay look after me."

Helena rolled her eyes. "Razor and I are perfectly capable of doing that ourselves."

"I don't want to be a burden to you, Helena."

"And I don't want to smother you," Helena retorted. "But we're family. And we're supposed to look after each other."

Jade sighed. She could see that Helena was going to be stubborn about this. Although, Jade did appreciate it. Helena felt a sense of loyalty to David, and she was fighting against anyone who opposed that. Jade had to respect that.

She took her scarf from her back pocket and wrapped it around her neck. Even after all this time, Jade still found the need to keep it close to her. It made her feel safe.

Jade lay on her back and attempted to fall asleep. Even after being up all night, she was finding it difficult to fall asleep. She tossed and turned on her cot for a while. She was getting frustrated. She was about to call it quits when Helena came over and lay beside her.

"Like this?" she asked as she wrapped her arms around her sister.

"Tighter, please," Jade sighed.

Helena held her tighter.

"Thank you."

"That's what I'm here for."

Jade smiled. She was happy to have her sister still. After a few minutes, Jade fell asleep.

**

The whole room was shaking when Jade woke up. She almost fell off her cot. Helena was rushing to gather up all their things. She threw Jade her combat mask, and Jade quickly put it on—along with her jacket. She had her boots in her hands when Razor and Clay rushed in.

"We need to get out now," Razor demanded. "The whole damn building is about to crash down."

They all made their way out the door and to the stairs. Clay lingered to help Jade because she kept losing her balance. Razor and Helena were halfway down the stairs. Clay went ahead of her a little. He was making his way down the stairs. Jade held onto the handrail to keep her balance as she slowly descended. The building shook even more violently. The stairs started to crumble underneath her feet. Razor, Helena, and Clay made it safely down to the bottom of the steps. Jade was halfway down the staircase when it crumbled. Razor, Helena, and Clay screamed her name.

Thankfully, Jade grabbed onto the handrailing just in time. She held on tightly, but it was moments away from being ripped out of the wall. Jade dreaded falling down the two stories. She probably wouldn't die but was positive she'd be severely injured. Her boots slipped out of her hand. Jade made the mistake of looking down. There was a loud thud as her shoes dropped to the ground. Jade couldn't help but envision herself being next. There was a ledge just above her. All Jade needed to do was pull herself up to it. She proceeded to do that when David reached over it and held out his hand.

"Come on, Jade," he said as he reached down to her. "Just grab my hand."

Jade nodded as she reached her hand out to his. She placed it firmly in his hand before she let go of the railing. Then his hand disappeared, and all Jade felt was air. Her scream was caught in her throat as she felt herself falling.

"Jade!" Helena shrieked.

Then something hard hit Jade's side as she was in midair. Someone grabbed her tightly. The next thing she saw was a sword being plunged into the wall. Jade slipped from the person's hold but was immediately caught by the wrist. She looked up to see Zara struggling to keep her grip on Jade.

"Just...hold...on...Jade," she gritted.

Jade locked onto Zara's wrist. She held on for dear life. The building continued to shake. Jade kept her eyes on the sword. She prayed that it would hold. Thankfully, the wall was concrete, so there was that. But still, it could only hold for so long.

After a few minutes of holding on and praying silently, the earthquake finally subsided.

"Grab ahold, ladies," Cole called out as he threw a rope across a ledge nearby. He, Tatianna, Keeper, Yoko, and a couple of members held on to the rope with Calvin as their anchor.

"You...first...Jade," Zara said as she gently swung her.

Jade quickly caught on to the rope and then reached out for Zara. She firmly took Jade's hand. She paused for a moment to get her sword out of the wall. Jade slowly climbed up the rope, with Zara following closely behind. Cole quickly helped her over the ledge, and Tatianna helped her to her feet.

"Thank you for saving me," Jade turned to Zara.

Zara got to her feet. "Don't worry about it."

Cole promptly pulled the rope up and began wrapping it. "We need to move quickly, Zara, before the ambulances start making their rounds."

Zara nodded and grabbed Jade's hand. "Let's head out."

They all followed Zara, who was rushing. Jade didn't understand the urgency. And she didn't understand Cole's comment about the ambulances.

When she reached the ground floor, Razor, Helena, and Clay immediately rushed to her.

"I'm ok," Jade held up her hand before they got any closer. "I'm ok. I just lost my grip."

Helena ignored her protests and examined Jade from head to toe. Once she was satisfied, she handed Jade her boots. Jade swiftly put them on.

"Grab everything that you can!" Cole ordered. "They'll be here soon."

Jade glanced around and saw how panicked all the Black Coats members were. She didn't understand it.

"Who'll be here soon? The ambulances?" Jade asked.

"Yes, a big part of the Radicals," Cole said as he gathered up some things that were on the ground.

"I don't get it," Helena chimed in. "They drive around in ambulances?"

"When everything went downhill, the Radicals took over many hospitals," Zara explained.

Razor frowned. "There had to be a lot of people to do that. Were there a lot of them already?"

"Apparently, they were a gang. And Liam was the leader of it," Zara quickly looked around for any valuables she had missed.

"Liam was always a bright young man," Cole added. "He saw early on how valuable the healthcare system and its resources would be in these times. So, he gathered up more people in his gang, and they hit some major hospitals. They managed to get more people on their side, and as resources started depleting, they began using ambulances to rob people."

"How?" Jade still didn't understand the use of them.

Zara paused. She turned around and looked at Jade. "I learned the hard way what they meant the day after my father, and I fled here from New York. There was an earthquake, and my father seriously got injured trying to save me. Once it subsided, the ambulances started making their rounds...I was so relieved when I saw them," her voice cracked.

Jade's heart raced. She knew that this story was going to be bad.

"Imagine my horrific surprise when a group of menacing, armed men came jumping out of the truck..."

"They sexually assaulted you, didn't they?" Tatianna demanded as she stepped up next to Jade. Anger was behind her voice, and Jade completely understood where it came from.

Zara nodded. "...right in front of my father. And they took everything we had once they were finished."

Helena gasped in horror.

"And that's only half of it," Cole said quietly. "So, we need to move."

Jade couldn't fight off the rage she was feeling toward this group. And by the look of Helena and Tatianna, they both felt the same way. Jade vowed to make their deaths painful—whenever she crossed paths with them.

"But you'd think after all this time, people would know about the scam," Yoko said.

Zara shook her head. "New people manage to flee here just about every day. And they've all heard the rumors about this place being the promised land. And because of this, they're still able to do it. And a lot of innocent people fall victim to them."

Cole looked around. "Do we have everything?"

Zara nodded. And so did everyone else.

"Then let's head out."

The group slowly made their way out of the store. Jade glanced around the shopping center. All the buildings still stood, but they were severely damaged. They went through the parking lot, with members actively looking out. A few members hurriedly carried Jackson's gurney through the parking lot.

Then they abruptly stopped.

"Radicals!" one of them called out.

"Three ambulances are heading this way!"

Jade pulled out her knives as Zara unsheathed another sword and growled. Both women were prepared for battle.

~12~

Razor

It took him a moment to respond as he watched Jade, Zara, Helena, and Tatianna meet a group of Radicals head-on. The women were vicious and quick. He saw their rage when the new girl, Zara, mentioned that a group of them sexually assaulted her. It didn't take a rocket scientist to figure out that these women would make sure the group would feel their wrath from here on out.

Razor watched as Jade plunged her knife into a guy's gut, twisted it, and yanked it out. Then Zara followed up by nearly taking his head off with her sword. The two women moved as one. Jade made the first attack, and then Zara finished them off. Razor turned to see Helena and Tatianna fighting with the same strategy. Helena struck first, and then Tatianna went in for the kill. He wondered if the two sisters coordinated this or if it was all just a coincidence.

Either way, Razor had to admire the women and their fight. And it was clear to him why Cole chose Zara as his number two. The girl was strong, fast, and, when needed, vicious.

Razor glanced around, making sure that no one was heading his way. The others stood on guard, waiting for some Radicals to attack them, but they never got past Jade, Zara, Helena, and Tatianna. Before they knew it, the three ambulance trucks filled with Radical members were all lying dead on the ground. Razor didn't think any of the women broke a sweat during the attack.

Razor chuckled.

And then someone came at them from behind. Razor turned when he heard someone from the group yell out for help. He saw that it was Junior who was being attacked. Razor didn't even bother to move. For one, it was only one guy. Junior should've had no problem handling him alone. Secondly, Razor was pissed at him, and his theory about Junior being the mole was correct.

The night they ran into Cole, Razor overheard him ask one of the members if he could use their radio. He told them a bullshit story saying he had a girlfriend in the States and gave coded messages to let her know he was alive and well. Razor had never heard that story before.

When Junior went off with the radio, Razor followed him. He heard Junior switching through various channels until he stopped on a certain one. Then he began to use Morse code. Razor instantly berated himself for not learning it the way he should have. He could only make out Bossman and Blackwell, but that was enough for him. Now, he just needed to confront Junior about it. But it was hard to do that when they were attacked so often.

It wasn't until Junior got slammed to the ground that someone finally decided to intervene. Reagan killed the guy with a quick arrow to the head. Jade had lent her bow to Reagan on their journey to Toronto because Reagan was currently out of ammo for her rifle.

"Thanks," Junior said breathlessly.

Reagan just rolled her eyes at him. Razor wasn't sure what that was about, but he guessed she didn't care for him for some reason. He looked around to make sure that those who mattered were all right. Everyone was fine. He sighed and made his way through the parking lot. The three ambulances had their doors open and keys still in the ignition. Razor smiled at that.

"Bright side," he said as he stood at one of the trucks. "We just found ourselves some rides to Toronto."

"Thank God," Yoko sighed. "I don't know how many of these attacks we can survive."

"All of them, if Jade stays angry enough," Danita joked with a smile.

"Point taken," Yoko admitted.

Razor didn't appreciate the joke. Especially since Jade recently had a close call. "Let's not press our luck."

"Agreed," Cole walked up, along with the members who were carrying Jackson. "Let's divide up between the trucks and head for Toronto."

Razor, Cole, Jackson, Helena, Jade, Zara, Clay, and Reagan rode in the back of one truck while a couple of members rode up front. The rest of the group was divided between the other two trucks. And the Black Coats members who couldn't fit in agreed to continue to walk while scavenging for supplies along the way.

"So," Jade looked over at Cole with blood splattered over the right side of her face. "How long was it before you found out the true meaning of the ambulances?"

Cole chuckled as he handed her a cloth to wipe her face. "When I arrived over here, it was night. And that was the only peaceful night I had. Because the next day, I found out the true horrors of this place."

Jade nodded as she cleaned her face.

"Seriously?" Helena asked, shocked.

"Seriously," Cole sighed. "I saw the trucks and was stupid enough to flag one of them down. I wanted to offer my services to the hospitals or whatever made up the healthcare system. But when they stopped, they immediately ambushed me. I wouldn't be here today if it weren't for Zara."

She shrugged. "I was just glad that you got one of them to stop. Made my job easier," she smirked as she remembered the altercation.

"I'm sure they suffered," Razor said. He could see the glee in her eyes.

"Indeed they did."

"So, nothing got any better," Razor sadly admitted, more to himself than anyone else.

"Sadly, no, old friend," Cole sighed and slowly smiled. "But you have to count the small victories. Like these trucks here," he knocked on the side of it for verification.

Razor smirked. "That is a win."

For once, he was finally happy that they were driving around instead of walking.

**

At some point, the good luck runs out, but Razor and the group barely had it, so it seemed unfair for it to run out now. But that's what it did—ran out. The first truck broke down a few miles out. However, everyone could pile in between the other two trucks and continue to drive. It wasn't until they arrived in Cambridge, Ontario, that both trucks ran out of gas simultaneously. The group looked around for any vehicles they could siphon gas from, but none were around.

Razor cursed under his breath.

"We're lucky to have made it this far," Cole was still optimistic. "We're 98.4 km from Toronto...or 61 miles."

"That's still a long way to walk," Razor countered. He was trying his best not to be annoyed.

"Don't be such a downer, old friend," Cole smiled.

"I'll take catching a ride over walking any day," Jade chimed in as she fiddled with her knives. Razor could tell that she was on edge. The group was vulnerable, standing around like this. And Jade hated feeling powerless.

"So, what's the plan?" Helena demanded. She could see her sister's antsiness too.

Cole sighed. "I guess find somewhere to rest up for the night."

"But I thought you said we should travel during the night?" Jade pointed out.

"Yes, but we should also be well rested," Cole looked around. "Did any of you get some sleep?"

Just about everyone shook their head.

"Then we should rest up and head out tomorrow evening," Cole confirmed.

"Sounds like a plan," Razor said. He began looking around the area. He saw an old, rundown, four-story apartment building. It sat just in front of a body of water. "We should hide out there."

"That's a good choice," Cole agreed.

"Wow, is that a small waterfall behind there," Jade said in amazement as she peeked around the building.

"It is," Zara confirmed. "That's Hespeler Mill Pond."

"*That's* a pond," there was disbelief behind Helena's voice.

"Believe it or not...yeah."

"Can we go sightseeing later?" Tatianna complained. "I'm exhausted."

"Yes, let's clear this building out fast," Razor was fighting off his bad mood, but losing the trucks wasn't easy to get over.

Since the women fought back at the safe house, Razor thought it was fitting for the men to check the building out. Plus, if something did happen, he wanted to ensure Junior became the casualty. So, he, Clay, Keeper, Junior, and a few more male Black Coats members went inside. Since Calvin was injured, he left him outside with Yoko. And Cole stayed outside to watch over Jackson.

The men cleared the floors in teams. Razor ensured that he, Clay, and Keeper were all on the same team. He let Junior be with the other Black Coats members.

The three men cleared the first two floors silently.

"Have you two seen anything suspicious with Junior?" he eventually asked.

"No," Clay sighed. "But honestly, I haven't paid him that much attention."

"Figures," Razor mumbled. He knew who was getting all of Clay's attention.

"Not since we've found Dr. Blackwell," Keeper glanced over an old jacket he had just found.

"What do you mean?"

"He just looks at him like he wants to kill him or something," Keeper shrugged. "I told Dr. Blackwell to be cautious of him...why? Have ya noticed it too?"

Razor sighed. "He's just been off to me since we crossed over."

"Wow, that long?" Keeper asked, shocked.

"We had a lot going on, and I didn't have the time to tell anyone," Razor said. He was still leery about telling them the truth.

"I'll keep my eye on him," Clay looked through a closet for anything valuable.

"Me too," Keeper shoved the old jacket into his bag.

"Still," Clay paused, lingering by the closet door. "Anyone throwing deathly looks at Blackwell has to be on the other side...right?"

Razor was secretly glad that Clay caught on to the warning. "My thoughts exactly."

"Ya don't mean, like a spy?"

Clay frowned. "What else could it be?"

Razor just shrugged.

There was a rumbling sound above them. He looked up. Junior and the other members were checking the two floors above them.

"I wonder if there's a problem up there," Clay looked at the ceiling.

"Well, these two floors are clear," Razor made his way out of the apartment. "So, let's go find out."

When they got to the third floor, there was a lot of yelling and cursing. Razor wondered if Junior had decided to make his move and attacked one of the members. But as he went down the hall, he saw that all the members were accounted for.

"The little fucker!" one of them shouted.

"What's going on?" Keeper asked.

Another member laughed. "Possum jumped out and scared the living shit out of Randel."

"Fuck off," Randel spat.

"Is this floor clear?" Razor demanded.

"All clear, boss," Junior said.

Razor eyed him. "Then let's clear the last floor."

Junior smirked. "Sure thing," he looked over at the members. "Let's go, boys."

Razor watched as Junior and the other members went up the stairs. He indicated for Clay and Keeper to stay back. They had done their jobs already—no sense in making them work extra.

"That little shit is definitely up to something," Clay growled once the group was gone.

"Just keep an eye out," Razor warned, still watching the stairs.

The building was clear. By the time everyone else got inside, they'd managed to scavenge up a decent amount of supplies. They all decided to rest in the apartments on the third floor. They divided up shifts for lookouts. Two would watch the back of the building from the roof, while another two watched the front from the lobby. Jade took a shift with him while Clay and Reagan took the roof.

They sat between the double doors, watching out for anything suspicious. Occasionally, Razor would catch Jade looking down at her hands, frowning. The last time, she saw him watching her.

"I lied to you and Helena earlier," she sighed.

Razor frowned, not understanding what she meant.

"Back at the safe house. I didn't lose my grip. I saw David," she looked back down at her hands. "He was there with his hand stretched out to me and told me to take it. So, I did, and it felt so real that I let go."

"Why didn't you tell us that?"

"Because I'm tired of the both of you looking at me like I'm crazy."

"We don't think that."

"Yes, you do, Razor. And it frustrates me," she snapped. "I'm well aware that I'm losing it. But it hurts to see you both thinking that too."

Razor sighed. "We don't mean to," it was no use arguing with her.

"We're just concerned."

"I know. I'm really trying here."

"I don't doubt that for a second."

Jade nodded as she began to pick at her hands. "There's something else I need to tell you."

Razor waited patiently for her to continue. She looked up at him.

"Just promise you won't overreact."

"I promise."

"I think there's a spy in our midst."

Razor looked at her in disbelief. He never thought she would catch on to that. Jade had been so out of it that he never thought it would even enter her mind.

"Ever since the day Bossman attacked the camp," she continued. "There was a moment in the woods when he mentioned me having a boyfriend. And ever since, I kept having this nagging thought. How did he know that? And how did he know we'd be at the river? And splitting up nonetheless."

"Did you share this with anyone else?" Razor asked.

"Just Reagan," she sighed. "But she won't say anything to the others."

Razor nodded. He knew this information was safe with her.

"So, what do you think? Am I just being paranoid?"

Razor looked into her eyes. He could tell that Jade was struggling to grasp reality and what wasn't. She was looking to know if this thought was real or not. Razor couldn't lie to her. Not about this. He sighed.

"Just keep an eye on Junior."

She stared at him with a blank expression for a moment, and then he saw the fiery rage behind her eyes.

~13~

Nick

Raina, Aiden, and Levi leaned casually against the stolen DC truck as Nick repeatedly punched its hood. He was pissed. The stupid thing broke down on them when he crossed the Pennsylvania and New York state lines. They were so close yet still far away from the Canadian border. Nick had to get to Blackwell first. That was the only way to ensure Chase's reign would come crashing down.

But that task was proving difficult with every passing moment because every DC officer and soldier was out scouring the streets for him. Chase had put the word out that Nick was a traitor to the country. He committed treason when he allowed Jade, Razor (his former right-hand), and the other rebels to escape to Canada. Nick was furious when he heard the order get called out over the radio. And he got even more enraged when his men quickly believed the lie. But what did he expect?

The program comprised nothing but deviants and people who sought it to survive. Never once did Nick believe that he had their full-fledged loyalty. But still. It's the principal of the matter. And he would've at least thought there would be a slight hesitation. But there was none. Every officer seemed ecstatic about the opportunity of having a hand in Nick's downfall.

Now here he was, stuck on the side of a rundown road with a broken-down truck and only a hallucination of a few dead children for company. Nick cursed under his breath as he punched the truck again, and the children jumped a little—startled by his reaction.

Raina sighed and rolled her eyes. "Hitting the truck won't make it work, *Nick*."

It was apparent that she was very annoyed with him. He couldn't help but find it a little amusing. She would've been getting into her early teenage years if he hadn't killed her. 12 if he wasn't mistaken. Her attitude was very fitting for that.

"You never know," he teased and flexed his hand. "It could help."

"Trust me, you only cause damage," she mumbled.

"Yeah," Levi chimed in. "You only destroy things. Not fix them."

"Point taken," he snapped.

Why did they always have to bring up what he'd done? He didn't need reminding. The fact that they were there with Aiden assured Nick that they were dead. But still, he thought he'd be allowed to joke around with them just a little. They were going to be with him forever, after all. They'd repeatedly tell him that they were there to haunt him, but they could at least enjoy a lighthearted moment occasionally.

"You can't be mad at them, Dad," Aiden frowned. "It takes a while to get used to death, especially when it's unexpected. And it's harder when you've been murdered."

"We sometimes still feel the pain," Raina admitted.

"Blood still comes out of my mouth," Levi complained as blood poured between his lips.

Nick looked away.

"Can't admire your handiwork?" Raina teased as the blade of a machete appeared out of her stomach.

"Stop it," Nick whispered as he shut his eyes.

"Why should we?" Raina asked angrily. "You certainly didn't."

"I get it! I get it, ok!" Nick screamed with his eyes still closed. "I'm a shitty person, and I did a shitty thing! How long do I have to apologize for that?!"

"I don't know...until we're *alive*," Raina laughed.

Nick opened his eyes then. Her laugh was so callous that it reminded him of his mother. Was she slowly seeping through Raina?

Nick shook his head. "You're not Raina," he whispered. "You're my mother. Get out of that sweet girl!"

Raina stopped laughing and then frowned at him. She looked confused but appeared more like herself. The machete blade quickly disappeared from her stomach.

"What's wrong, Nick?" she sounded more like herself. Nick sighed with relief.

"Nothing," he looked over and saw Levi staring at his fists. Traces of blood still lingered on the boy's lips.

"How do you do it? Just kill people?" Levi frowned and looked up at him. The blood became more prominent as he talked. "Do you ever feel guilty about it?"

"No, not with most of them," Nick looked away and then back at them.

"I only feel guilty about killing the both of you."

Aiden shook his head. "You're a monster, Dad."

"An evil monster," Levi agreed.

"You've all made that fact known already," Nick glanced around the surrounding area, ensuring no one was lingering by. His conversations with the children sometimes got repetitive. But what did he expect with dead children? Their conversation topics were minimal.

"We'd thought we'd make it known again," Raina smirked. She glanced around. "So, what's the plan, Nick? Now that every DC officer in the country is looking for us."

"Not us, young Raina, me."

"We've been through this. We go where you go."

Aiden's eyes widened as he looked down the road—clearly seeing something Nick couldn't see. "We should get off the streets, Dad."

Just then, the sound of trucks roared in the distance. Nick didn't see them but knew they were DC trucks. There was a thicket of bushes and trees right off the road. Nick retrieved all his supplies and weapons from the truck and proceeded to the forestry.

"Let's go, children," he called over his shoulder as he entered through the trees.

As soon as he broke through the tree line, a cluster of old restaurants and convenience stores were just a few feet ahead. Nick paused as he glanced at which building would be suitable for them. He settled for an old store-restaurant that was housed together. It was in the far back, so he figured it would be the last building they would look in.

Once he broke inside and secured the doors, Nick checked to ensure no one else was hiding inside. No one wasn't. Levi and Aiden hid in an aisleway while Raina lingered beside Nick. He pulled out his radio and turned it down to a point where he could hear, but the volume couldn't give his location away. He also pulled out a knife and binoculars and crouched near a boarded-up window. There was enough space between the boards that he could peek out through.

Nick sat the radio down beside him and looked through the binoculars. There was no one in sight. But that didn't fool him. He was sure that there were DC officers lingering nearby.

"This is team Echo, New York," someone radioed. "Let the commander-in-chief know we found the traitor's stolen truck near the state line, over."

"Has the vehicle been searched, over?" someone else radioed.

"Negative, team Echo, New York is approaching vehicle now, over."

"Copy that."

Nick waited patiently for the team to give an update. He knew that they would be searching the surrounding area eventually. He glanced around the store to see if there was anything he could use to tie someone up. At least one of the officers needed to be kept alive. He needed to know what Chase was up to. He spotted an old telephone cord lying nearby. He quickly retrieved it and went back to the window.

"The vehicle is empty, but we are preparing to search the surrounding area, over," team Echo updated.

"Copy that, team Echo, New York. Stay sharp and safe, over."

Nick looked through the binoculars and waited for the officers to walk into view. After a couple of minutes, four officers walked into eyesight. He watched them. One officer instructed the others to search the nearby buildings. One went to explore the fast food restaurant at the front. Another went to a gas station and rest stop combination to the far left. The third officer was heading his way, while the fourth officer lingered up front, acting as the lookout.

"Team Echo, New York is now searching nearby buildings, over," the fourth officer radioed.

"Copy that."

Nick clutched onto his knife as the third officer approached the convenience store. Raina gently touched his hand and shook her head.

"If you kill him, they'll know where we are," she whispered.

Nick sighed. "Would you stop whispering? No one else can hear you."

Raina rolled her eyes. "Just take my advice for once."

"When have you ever given me advice," Nick chuckled. He immediately fell silent when the officer got closer.

Nick quickly hid behind the counter. He heard the officer enter the building. The children crouched down next to him—fear clear in their eyes. Nick couldn't help but roll his eyes. Why were they so fearful? Didn't they know it was pointless to be afraid when they were with him?

The officer slowly made his way through the store. His steps were gradual and deliberate. Nick waited for the officer to get closer to his hiding spot. He peeked behind the counter and saw the officer looking down an aisle Levi and Aiden had hidden in. The officer was just a few aisles away from the counter. Nick quickly retreated to his hiding spot.

Raina shook her head as soon as he made eye contact with him. "Don't do it," she mouthed.

Nick shook his head. He had to do it. He *wanted* to. This was the only way he could find out what was happening with Chase. This was the only way he could get updates that involved him.

The officer was getting closer. Once it sounded like the officer was just above him, Nick jumped out, sliced the officer's throat, and pulled his body over the counter. The officer lay behind the counter, quickly bleeding out. Nick tried to no avail to clean up the blood that spilled on the counter.

"I told you it wasn't a good idea," Raina sighed.

"Shut it already."

"Rookie!" someone called out, followed by a whistle. "Rookie!"

Nick struggled to look out the window since he was far away from it. But it sounded like one of the officers was looking for his comrade.

"What's the problem?" someone else, who sounded further away, asked.

"The Rookie hasn't reported back yet."

"Did you see what building he went into?"

"Negative, but I saw him head this way."

"Well, let's check the surrounding buildings."

"Copy that."

Nick went back to his hiding spot behind the counter. He made sure the officer's dead body wasn't in the line of sight. Another officer made their way into the store. Nick waited for them to get closer to his hiding spot.

"Rookie," the officer whispered. "Are you in here?"

The new officer walked a lot louder than the rookie. He quickly made his way to the counter and then paused. Nick knew the reason for that. It was the blood he couldn't get off the counter. He had to strike fast.

"I've found—" the officer managed to get out before Nick stuck a knife into his chest.

Nick struggled to pull this officer's body over the counter.

"Something's wrong!" another officer called out as he approached the store.

"Fuck," Nick whispered as he barely hid in time. Raina shot him a look that said, *I told you so.*

"Rookie, Senior, report," the officer demanded.

Nick looked at his radio and immediately turned it off.

"Alpha, we have a problem at the convenience store, over," the officer reported, just like Nick predicted.

"Copy that, on the way."

Nick waited until the officer was a few feet away from the counter before he attacked. However, it wasn't silent like the others. The officer put up a good fight, but Nick still managed to get his arm around his neck before the officer could make a sound. He quickly snapped his neck. The officer dropped to the floor. Nick didn't even bother trying to hide the body.

He made his way to the door with a baton in his hand. The leading officer was approaching the door. Nick crouched down and waited. As soon as the officer opened the door, he struck. He immediately hit the officer on the head with the baton, but he didn't pass out. Nick had to hit him several times before the officer fell unconscious.

Raina stood in front of him shaking her head.

"Don't just stand there," Nick teased. "Grab his feet."

Raina did. "This is going to be bad, Nick."

"I don't see how things can get any worse."

"Trust me," the warning was clear in her eyes. "It can always get worse."

~14~

Jade

As she looked at Razor, Jade struggled not to stab him. She was furious at him. He'd known about the spy way longer than she did, and he'd done nothing about it.

"Don't do it, Jade," Raina pleaded as she stood beside Razor.

"Don't be like the mean man," Levi cried.

Jade closed her eyes as she clutched onto her knife. *Please don't do it. Please don't do it. Please don't do it.* She couldn't give in to her impulses. It seemed like Razor didn't notice her struggle.

"How long have you known?" she asked, her eyes closed.

"I had a suspicion after the camp was attacked," he said. "And then I narrowed it down to Junior once we crossed over."

"Don't do it, Jade," Raina warned. "We have to know how he narrowed it down to Junior."

Jade nodded and took a deep breath. "How did you know it was him?"

"He kept saying he broke out with the prisoners, but I never saw him in my prison."

"So, that automatically makes him the spy."

"No, I did a background check on everyone, even those who died on the river, and he's the only one who had no information on him."

"And *that* makes him the spy."

"It makes him suspicious."

"Why did you wait so long to say something?" she gritted.

"I haven't exactly had any free time to do so, Jade," there was a little bit of annoyance in his voice. "Besides, I wasn't 100% sure, and I didn't want to add further discourse in the group."

"That wasn't your call to make!" she snapped. "You've allowed us to rest our heads with a snake!"

"I've been watching him closely," Razor shot back.

"He got Raina, Levi, and David killed, Razor," the grip on her knife got tighter. "And you've been protecting him."

"I wanted to be certain before I condemned a man to death."

"Like you've cared about a man's death before!" Jade rose to her feet.

Razor looked hurt for a second. "I've made the right call. And I just warned Keeper and Clay to keep a watch on him."

Jade shook her head. This didn't convince her at all. Razor was a traitor and betrayed her when he kept this information away from her for so long. *Please don't do it. Please don't do it. Please don't do it.* She repeated over and over in her head.

"You're not like the mean man," Levi said.

"Fight it, Jade," Raina encouraged. "Be yourself again."

"Don't do it. Don't do it," Jade repeated under her breath.

"Look, I understand you may be pissy with me," Razor sighed as he stood. "But I promise you. I was trying to do the right thing. I didn't want to add any further stress on you."

That only made Jade angry even more. She glared at him. All little control she had quickly fleeted.

"You traitor!" she yelled as she jumped on him.

Razor looked briefly shocked as he fell on his back—Jade falling on top of him. But he instantly composed himself as he held tightly onto her wrist. Jade tried with all her might to get the knife to his throat. He was a traitor. And traitors needed to be dealt with.

"Stop...it...Jade," he gritted. There was sadness in his eyes.

"You betrayed us!"

"Jade!" Helena quickly wrapped her arms around her sister and pulled her off Razor. "What the hell is wrong with you?!"

Jade tried to get out of Helena's hold. But at this point, she had her pinned against the glass doors, and Keeper was there to help Helena.

"He's a traitor, Helena!" she glared as Razor rose to his feet. "He knew there was a spy in our midst, and he's just now saying something."

"What?" Helena glanced at Razor.

"It's Junior," Keeper confirmed. "But Razor confided in Clay and me, and we've been watching him."

"He's still a traitor!"

"Enough, Jade!" Helena screamed as she looked at her sister. "Razor is no traitor. God, listen to yourself! You sound paranoid."

Jade glared at her sister and then at Razor. Raina and Levi huddled up in the corner just behind him, looking terrified of her.

"Do you honestly think that he would betray you?" Helena's voice cracked, and it was clear that Jade's accusation hurt her. "He loves you more than anything and would lay down his life for you, Jade."

Her glare softened as she continued to look at Razor. He was frowning, but it wasn't from anger. It was from pain. Jade remembered that look the night they had crossed over—the night he had cried because he failed her. That look completely shocked her. And it hurt her to know that she was the cause of it. She had vowed never to make him feel that way again. And now she had broken it.

Jade dropped her knife. "I'm...I'm so sorry, Razor."

He didn't meet her eyes.

Helena still had her pinned. She glanced over at Keeper. He nodded.

"Come on, Jade," he said, grabbing her elbow. He opened one of the doors leading to the apartment lobby. "Let's go help Cole with Jackson."

Jade looked at Helena and then back at Razor. She had hurt them both immensely. Shame and regret instantly filled her. She could no longer be in their presence. She looked over at Keeper and nodded. He pulled her into the lobby and quickly shut the door, and Helena barricaded it by leaning against it in case Jade tried to attack again at the last minute.

The action made Jade feel like a monster. Her sister no longer trusted her not to hurt them. How could she do that? And to Razor, nonetheless? Jade knew that Razor had an unfaltering loyalty to her. So, how could she accuse him of being a traitor? Of all things? He had proven time and time again that he loved and was loyal to the Willer sisters. And how does she thank him for that? By calling him a traitor.

Jade was silent as she slowly followed Keeper to the staircase. Once they were inside and climbing the stairs, Jade instantly shoved her hands in her pockets. She didn't trust herself and didn't want to do something horrible like suddenly attacking Keeper too.

Their journey to the third floor was a silent one. But they made it to the floor quickly. Since Cole was looking after Jackson, he took the apartment at the very end of the hall. It was the furthest away from the stairs and less vulnerable to intruders.

Cole greeted them with a smile as they walked in. "A shift change already?"

"Yeah," Keeper smiled as he sat beside Cole on the living room floor. Zara and a few Black Coats members were there as well. "Jade and I wanted to check and see if you needed help before we went to rest."

Jade appreciated Keeper being discreet about the incident downstairs, but she thought he should've at least warned the others about her instability.

"I was just about to do his stretches," Cole looked over at her. "Jade, do you mind helping me?"

Jade walked over to him but stopped by Zara first. She surrendered her weapons to her without a word. Zara took them without any questions. Jade was overly grateful for that. Then she walked over and kneeled beside Cole.

"Hey," Tatianna greeted as she walked in. She was looking at Keeper. "Are you ready?"

He smiled. "Yeah, I'll be right there," he looked over at Jade. Concern filled his face. "Are ya going to be ok here?"

Jade nodded, too ashamed to talk to him.

"Ok," Keeper slowly stood. "Make sure ya get some rest."

Jade focused on the stretches that Cole was doing. They started with Jackson's legs and moved to his arms. Jade recalled doing these same stretches on David when he fell into a diabetic coma. That felt like ages ago. She was a mess then. And she was even a bigger mess now.

It took them no time to finish the stretching exercise. Cole stood up and walked to the kitchen. Jade sat beside Jackson—staring at his unconscious body. She wondered if he would ever wake up. She couldn't imagine how he would handle the loss of his sister. He and Beverly were twins, and that was a connection that she could never understand. But she could only imagine the hole and emptiness it would have. It seemed like Cole was handling the loss of a child pretty well. Better than she was.

Cole walked back into the living room with two cups of tea. He handed one to Jade, and she took it and smiled. Cole sat beside her on the floor.

"I hear you're having a tough time."

Jade nodded as she blew on her tea.

"I completely understand. The loss you've experienced, it's a tough one. My condolences."

Jade remained silent as she sipped on her tea. She didn't know what to say to him for some strange reason. At this point, she felt she was repeating herself to everyone she met. It felt like she was going crazy. And everyone told her that she wasn't. She was grieving. But after the incident with Razor, Jade came to a scary conclusion. She wasn't *going* crazy. She *was* crazy. The transformation happened without her realizing it. How else could she explain her attacking Razor?

"I'm a monster," Jade finally admitted after a while. She stared into her empty teacup. "I attacked someone that I really love and care for."

"Grief sometimes makes us do some terrible things."

"It wasn't grief!" she snapped. "It was madness. Anger. Rage."

Jade looked up to see Cole frowning at her. Zara stood alarmed—her hand hovering over the handle of her sword. Jade sighed. At least there was one person who would respond to her appropriately. Zara had no loyalty to her, only to Cole.

"Sorry, I'm just tired of people excusing my behavior," Jade stood up. "I'm becoming the very thing I've fought so hard against. I can feel it. I have these urges, and I give in to them."

Cole's frown deepened at her words. "That's definitely unfortunate," he sighed and looked up at her. "Look, Jade. I won't sit here and pretend I know you. I don't. But I can say that you must fight to remain who you are. If you feel like you're changing for the worst, then fight to hold on to what grounds you and made you the person you once were."

"That's the problem, doc," Jade handed him the teacup. "Those who grounded me were killed. I don't know what to hold on to anymore...thanks for the tea."

Jade made her way to the door. She stopped in front of Zara for her weapons. Zara walked into the hallway before she gave Jade her weapons back. Jade didn't find the action insulting. Zara was doing her job of protecting Cole.

"Where's Clay's room?" she asked.

"302," Zara smiled. "Get you some rest, Jade."

Jade nodded as she headed back to the end of the hall. The apartment Clay was in was near the staircase. For some reason, Jade preferred that location. If intruders happened to wander in, she'd be among the first to greet them.

The apartment was empty when she walked inside. She thought Reagan and Clay would be off their lookout duties by now, and she certainly couldn't go anywhere near Razor and Helena. Jade didn't trust herself yet. Besides, she was still too ashamed and embarrassed. Since she didn't know what room Clay was sleeping in, Jade sat on the coffee table in the living room, glaring at the wall.

At that moment, she hated herself. How could she turn into the very thing she hated? She was tarnishing Raina, Levi, and David's death being the way she was. She thought that still having Helena and Razor in her life would be enough. But she'd quickly turned on Razor as soon as he angered her. That was proof that they weren't enough. Maybe she should leave. Just leave and become the monster she was meant to be.

"Hey," Clay said in the doorway. He had a smile on his face. Obviously, he hadn't heard what she had done yet.

She smiled weakly. "I didn't know which room you were sleeping in."

Clay walked in and sat down beside her. "I'm not even sure yet."

"I guess I should've picked one then."

"Honestly, I thought Helena would've had you with her and Razor."

Jade looked away from him and frowned at the wall. "I don't think they'll want me around them right now."

Clay frowned at her.

"Razor told me about Junior," a few tears fell down her face. "I called him a traitor and tried to slit his throat. Helena and Keeper stopped me," she instantly looked over at Clay. His face was blank. An uncomfortable silence lingered between them.

"That was a very shitty thing to do," he finally said. "Razor is far from a traitor."

"I know," Jade cried. This was what she needed. Someone to call her out on her poor behavior. "I can't believe I did that."

"He had his reasons. And I completely understand them."

"I don't know if apologizing to him is enough," she was worried that he and Helena would never forgive her.

"Just give them a little space. They'll forgive you, Jade," Clay stood, grabbed her hand, and pulled her to her feet.

Jade looked into his eyes. "How can you be so sure?"

"Because you're family. And they love you more than anything," Clay turned and led her to a bedroom.

They went into the first bedroom on the left. There was a full-sized bed, a dresser, and a nightstand. It all was covered in dust. Clay spent time clearing the dust off the bed. Jade was thankful that she still had her mask on. Her asthma got agitated, and her mask swiftly delivered a breathing treatment to her. It took Clay about ten minutes to completely dedust the bed.

"I should've had you wait in the living room," he said as he cleared the nightstand from dust. The sound of her mask giving her another breathing treatment filled the room.

Jade shrugged out of her jacket as she inhaled the medicated air. "I feel safer here with you."

Clay looked at her over his shoulder. There was a strange look on his face that she couldn't decipher. She decided not to linger on its potential meaning. He turned back around and moved to the dresser.

"You should probably keep your mask on," he suggested—his back still turned to her. "Or at least sleep with your scarf."

Jade looked around the room. Clay did a good job removing all the dust, but she understood what he meant. The room didn't appear completely dust-free. And it was better to be safe than sorry. Jade waited until her treatment was done before she switched to her scarf.

"It's all clear," Clay sighed as he sat on the bed.

Jade sat on the edge of the bed and removed her boots. She felt Clay move on the bed. She turned to see him lying on his back, staring at the ceiling. Jade quickly joined him and rested her head on his chest. Clay wrapped his arm around her, never taking his eyes off the ceiling.

"Hey, Clay," Jade said after a while. "If I ever try to attack you, will you promise just to kill me?" She looked up to see the many emotions appear on his face. First, it was anger and then pain, and then conflict. Finally, he settled on amusement.

He looked down at her with a smirk and stared into her eyes. "Most definitely," he said with conviction.

Jade smiled at him. And then quickly drifted off to sleep.

**

Sounds from the hallway woke Jade up. She was wrapped tightly in Clay's arms. He was in a deep sleep—snoring very heavily. Jade wiggled her way out of his grasp. Clay just turned to his side once she was out of his arms. She grabbed her mask and knives as she went to the bedroom door. Once she opened it and peeked out the door, she saw Reagan and a Black Coat member standing in the living room. Jade slowly walked out—confused.

"What's going on?" she asked.

Reagan turned to her. She looked a little alarmed to see her up.

"Just asking for volunteers to go out on a quick scavenging mission," the member said.

"You should go back to bed, Jade," Reagan said.

"Are we low on supplies?" Jade asked, ignoring Reagan.

"Not yet," the member answered. "But the doc thinks we should stock up while we have a temporary base."

"Makes sense," Jade mumbled.

"So far, it's just two volunteers from our group and one from yours."

"Who?"

The member frowned as he tried to recall the name. "I believe his name is Junior."

"I'll go," Jade quickly said.

~15~

Jade

If he knew that she was on to him, Junior did not indicate it. When she and the Black Coats member met him and the others in the lobby, he appeared happy to see her.

"All right," Junior smiled. "Grade-A badass, Jade, is coming with us."

"More like crazy, unstable, Jade," she admitted as she looked into his eyes. It gave nothing away.

"Aww, don't say that," he frowned a little. "You're still a badass to me."

Jade nodded and turned to one of the Black Coats members. "Where are we going?"

"Just a few buildings a couple of miles away," she answered.

"Sounds great. Lead the way," Jade hung back as the three members, and Junior walked out the doors.

"Be careful, Jade," Raina warned as she appeared beside her. "You don't want to give yourself away too quickly."

Jade looked over at her. She hadn't really talked to Raina since she yelled at her. She thought that Raina would've stopped visiting her by now. But here she was. Loyal as ever. Jade nodded as she proceeded out the doors. She didn't plan on confronting Junior. She just wanted to see the suspicious behavior for herself. That had to be why Razor zeroed in on him in the first place because he was acting suspiciously.

The small group was just a few feet ahead of her. Jade lingered on purpose. She watched very closely how Junior interacted with the members. For the most part, he was very friendly. He joked around with them and occasionally made the female member laugh. Jade could tell that the young woman was very into him.

Raina walked beside her—glaring at Junior. His behavior didn't fool her. Raina found him to be very distrustful. Jade couldn't help but smile at her reaction.

"I don't know if I said this, but I'm sorry for yelling at you," Jade said in a low voice. No one in the group heard her, which she was grateful for. She glanced over at Raina to see that she was still frowning in Junior's direction.

"I know you just want me to be strong," she said. "But I can't be strong that way."

"You don't understand how guilty I feel. I promised to keep you safe in this world and failed you."

"You didn't fail. You've kept us safe for as long as you could," Raina stopped walking and looked at her. "I was dying either way, Jade. If Bossman hadn't gotten to me, my disease would have."

"But it would've been more peaceful that way," Jade hated to think of

Raina dying at all, but she had a point. Either way, Raina would die, but Jade just hated that she went so violently.

"And do you really think Levi could've lived on without me?" Raina resumed walking. "At least now we can be together forever. And I get to watch over him."

Jade looked at her in awe. That was such a mature assessment. But the pain from it all was still there.

"I'm just having a really tough time living without you two," Jade admitted. "*I* can't survive without you."

"You have to," Raina said forcefully. "There are other children out there who need someone like you watching over them."

Jade's heart raced as she thought about the possibility of coming across other children. That was the last thing she needed. Her breathing sped up and began to become shallow. She couldn't handle an encounter with other children. There was no way she could protect them. They would die for sure. And what little was left of her would undoubtedly die.

"You can do this, Jade," Raina encouraged. "I have complete faith in you. But they need the old Jade and not this new version...the version *he* wants you to be."

Oddly enough, Jade calmed down at the mention of Bossman. It brought her back to the task at hand, Junior being the spy. She noticed they were coming up on an old building. It appeared to be an old storefront complex. Two of the Black Coats members went to check out the back of the building while Jade, Junior, and the young woman who was into him stood guard out front.

Jade couldn't help but stare at him. She was trying to decipher every movement he made. Sadly, it gave nothing away. Junior kept his attention on the young woman. Occasionally, Jade did glance around the surrounding area. To ensure no one was trying to sneak up on them.

Everything appeared to be clear. After a few more minutes, the two Black Coats members came from around the back.

"All clear," one of them said.

"Good," Jade said. "We should split up. Junior and I will stand guard out here while you three check the inside."

"Sounds good."

The young woman reluctantly went inside with her fellow members while Jade and Junior hung back. Jade noticed the way Junior smiled at the girl. She couldn't tell if he was really into the girl or just trying to get something out of her. It left her confused and very frustrated. She reminded herself to be calm and was only there to watch him—not confront him.

Junior turned and smiled at her. "Like what you see?"

Jade frowned at him.

He chuckled. "You've been staring at me all night, Jade."

Her frown relaxed some. She didn't notice that she was being *that obvious*.

"I'm flattered, really," he went on. "I thought it was Clay you were into."

"I'm not into Clay," she said defensively, but the statement didn't seem convincing. Not even to her.

Junior shot her a look.

Jade sighed and then shrugged. "All right, I'm sorry. I didn't realize I was staring."

Junior shrugged. "I don't mind it. A pretty woman like you, staring at a guy like me. It gives a guy a real ego boost."

Jade rolled her eyes. That was far from the reason why she was staring at him. But she couldn't tell him the real reason. "Is that all you care about? An ego boost?"

"Life is shorter than ever, Jade. We all need to take in the good while we still can get them."

"Point taken," she paused and glanced back at the building. "That girl seems to be really into you."

A smile spread across his face. "Yeah...do you know how long it's been since I had sex?"

Jade frowned. She really didn't expect the conversation to go that route. "I prefer not to know."

He chuckled. "Aww, come on, don't be like that. Besides, the only one who's been getting it regularly is Razor...lucky bastard."

"That's my brother and sister you're talking about," Jade gritted.

Junior found her anger to be amusing. "Just saying. I'll like to be the lucky one for once."

Jade sighed in annoyance and rolled her eyes. She was starting to regret entertaining a conversation with him in the first place. Just then, the three members came out of the building. She was immediately grateful. It appeared that the building was a bust. There were only a few things in one member's hands.

"We should try the next building," the young woman said. She was looking at Junior, all dreamy-eyed.

"Sounds good to me," he had a smirk on his face.

Jade rolled her eyes again. The whole interaction made her want to gag. She wished that they flirted on their own time. Like before, she hung back and tried to be more discrete about how she watched Junior. He appeared busy chatting up and flirting with the girl.

The next building they stopped at was a fish and tackle store. Again, two members scouted the building while Jade, Junior, and another member hung out front. This time Jade volunteered that she and Junior should head inside since this store was smaller than the previous one.

"You still can't keep your eyes off me, huh?" Junior asked smugly once they were inside.

Jade ignored him and focused her attention on the things that were scattered around the cash register. It was just some odd knickknacks, but she stuffed them in her bag anyway. She knew that Keeper could find some use for them.

"I must admit, Jade, you're really making my night here," Junior continued. "What is it? Jealousy of another woman's attention."

Once she had taken everything from around the register, Jade turned to the counter on the back wall.

"I would be cautious if I were you," she said over her shoulder. "The last guy I was with ended up with a death sentence."

To her surprise, Junior grimaced at the statement. Was Razor wrong? But then the look quickly went away, and Junior smirked.

"No offense," he said. "But I think I'll be luckier than him."

Jade turned around then. She had to fight off the rage she was feeling inside. "Is that so? What makes you so sure?"

Junior shrugged. "Just a feeling."

Jade literally bit her tongue, and she could taste the blood in her mouth. She turned her back toward him as she glared down at the counter. *Please don't do it. Please don't do it. Please don't do it.*

She looked over and saw Levi standing next to her. Blood poured out of his mouth as a machete stuck out of his stomach. Jade shut her eyes and took deep breaths.

"You know what's really bothering me?" she blurted out as she turned around to face Junior. He had been watching her the whole time. "How did Bossman know we'd split up at the river?"

Junior gave her a blank look.

"I mean, that was some key piece of information there," Jade fiddled with a random item in her hand—blood gliding down her throat. "One would think that we *all* were planning to escape over here. But how in the world did he stumble across *that* group? With the children, nonetheless."

"That's a valid question."

"You know what I think," Jade slowly walked toward him. Junior raised an eyebrow. "I think we have a traitor in our group."

"Really?"

"Really," she closed the gap between them. She looked into his eyes. "Do you have any guesses who that might be?"

Junior looked down at her like he wanted her very differently. "No clue."

Jade moved in closer to him. His body pressed against hers. Junior stiffened. "Razor has a theory."

Junior leaned down, his lips hovering over hers. "Is that right?"

Jade nodded. She waited patiently for him to make a move. He brushed his lips against hers. Jade held in her revulsion. She wanted him to slip up—for him to confess, and she would play into it if his loneliness got him to do that. She *had* to know and couldn't live on with just guessing.

"Tell me," he murmured.

The door burst open just then, and the young woman walked in. Jade and Junior jumped away from each other. The girl looked shocked as she glanced back and forth between them.

"Find anything?" she asked in disappointment.

Jade sighed and shook her head. "This place is a bust," she quickly brushed past Junior and headed for the door. The young woman followed, along with Junior.

The last building they were heading to was a lot further than the others. Again, Jade lingered behind. This time Junior had his arm draped over the girl's shoulder. She giggled and leaned into him the whole way.

Jade couldn't figure out what Junior was getting at with this whole charade. Did he really think he was making her jealous?

But then everything went horribly wrong.

Very suddenly, Junior spun the girl around so that they would be facing Jade. Out of nowhere, there was a knife at the girl's throat. Junior looked into Jade's eyes with a menacing look as he sliced the girl's throat. Jade stood there frozen and in disbelief. It all happened so abruptly. She felt like her eyes were deceiving her.

One of the members screamed as they charged at him, but Junior was fast. He turned around and shoved the knife into the guy's gut. The member dropped to the ground instantly. She wasn't sure when she did it, but Jade had her bow out, arrow at the ready, and pointing it at Junior when he took the last member hostage.

"Drop it," Jade demanded.

"Who's the traitor, Jade?" there was an unfamiliar look to Junior. She thought she knew him, but she had no clue. The cultivated façade he put on with them was all crumbling down. Even when he was fighting, Jade never saw this side of him, and it was very eerie.

"You already know who."

Junior smirked as his knife slowly went to the guy's throat. "Don't get shy on me now. Say it."

"It's you," she clenched. She was trying so hard not to release the arrow prematurely. But she wanted to kill him so badly.

"That damn Razor, always being so perceptive," he mumbled.

"Does Bossman know that Blackwell is alive?"

"He does, so your little plan won't work."

"I don't care about the plan," she said as a matter of fact. "I care about my revenge."

"That'll get you killed," he stated. "And you're just way too beautiful to die like that."

"Don't try to flatter me...my loved ones are dead because of you!"

"They've picked the wrong side, Jade...come on, don't be like that," he smirked even wider when she glared at him. "Suit yourself."

Junior moved in to stab the guy, but Jade was quick. She shot off an arrow, and it hit Junior in his hand. He yelled out in pain. The captured member took that opportunity to elbow Junior in the gut. He tried to run off, but Junior grabbed him. Jade charged at him and tackled Junior to the ground before he could do anything.

The two of them tussled for a moment. Even injured, Junior managed to get the upper hand on her.

"All I wanted was to fuck, Jade," he grunted as he tried to wrap his hands around her throat.

Jade quickly began to hit his injured hand. Junior winced out in pain. He struggled to pin her arms down. There was enough space between them that Jade managed to knee him in the groin and again in the stomach. Junior lost his hold on her. She managed to retrieve one of her knives from her thigh strap. Junior saw the weapon. He quickly snapped the arrow in half to move his hand more freely. But the blade still stuck out of his palm.

He tried to pin Jade down again, but she was quick. Unfortunately, Junior was quicker. Jade aimed for his gut, but Junior moved at the last minute, so she got his upper thigh. Still, Junior groaned out in pain all the same. The member came and began pulling Junior off her. Then Junior shocked them both again. He suddenly pulled the rest of the arrow out of his hand and stabbed the guy.

Jade screamed out in shock as she kicked Junior with all her might. He went flying back a few feet away from her. Blood was pouring out of the member. Jade rushed to his side. She applied pressure to his wound. It was in his chest.

Junior grunted as he rose wobbly to his feet. Blood was gushing down his leg. He and Jade locked eyes for a moment. Jade went for another knife, but Junior made his retreat. She thought about going after him when the member moaned in pain. Fear was covering his face. Jade didn't want to see another one of them die. Junior would have to be dealt with later. He was severely injured. How far could he get?

"It's ok," she reassured the member. "I got you."

Jade rose to her feet. She kept the pressure on his wound as she began to drag the member back to the apartment complex. How was she going to explain this to everyone? Razor was sure to be pissed at her. She glanced in the direction that Junior fled. It was all clear. Jade vowed to end his life if he wasn't bleeding out already.

It was only fitting.

~16~

Razor

As he watched Keeper pull Jade away, Razor couldn't help but feel heartbroken. It was worse than he thought. Being around Jade was slowly starting to feel like being around Nick. How could he let it get that bad? Not once did he ever believe that Jade would turn on him. But she did. And so quickly at that.

Yes, he shouldn't have kept his suspicions about Junior to himself for so long, but he had to be sure. That was a serious accusation to be throwing around carelessly. Razor needed facts before he brought it to the group. He still felt like there wasn't enough for him to go on—just a gut feeling. But as of now, that was enough. Besides, Jade was already worried about a spy in the group, and Razor couldn't lie to her, not on this. So, he told her the truth. And Jade called him a traitor and tried to kill him for it.

Razor avoided her gaze as she looked at him one last time before entering the lobby. Keeper quickly shut the door, and Helena barricaded it with her body. Once they were out of sight, Helena turned to him.

"Junior's a spy?" she frowned.

"I'm sorry," he sighed. "I was going to tell you. I just wanted to be sure first."

Helena looked back at the door.

"She's been thinking about a spy being in our midst," he quickly answered her unasked question.

"Why?"

"Because of Nick showing up at the river and capturing the group who were escaping. How did he know that, if someone wasn't feeding him information?"

Helena frowned as she put the puzzle pieces together. After a few seconds, she shook her head. "I still don't understand why she would attack you."

"She's angry I didn't tell her sooner," Razor paused as he looked at her face. "Are you angry with me?"

"Why would I be? You would've told me eventually...when you were sure."

Razor walked over to her and took her into his arms. Helena rested her head against his chest and sighed. Razor buried his face in her hair. He took in her smell. He loved how her hair smelled and couldn't recall it ever smelling bad. No matter what, Helena always managed to get her hands on different kinds of oils that made her hair smell amazing. She had a knack for that kind of stuff.

As he kissed the top of her head, Razor sighed with relief. Helena always calmed him. And right now, Razor was very worked up.

"She's worse than I thought."

Helena frowned as she looked up at him and glanced at the door. "I think you're right."

Razor gently turned Helena's face back to him. He stared into her eyes for a moment. "There's something else," he had to look away from her gaze for a second. "I lied to her. The night our camp was attacked, David came to me, and he wanted to try to ambush Nick so that he could free Jade. She asked me what we discussed, and I told her I never talked to him."

"Oh, no, Razor," she whispered.

"I know. I don't know how I'm going to tell her."

Helena shook her head as she slowly walked out of his arms. "You can't tell her."

"I'll have to eventually, Helena. She deserves to know."

"Not in this state, she doesn't!" she frowned at him. "What would've happened if Keeper and I didn't get here when we did?"

"I would've been all right."

"No! One of you would've gotten hurt, Razor. And just imagine how she'll react to the news about David."

Razor frowned. Helena was right, of course. But he really didn't want to keep lying to Jade, and he knew the reaction would be bad the longer he waited to tell her.

Keeper and Tatianna walked into the lobby. It was their turn to take watch. Razor was a little relieved about that. Although, he did wonder what Jade was currently up to.

"Ya good?" Keeper asked as he walked in. Tatianna was right behind him.

Razor nodded.

"Well, I left Jade with Cole, and she's helping him with Jackson. She seems calm enough," Keeper added. "But I guess as a precaution. She surrendered her weapons to Zara."

Razor nodded again.

"My guess is she'll be resting with Clay and Reagan tonight. They tend to do a good job with handling her."

"Well, I won't protest her being with him tonight," Helena admitted.

"It's been quiet here," Razor told them.

Keeper nodded. "Sounds good. We'll be here until two Black Coats members come to relieve us. Rest up."

Razor nodded for the last time as Helena pulled him to the door. They silently left out and walked into the lobby. Razor needed help with what to do with Junior. He was sure that by now, most of the group knew about Junior potentially being a spy. Jade must've spread the news by now. But Tatianna did not indicate that she knew anything. And as he and Helena made it to the third floor, Yoko, Danita, or the others gave no inkling that something was afoot. Maybe Jade didn't say anything after all.

Helena led him to an apartment at the end of the hall, just across from Cole's residence. Zara was standing just outside the door, and she smiled when she saw them.

"Just so you know, Jade took up residence with that guy Clay," she smirked. Razor noticed that she was looking at Helena.

Helena smiled weakly. "That's all right."

Zara nodded and then turned to go inside Cole's apartment.

Helena turned to him as she opened the apartment door. "We have this place to ourselves tonight."

"Really? Why?" there weren't enough apartments on the floor for them to get their own.

"I requested it," Helena shrugged. She led him through the kitchen and the living room. It all was tiny. "Besides, this place is only a one-bedroom."

Helena guided him down the narrow hallway, and at the end to the left, there was a small bedroom. It appeared to have already been cleaned and tidied.

"You did all this," he lingered in the doorway as Helena went inside and began to take off her jacket and boots.

"Yeah, I didn't want you trying to clean after a long shift."

Razor walked inside. Helena was about to take off her shirt when Razor took her hand and pulled her to him. He kissed her softly on the lips.

"Thank you," he said once he pulled away.

Helena didn't say anything. Instead, she pulled him toward the bed. She quickly took off her shirt once they were near the bed. It never failed. Razor was always in awe of her beauty. Helena smirked when she noticed the way he was looking at her. She took off his shirt and began to undo her pants.

A small voice in his head told him that he should protest. They'd been having sex a lot lately, and he was worried that Helena wasn't processing her feelings correctly, but as he looked at her, he knew it was a struggle to deny her. So, ignoring that voice, Razor undid her pants.

Once completely nude, Razor swiftly picked her up and laid her on the bed. He kissed her lips and her neck. And then he moved down to her breasts. Helena's breath increased.

"Aren't you glad we're alone?" she moaned.

Razor responded by kissing her deeply. Helena dug her nails into his back as she pulled him closer. He loved how soft her body felt against his. The feeling never changed, no matter how much time had passed. And no matter how much stress he felt. It always melted away when he was with her. Razor was instantly relieved as he listened to his wife's moans all night.

**

There were a series of rapid knocks at their bedroom door, followed by some incoherent yelling from outside. Razor jumped out of bed. He was heading toward the door when he realized he was still nude. He quickly found his pants and put them on. Reagan was on the other side of the bedroom door when he opened it. She looked worried.

"It's Jade," she said and then swiftly walked away.

Razor turned to see Helena rushing to put her clothes on. Once she was decent, they both rushed out of the apartment. When they got out into the hall, it was pure chaos. Cole, Keeper, and Zara ran down the hall, heading toward the stairs. Reagan was waiting for them by the staircase door.

"What's going on?" Helena panicked.

Reagan opened the door and began heading down the stairs. "Something happened with Jade and Junior."

"What?!" Razor was furious as he followed her down the stairs.

"Members were taking volunteers to go on a scavenging mission," she said over her shoulder. "They stopped at our place. She heard that Junior was going, and she volunteered. I tried to stop her, but she wouldn't listen," they had gotten to the main floor. Reagan paused before she opened the door. She looked Razor in the eyes. "I made her promise that she wouldn't confront him. And she did. She just wanted to see what you saw."

"So, she told you her theory was correct?" Razor asked. Although, he wasn't worried. Reagan knew how to keep a secret.

She shook her head. "My brother told me about your suspicions."

Reagan opened the door, and there was chaos in the lobby. Keeper and

Cole were attending to an injured member. The guy was bleeding from his chest.

~17~

Nick

Raina stared at him in disgust as Nick sat in the chair, gazing into nothingness with his bloody hands. The captured DC officer wiggled in his chair as he struggled to escape his bondage. Nick ignored him. There was no way the guy could escape. He had been trying most of the night but with no success.

Nick locked eyes with Raina. She rolled her eyes and shook her head in disapproval. Nick smiled. The girl was growing braver. She stood right before him while Aiden and Levi huddled in the corner. Nick was impressed that she was growing more comfortable around him. How could she not? She was there with him forever, after all. And he appreciated that she was at least trying to save him from himself.

Although he usually ignored her.

When Raina warned him that things could always get worse, Nick briefly considered her words—*briefly*. But then his mother's voice crept through his head, and any thoughts of following the girl's advice quickly disappeared.

The captured DC officer moved in his chair again. The legs scrapping across the floor brought Nick back to his current situation. He was torturing the guy to see what he knew about Chase's current plans. Unfortunately, the officer gave him nothing, leading Nick to perform very unpleasant acts in front of the children. Nick looked down at the knife that was in his bloody hands. He had done a lot of cutting and chopping through the night.

Raina frowned as she looked down at the floor. "How can you do this?"

Nick followed her gaze. She was grossed out by the fingers that lay scattered across the floor. As his first form of torture, Nick thought relieving the officer of some of his extremities was a good idea. Whenever the officer was defiant or refused to answer a question, Nick took the liberty of relieving him of a finger. Eventually, he had to stop, or else the poor guy wouldn't have any fingers left.

By the time Nick took off the fourth finger on the officer's right hand, he had decided to change things up a bit. He then moved on to very meticulously removing layers of skin from the officer's arms. This had proven to have more of an effect on the officer. The deeper he sliced, the more the officer screamed and cried. As each layer was removed, more nerves and sensitive areas were exposed. The officer was going to crack soon. Nick just needed to wait him out a little.

"I think I'm going to be sick," Levi groaned. He had finally opened his eyes, and it looked like he was instantly regretting it.

"You can't get sick," Nick sighed. Why was the boy so weak? But then he noticed that Aiden had his eyes covered too. Nick sighed even louder.

Levi began throwing up blood. Nick was a little horrified at the view. He really didn't expect to see that.

"I stand corrected."

"What are you talking about?" the DC officer spat. "I'm not getting sick."

"No one was talking to you," Nick rose to his feet and walked to the corner where Levi and Aiden were huddled in. He gently pushed Levi aside and grabbed Aiden's hands, and he removed them away from Aiden's eyes. "Open your eyes, son."

Aiden shook his head in refusal. Nick swallowed his frustration. He didn't want to get angry with his son, but he needed him to be braver— stronger. He could not survive in this world if he weren't strong.

"There's nothing to fear. Just open your eyes," Nick calmly encouraged.

"I'm afraid of you, Dad."

Nick stood there frozen and in shock. How could Aiden be afraid of him?

"Look at what you've done to that poor man."

"How do you know what I've done if you haven't opened your eyes?" annoyance dripped through Nick's tone.

"I don't need my eyes open to see the damage you've done."

"He was going to kill me."

Aiden remained silent—eyes still closed.

"What I'm doing is necessary."

"Keep telling yourself that, Dad."

"Who the hell are you talking to?" the officer demanded. He was looking at Nick like he was crazy.

Nick glared at him. "Shut it," he returned his attention to Aiden, who still had his eyes closed. He stood there speechless for a few seconds, unable to find the words. Aiden was afraid of him. His own son. Maybe he really was a monster.

Nick sighed as he turned his back to his son. Raina was resting against the back of his chair. She had a look that read, *I told you so*. Nick sighed again. He walked back over to his chair and sat down. Raina stood beside him. She looked over at the officer and shook her head. The officer still looked defiant—despite the missing limbs and layers of skin. Nick didn't bother with questions. Instead, he took his knife and resumed slowly slicing off another layer of the officer's skin.

The cries and screams from the officer filled the small store. Everything was falling apart, and Nick was trying his best not to fall apart with it. He was always able to adapt to the situation. But if Nick was frank with himself, he struggled to adapt to this. He tried not to show it, but the children being with him constantly was getting to him. Even before, he had never seen Aiden as much as he did now. And it was a struggle to look at Raina and Levi, knowing what he'd done to them. No wonder Aiden was afraid of him.

"Nick...Nick," he heard vaguely.

It wasn't clear how long he'd been going at it. Apparently, he had blacked out. There were small rays of light peeking through the boarded-up windows. When he became aware of himself again, the officer's arm looked mutilated. Levi was in the corner throwing up blood again. Aiden was crying. And Raina looked horrified. The officer was passed out—most likely from the pain.

"Where did you go, Nick?" Raina asked with concern.

Nick looked down at his hands, which were soaked in blood and pieces of flesh. He tried flinging some of it off, making Levi sick even more.

"I'm not sure."

"Well, I don't think you'll get anything out of him tonight."

Nick rubbed his hands against his pants. "Perhaps you're right," he sighed and stood. "This is a dead end."

"I think it's better if we just get out of here."

"I want to see Jade," Levi groaned.

Raina nodded. "We should just take one of their trucks and head for the border."

Nick looked over at the unconscious officer. He was slumped over. Nick debated whether to leave or kill him, putting him out of his misery. After a few seconds of pondering, he decided to let the officer be. He wanted the other officers to find him. That way, Chase would know what he was doing.

"Let's go, children," he said as he gathered his weapons and supplies.

Raina grabbed Aiden and Levi's hands and led them out of the back room. Nick followed them out. Aiden was still determined not to open his eyes. And Levi was struggling not to get sick again. Once they were clear from the back room, Raina encouraged Aiden to open his eyes.

"You won't see anything bad here," she assured.

Aiden slowly opened his eyes and then smiled at her. "Thank you, Raina."

She smiled back and led them to the door.

Nick slowly followed them. They paused at the door, waiting for him to go out first. Nick's hand rested on the doorknob. He was listening out for anything suspicious. He didn't hear anything unusual, so he cautiously opened the door. Although the sun was gradually rising, there was still enough darkness to provide them with some cover.

Nick moved quickly through the thicket of trees and bushes. The children had to run to keep up with him. They needed to get closer to the border. They were now at what used to be Alma, New York. The small town was now overrun with forestry. They were just about 100 miles from the Canadian border. And that felt like worlds away. Even with a stolen truck, that was much ground to cover. And many opportunities for things to go horribly wrong.

They'd finally crossed the tree line to the road. Nick was leery about traveling at first. He wanted to be sure that there wasn't anyone nearby waiting. The captured DC officer never told him if more of them were lingering by. But after a few minutes of waiting, he decided to go for it. Nick took the truck with the most gas and raided the other truck for supplies and weapons.

"You did the right thing, Nick," Raina said from the backseat. She was between Levi and Aiden, and they held her hand for comfort.

Nick didn't say anything to her. He didn't think he did the right thing. He just didn't see the point of torturing that officer any longer. The officer was very rebellious and wasn't easy to break. The best thing was to walk away. He was sure he'd stumble across another officer to get information from sooner than later.

They were about 20 miles from their previous location when they heard trucks roaring. The sound was getting louder, and it sounded like many of them. Nick sped up a bit, even though the trucks weren't in his view.

"Faster, Dad."

Nick was about to tell him that he was going as fast as he could; when a couple of DC trucks came barreling out of the trees from the right side of the road. They nearly crashed as Nick quickly swerved to avoid the trucks. They tried to create a blockade to stop him, but Nick got through a small gap before they could block it.

"How did they find us so quickly?" Raina pondered as she turned to look out the back window.

Four trucks were chasing after them. Nick floored it. They sped through the narrow highway. The twists and turns of the road were treacherous.

"Fuck," Nick mumbled as the truck tilted slightly as he abruptly turned. The children screamed from the backseat.

How did they find him so quickly? There was no way that the captured DC officer contacted the others so quickly. No. They had to be lurking around already. That was the only logical explanation. Nick needed to think of something fast. If he stuck to the road, they would catch him eventually. It was only a matter of time.

Two trucks came speeding at him head-on while the four trucks behind were gaining on him. Thinking quickly, Nick quickly turned left and went racing through the woods. One truck crashed into a tree. Nick saw the accident from the rearview mirror. The other trucks struggled to follow him through the woods.

"I told you, it could always get worse," Raina reminded him.

"Yeah, yeah," he mumbled as he weaved in and out between trees.

There was the sound of another truck crashing. This time it was more severe than the last one. Some flames shot up in the air. Nick was back down to four trucks chasing him. He would be in the clear if he could somehow get rid of them. But the forest was getting thicker with trees. Soon there would be nowhere to go, and he would have to go on foot. And it wasn't exactly clear if he could outrun them for long.

"What's the plan, Nick?" Raina demanded as she looked out the window.

"I'm working on it," he growled. He couldn't get captured again. If he did, he was certain it would be his end.

Chase probably wouldn't want to torture him. If he was captured now, a death sentence was sure to follow. And Nick didn't want that. Not just yet. He needed to see Jade first. After all, all of this was for her. So they could be together.

A large branch barely missed his truck and fell onto the one behind him. The vehicle screeched to a halt, and the one behind it crashed into it, causing a ripple effect to the other trucks behind them.

Nick sighed with satisfaction as more and more distance was made between him and his pursuers. And then his heart stopped as they suddenly approached a steep slope. Nick slammed on the brakes, but he was too late. They flew off the hill for a few seconds, crashed-landed on the wheels for another second, and then the truck tumbled down the rest of the way.

By the time they descended the hill, Nick was hanging upside down. The seatbelt had him suspended in the air. Blood was dripping from his head, and a searing pain was in his arm. Raina rushed to his side—panicked. The machete was sticking out of her stomach.

"We need to move, Nick," she looked around as blood poured out of her mouth. "Someone's coming!"

As the sound of footsteps approached, Nick slowly blacked out.

~18~

Jade

It felt like everything was going in slow motion. Cole and Keeper worked aggressively to stop the blood from pouring out of the member's chest. The member looked so frightened. Jade recognized that look. The look of death and the knowledge that it was lingering close by. She remembered Lang had that same look as the bullet from Bossman's rifle penetrated his skull, taking his life out of him. For a brief moment, she recalled David having that same look.

And she was the cause of it all.

No. Junior was the cause of it all. He was the traitor. The spy. The mole. Their blood was on his hands...but Jade couldn't fight off the sense of responsibility. If only she had just kept her mouth shut.

The journey back to the safehouse was an agonizing one. Jade struggled to drag the member's body back while keeping pressure on his wound. To make matters even worse, Jade was paranoid about someone coming up to attack her—mainly Junior. But Jade was determined to get the member back to Blackwell, and she wouldn't let another one of them die on her watch.

Now, as she stood stunned in the lobby, she couldn't help but think that it all was a lost cause. There was so much blood pouring out of him. Jade hadn't really noticed it before. She looked down at her hand and saw it was drenched in blood. Her mind was so preoccupied with getting them back that she didn't notice how much blood was being lost.

"What happened?" Razor growled.

Jade looked at him, startled. She hadn't registered his presence. Nor Helena's or Reagan's. Razor scowled as he looked at her. Jade couldn't tell if he was angry at her or the situation. It was probably both.

"We need to get him upstairs," Cole demanded. "You two, help Keeper and me with him."

Two stunned members quickly went to help their leader. The injured member groaned in pain even more as his comrades attempted to move him.

"It's all right," Cole tried to comfort him. "It's going to be all right."

Jade watched as the member continued to cry and scream out in pain. Cole and the others tried their best to be gentle with him, but any movement seemed agonizing.

Zara walked up behind Razor—a frown prominent on her face. "What happened?"

Razor turned to look at her. "That's what I was trying to figure out."

Zara and Razor both looked at Jade, but she was focused on Cole and the injured member. Helena held open the door to the stairway as Cole and the others gently carried the member. His cries echoed through the building.

Once they were gone, Helena shut the door and walked over to Zara, Razor, and Jade. Reagan lingered by. Helena looked at her sister closely, and Jade could tell she was examining her for any injuries.

"You're all right," Helena sighed.

Jade just nodded even though it didn't sound like a question—more like a statement. Slowly, Jade met Razor's eyes. She wasn't ready to face him yet, especially after what had happened between them earlier. But she couldn't put it off any longer. She had to let them know what was going on.

"I didn't intend to confront him," she started. Jade kept her gaze on the wall just behind Razor—too fearful of his reaction. "I just wanted to see what you saw."

"I don't understand," Zara frowned.

"Junior," Jade sighed. "He's a spy for Bossman."

Zara's reaction frowned at the news. "And the other members..."

"Dead...he killed them."

"What did you do, Jade?" Razor sighed.

"Nothing, I was just watching him most of the night. Eventually, he noticed. But at first, he thought that I was checking him out. So, I went with that. And then he brought up David," Jade paused as she recalled how smug and confident Junior seemed when he told her he wouldn't experience the same fate. "I just got so angry that I mentioned how we thought there was a mole in the group."

"And that's when he attacked," Helena guessed.

Jade shook her head. "We were heading to the last building when he did that. It all happened so quickly...it took a moment for everyone to react."

"Where did you lose him?" Razor asked.

"About half a mile from the fish and tackle store."

"We need to assemble a search team," he said, looking at Zara. She nodded at him and proceeded to leave.

"He couldn't have made it far," Jade mumbled.

Zara turned and looked at her. Razor raised an eyebrow.

"I managed to stab him in his upper thigh," Jade continued. "He was bleeding out pretty bad."

Razor nodded at this. He looked over at Zara.

"I'll get a team assembled," Zara stated. She rushed out of the lobby.

"Jade, you'll need to come with us," Razor demanded once Zara was gone.

Jade shook her head. That was the last thing she needed to do. She still didn't trust herself around those she loved. And her attempted attack on Razor was way too fresh for her to be near him.

"Don't be silly, Jade," Helena said as she approached her. "We need you."

Jade took a deep breath and looked at Reagan, casually leaning against the wall. She looked indifferent but smiled a little when Jade caught her eye.

"You can stick by me," she said, answering Jade's unasked question.

Instantly, Jade was relieved by the notion. She knew if anything happened, at least Reagan could stop her.

Zara quickly returned with a few members, along with Clay and Danita. They both looked confused.

"Is it true?" Danita asked when she approached them. "Junior's really a traitor?"

"It is," Razor sighed. Jade could tell he was tired of relaying this information to everyone already.

"The bastard," she mumbled.

"Tatianna is staying behind to help Keeper and the doc," Zara stated. "And Yoko is watching over Calvin. He's still too tired to do anything."

"This is fine," Razor looked over the people Zara brought. "What about the lookouts here?"

"They're already in their positions," Zara stated. She looked over at Jade. "Lead the way."

Jade nodded as she slowly made her way to the lobby doors. She avoided eye contact with everyone, especially Clay. The thought of admitting that she messed up yet again was too much to handle. Jade was thankful for the slight breeze that hit her face as she pushed open the main door. The sound of the rushing water from the pond was loud. It didn't seem that loud to her before. But then again, her mind was elsewhere the last time she was out here. The rushing waterfall sounded peaceful.

As they slowly left the apartment complex's sights, someone handed Jade an old rag. She looked over to see that it was Clay. He didn't say anything, and his face was expressionless. Jade stared at the rag momentarily—unclear what to do with it. Clay gestured to her bloody hand. Finally, she took the rag and tried to wipe all traces of blood away.

Once her hand was somewhat clean, Jade took out her bow and an arrow. She quickly sped up her pace so she was nowhere near anyone. She wasn't in the mood to talk. And she certainly wasn't in the mood to answer questions. Right now, she needed to redeem herself. She needed to right her wrong. Jade had allowed Junior to get to her. And in turn, she gave away their position prematurely—a stupid, stupid mistake.

Since the horrors on the Detroit River, Jade has acted irrationally and foolishly. It was time for her to get it together. If she was ever going to get her revenge, she needed to play smarter. They needed to find Junior and torture information out of him. And then kill him. That was her plan. And she needed more than anything to execute it.

Find Junior.

Torture.

Kill him.

That was what needed to be done.

Before she knew it, Jade approached the fish and tackle shop. She instantly slowed down a little. Her heart began pounding in her chest. This wasn't the crime scene, but this was the start of it. This was where Jade slipped up and gave too much information away. And she was sure this was the place where Junior began panicking.

Jade kneeled to the ground and tried to find any traces of blood. There were no fresh tracks that she could see.

"I thought you said half a mile away from here," Reagan stood over her.

Jade was startled for a second. Reagan was so eerily quiet when she walked.

"Just making sure he didn't double back this way," Jade glanced at the surrounding area. Razor and the rest of the group were looking around too.

"I don't think he would if he was injured."

"Yeah," Jade stood and sighed. "But who knows what traitors do nowadays."

Reagan chuckled as she walked away.

Jade followed her. She was right. It was improbable that Junior would double back when injured, but Jade just wanted to find him quickly. She rushed past the others and continued to lead the way.

Find Junior.

Torture.

Kill him.

Find Junior.

Torture.

Kill him.

Jade could picture it. Junior strung up by his legs. She and Razor taking turns beating him. Junior confessing and telling them everything that he did. And finally, her knife quickly sliding its way across his throat. Or maybe his gut. Or his black heart. Either option was perfectly fine with her as long as he stopped breathing.

"Oh shit," Zara moaned.

The group had finally come to the scene of the crime. Jade was so caught up in the pleasures of killing Junior that she hadn't noticed. The two member's lifeless bodies still lay on the ground. Zara hovered over the girl's dead body—crying. Instantly, Jade felt regret and shame. She had forgotten all about them. They would need to take their bodies back.

"Her sister is going to be devastated," Zara looked at Jade with tears. "I didn't even know she volunteered to go. I wouldn't have let her."

"I'm so sorry," Jade mumbled. She could imagine the sister's pain now. Jade was all too familiar with that grief when she thought Helena was dead.

"I got a trail of blood over here," Razor called out.

The group quickly rushed over to him. Sure enough, there were specks of blood leading in the direction Junior fled off to.

"He can't be too far," Jade looked around, wondering if he was nearby.

Zara looked at the members that were with them. "You think you can take their bodies back?"

"We can."

"Stay sharp out there," Zara ordered. "I'll stay with them."

The members quickly attended to the bodies as Zara, Jade, Helena,

Razor, Reagan, and Clay followed the blood trail.

This time Razor insisted on leading the group. Jade didn't argue with him. Instead, she hung back and brought up the rear. If Junior were to attack anyone, she figured that it would be her. So, she made herself appear vulnerable, so the opportunity would be too good to pass up.

Jade was thankful that the others were giving her space. Although, she could tell that Clay wanted to talk to her but was refraining from doing so. She didn't need any distractions right now. She just needed to focus on her plan. And more than anything, she needed to redeem herself.

Find Junior.

Torture.

Kill him.

Just then, David appeared beside her—a frown on his face. Jade ignored him as she struggled to scan the trees and bushes behind him. Instinctively, she slowed down as the others went ahead. She knew that she wouldn't be able to ignore David for long, and she didn't want to feel the concerned gaze of the others as she talked to herself.

"You shouldn't be here," she said in a hushed tone.

"How could I not?"

"Just stop it, ok," Jade stopped walking as she squinted to get a better view of the trees behind David. There didn't appear to be anything unusual. "I have to do this."

"No, you don't."

"Ok...I *want* to do this."

David sighed. "Jade."

"He's the reason you're dead, David."

"And killing him won't bring me back."

"But it'll make me feel better," Jade resumed walking once she saw the group slowly leaving her line of view.

"And it's all about you, right?"

"Stop it, David."

"No! I have a right to have a say in this."

Jade rolled her eyes but didn't say anything else. Her hallucinations were starting to get ridiculous. Nothing was going to stop her from getting to Junior. He had a part in David, Levi, and Raina's death. That was unforgivable. And it deserved the cruelest punishment. No one was going to stop her from achieving that. Not even her own mind.

"So, that's it, huh," David said, reading her mind. "Whatever you say goes."

Jade glared at him. "You're not *here*, David."

"Got something!" Razor called out.

Immediately, Jade was thankful for the interruption. She didn't need to look over to see if David was gone. It was clear that he was.

The group was huddled up in a nearby building—a garage. It was small and ran down. As Jade approached them, she saw the faint blood trail that led to the door of the building.

Razor looked over at everyone with a stern look. "Stay sharp in there. He's backed into a corner, so he's liable to do anything to save his skin."

Jade's grip on her bow and arrow instantly got tighter. Razor went in first, followed by Helena and Zara. Reagan and Clay hung back near Jade. Her heart raced once they went inside. She wanted nothing more than for him to be inside, and she wanted nothing more than to see the life slowly drained out of his eyes.

She *needed* it.

The strong urge in the pit of her stomach desperately needed satisfaction.

By the time she fully got inside, the rest of the group was at the back of the building, wearing a look of defeat. Jade began to panic. Her moment of satisfaction was entirely fleeting. As she approached, Razor kneeled and looked at the area near the corner.

"It looks like he attended to his wound here," he held up a bloody cloth for the group to see.

"Maybe he made a tourniquet," Helena suggested.

Razor sighed as he threw the cloth down. "Yeah, maybe."

"Tracks are moving out this way," Zara pointed to the back door leading to the massive tree area.

Reagan frowned as she got a closer look. "These are drag marks."

"And four different sets of footprints," Zara added.

"That doesn't sound good," there was agitation in Razor's voice.

"The Radicals," Jade came to the scary, horrible realization.

"It looks like it," Zara admitted. She didn't seem as panicked as Jade felt.

"We need to get back now," Razor ordered as he headed toward the front exit.

"Shouldn't we see how far the tracks go," Reagan frowned.

"It doesn't matter," Razor said from over his shoulder. "Our group is now vulnerable."

The rest of the group quickly followed Razor out. Jade was furious that the Radicals got to her target before she did.

**

The mood was a somber one once they all got back. People were grieving over the members' bodies that were brought back. And people were grieving over the member that they'd just lost. Jade and the others walked into Cole's apartment only to find everyone mourning and crying. Cole looked defeated.

"His injury was worse than I thought," he whispered. "There was nothing I could do."

"I'm so sorry, Cole," Jade fought back the tears.

"Please tell me that you found him."

"No," Razor stated. He looked at everyone in the room. "Pack up. We're leaving. The Radicals got to him before we could."

"Christ," Cole mumbled.

The members began to gather up their things frantically.

Cole looked at the member's dead body in front of him. He sighed. "I really don't want to leave their bodies."

"It'll slow us down," Razor stated.

"They shouldn't be left behind," Jade mumbled. She didn't deserve to argue with him, but she couldn't leave these members' bodies like that. They deserved better. They deserved to be with their families and friends. Jade at least owed them that much.

Razor sighed. "Fine."

"Bright side to all of this," Cole stood. "At least Junior can't give away our headquarters position."

"Besides," Zara added. "I don't think the Radicals are listening to him anyway."

"You think they're torturing him," Jade was a little hopeful at the notion.

"I don't think they're pampering him."

"Yeah, but it's only a matter of time before he gives them something they can use," Razor added. "So, we need to be far away from here before that happens."

"You have a point there," Zara said. "Let's get packing."

Everyone dispersed to gather up their things.

Jade headed back to the apartment she shared with Clay and Reagan alone. She quickly gathered up her things. It wasn't that much. Once she was done, she sighed and lay across the bed. Someone would come and tell her that they were ready to leave. In the meantime, Jade focused on her breathing. She really needed to get her emotions under control. Not only did she allow Junior to get away, but she also allowed him to be captured by her enemy. That was unacceptable. There was no telling what information Junior was giving them.

Jade wrecked her brain, trying to determine if any sensitive information had been exposed to Junior. Nothing came to mind. But that didn't mean anything. And it certainly didn't bring her any comfort.

"Wallowing, I see."

Jade sat up to find Clay leaning in the doorway with his arms folded. She sighed and lay back down. "I'm just thinking."

"On where Junior could be?" Jade felt him sit on the bed.

"On what information he could be giving up."

"You heard the doc. Junior doesn't know the location of their headquarters."

"We don't know what Junior knows, and that's the scary part."

Clay sighed. He and Jade sat silently for a moment. "How are you feeling?" he finally asked.

"Peachy," Jade responded sarcastically. She was getting tired of people asking that question.

"I'm sorry. I'm just a little worried about you."

Of course, Jade was starting to regret her initial reaction. Clay has been supportive and patient with her, and he certainly didn't deserve her lousy attitude. She sighed as she sat back up.

"I'm just angry with myself," she admitted. "Lately, I've been letting my emotions control me. I should've been smarter when it came to Junior."

Clay didn't say anything. Instead, he looked Jade over—checking for any cuts or bruises. Once he saw that she was fine, he released her from his gaze.

"Thank God *you* weren't killed," he sighed.

"It's what I deserve."

"Come on now, Jade."

"You seriously think I deserve to be alive."

"You're not some evil, shitty person," Clay rose to his feet. "A lot of shitty stuff happened to you...it happened to all of us. And we all have our way of getting through it. Your way is a little more difficult, and that's understandable. But it doesn't mean you deserve to die."

Jade shook her head in disbelief. Clay gave her more credit than she deserved.

"Look, everyone is still packing," he sat back on the bed. "How about you lay down and get yourself some rest? I'll wake you when it's time to go."

Jade didn't say anything. She just did what she was told. It didn't take long for her to drift off to sleep.

The sun had been up for a few hours by the time they'd hit the road. Everyone was silent as they made their journey. The mood was a very gloomy one. Jade had pulled Jackson duty with Keeper. She had the front of Jackson's gurney, while Keeper had the rear. Clay and Reagan were a few feet away from her. Jade could see the back of Razor and Helena's head up front. They were talking to Cole and Zara. More than likely, they were going over some plan.

Jade made it a point to cut them a wide berth during this journey. Shame and embarrassment still hunted her. Plus, she was just too disappointed in herself to be anywhere near them right now.

"It's natural, you know," David said.

Jade sighed as she looked over to see him walking beside her. She quickly looked around to ensure the others weren't paying her any attention.

"What is?"

"The need for vengeance. It's perfectly natural."

"But?"

"It could kill you too."

Jade stared ahead. "I see nothing wrong with that."

"Come on, Jade. Please, don't do this."

"You don't understand what it's like to be here without you...without them."

"Do you think we want you like this?" he gestured at her in disgust. "You're becoming the person he wants you to be."

Jade ignored him. Nothing David said was going to sway her. Jade was determined to stick to her plan.

"I just don't want to lose the woman I love."

"You lost me that night on the river, David. Bossman did that. And I plan on making him pay for it."

"There will be no coming back from this."

"Who said that I want to come back?"

~19~

Razor

According to the small, faded, beat-up sign they'd passed about 35 minutes ago, they were in Puslinch, Ontario. They'd been on the road since the morning, and the group's mood became bleak as it got into the afternoon. But how could it not? A traitor was among them, and he killed four Black Coat members. He'd managed to escape and was now captured by their enemy. The situation was grave. And Razor was beyond frustrated.

"How long do you think we should stay on the road?" one of the members asked.

"I'd like to put some more distance from us and the hideout," Razor looked around, wondering if there were eyes on them right now.

Cole sighed. "He's right. We're only about 23 kilometers out, and I'd feel more comfortable if we could make that number a little more."

The member sighed in disappointment. Clearly, he didn't feel comfortable being on the road much longer.

Razor glanced behind him to see how the others were doing. Helena, Tatianna, and Zara appeared to be in an intense conversation. Danita and Reagan were scouting ahead, along with a few members, ensuring no surprises were heading their way. Yoko was walking arm and arm with Calvin. He seemed well-rested and was counting his steps. Clay was keeping a close eye on Jade, who was on Jackson duty with Keeper. Her gaze was on the ground. She seemed out of it. Razor didn't know if she was just tired or still beating herself up over what had happened with Junior. Still, he was concerned about her well-being.

Once they've gotten somewhere safe, he'll figure out what to do with Jade. He'll figure out how to bring her back. What she desperately needed right now was revenge. If they could find Junior, he could give her that. Maybe then, she'll calm down a little. Razor knew she wouldn't be back 100 percent, but it'd be something. They just needed to get somewhere safe so he could think properly.

"You don't need to worry, old friend," Cole encouraged. He'd been watching Razor the whole time. "Junior can't give them anything useful."

"It's not that," Razor sighed.

Cole glanced in the direction of Jade. He lingered for a moment before turning his gaze back to Razor. "You can't help those who aren't ready to be helped."

"She does want help."

"Does she?"

Razor glared at Cole. He didn't appreciate what the doc was trying to say about his sister.

Cole shook his head. "Sometimes, when so much pain and evil are put on one person, that person eventually wants to do the same thing back."

Razor looked back at the road in front of them. He didn't want to hear anything that the doc had to say.

"We've all heard the stories about abusees killing their abusers," Cole continued, ignoring Razor's denial of this conversation. "This case doesn't seem to be any different."

"So, what do you expect her to do? Turn the other cheek?" Razor said defensively. "I don't see you doing the same doc."

Cole chuckled a little. "I'm not saying what Jade is doing is wrong. I'm just saying that right now, she might not want to be saved. And that's perfectly ok," he looked over at Razor. "You, my friend, just need to find a way to be ok with that."

"Keeping Helena and Jade safe is my mission. And I will always find a way to save them...even if it's from themselves."

"That's one way to guarantee failure, my friend," Cole glanced around and sighed. "I think we're losing the group. It might be better to scavenge for a bit and find a place to settle in for the night."

Razor looked around too. The group's energy decreased with each step they took. "I think you're right."

Both men stopped walking, and Razor let out a quick whistle. Everyone stopped walking and turned to look at them, even Reagan, Danita, and the few members who were up ahead. Razor waited until they got into hearing range before he delivered the plan to the group. He did a quick glance at their surrounding area and noted what was nearby. It was a heavily wooded area. Before the new world, the area used to be farmland. There were a few barns nearby and, surprisingly, two huge houses. One of them looked like a mansion. That was the one he decided they would rest in for the night.

"All right," Razor began. "Although I would like to put some more distance between the Radicals and us, I think it's time to find somewhere to rest up for the night. It'd be useless if the Radicals caught up with us, and we're all too tired to fight."

A few of the members mumbled in agreement.

"So, we're going to split off in groups to look for supplies nearby and clear the house that we'd be staying in," Razor looked over at Jade. She did not indicate that she was listening. "Keeper and Jade will stay on Jackson duty with Zara and the doc."

"Copy that," Zara said.

Jade still had a blank look on her face. Razor continued.

"Reagan, Danita and a few members will scout the barn and house to the west. Helena, Tatianna, Yoko, and Calvin will take the barn and house to the south."

"Got it," Helena stated.

"The rest of the members will take anything else to the east. Clay and I will clear the hideout before joining the rest of you."

"Sounds like a plan," one of the members stated.

"Everyone is to be back before sundown," Razor slowly glanced around. "If you haven't reported back by then, you'd be presumed dead."

"Wait, you won't come looking for us?" another member asked, shocked.

"We can't afford to waste any more time out here on the road."

"Sadly, he's right," Cole stated. "We've been on the road too long already."

"So, stay sharp out there. Move out!"

A few members grumbled their disagreement as they all dispersed. Helena and her group lingered behind. Once everyone was gone, she walked up to Razor and kissed him.

"Be safe."

"You too," he kissed her forehead. "I'll meet up with you once the hideout is cleared."

She nodded. Helena was about to leave when she paused and turned to face Jade. "Don't give them any trouble, ok?"

Jade didn't say anything. She just nodded.

Razor watched Helena and her group off before focusing on those remaining. "All right, Clay and I will start with the garage. Once we've cleared that, you all can hide out in there as we clear the house."

"Copy that," Zara unsheathed her sword.

Razor looked over at Jade. She and Keeper had just laid Jackson on the ground, and Cole had kneeled to look at him. Razor and Jade locked eyes for a moment.

"You good?" he asked.

"Yeah," she spoke for the first time. "Just be safe."

Razor nodded. "Stay sharp, everyone," he looked over at Clay. "Let's go."

As they headed toward the house, Razor looked back at Jade one last time. Her back was to him, and she was pulling out her knives—preparing for an attack, should it ever come. Razor sighed as he turned his attention to the road before him.

The area in front of the house was overrun with bushes, high grass, and trees. He and Clay slowed down as they got closer to it. Razor pulled out his trustee machete, and Clay retrieved his crowbar. Razor went ahead of him and started attacking the high grass with his machete. Nothing but small animals and bugs retreated. Razor made a mental note to return to hunt for small game later.

It took them about five minutes to clear the house's front yard. It appeared nothing was hiding in there besides small wildlife. The two men carefully approached the entrance of the three-car garage. The doors were damaged. It looked like the bottom half was pried open. Razor was positive that this house fell victim to marauders numerous times. He was just hoping that none of them were hiding out there at this moment.

Clay looked at the garage door, which was heavily damaged. "That doesn't look comforting."

"You hold it open while I go inside."

Clay nodded. He slowly approached the garage door—each step deliberate. He pulled it back as far as possible and then signaled Razor to proceed.

Razor quickly made his way through. He mentally prepared himself for any sudden attacks. Nothing happened. He glanced around and saw that the place was empty. Literally, there was absolutely nothing there. Not even a nail. The area had been picked clean. Razor shouldn't have been that shocked. A place like this is a huge target for looters. He wouldn't be surprised if they found the inside in the same position.

"What's the verdict?" Clay asked from underneath the door.

"It's all clear. Let them know they can proceed on."

"Roger that."

Razor took another look around the garage. He hoped to spot something he had missed the first time. Nothing new came up. The garage was clean. Unusually clean. The concrete floors looked like they'd been swept. Was it ever used? That'd be disappointing if the original owners never got the chance to try the house out. He could never picture himself in a home like this. It was way too much. It was just him, Helena, and Jade. They would never need that much space. The only way he could even consider living in a place like this is if he had kids. And that was so far from his mind. Who would even think about bringing a child into this chaotic world?

But if this was before. And if he'd met Helena before. Then Razor could definitely see it. A little girl with Helena's beautiful brown eyes and the Willer sisters' stubbornness and fierceness—times ten. He would be wrapped around her little finger. There'd be nothing in this world he wouldn't give her. If only it were before. Then Razor knew that he could protect her from anything and anyone. That wouldn't even be a question.

But this was now.

Razor was barely succeeding at protecting Helena and Jade in this crazy world.

And he failed miserably at keeping Raina and Levi safe. Their death just solidified one thing—this new world wasn't safe for children.

So, the thought of bringing in one and eventually losing them put Razor in a grim mood. That could never happen, and that would be the most selfish thing he'd ever done.

"Hey, umm, Razor," Clay called out.

"Yeah," Razor's tone was slightly harsher than he intended. It took a few seconds for Clay to respond.

"We're trying to figure out how to get Jackson in there."

Razor cursed under his breath. None of the doors lifted enough for someone like Jackson to get through. Razor sighed. "Give me a minute."

He was frustrated. It was best if he took it out on the door. Razor pushed, kicked, and punched on the door until it bent far enough for Jackson, and his gurney could get through.

"So much for trying to stay discreet," Zara stated as she entered.

"To hell with discreet."

"Are you all right, Razor?" worry was in Cole's tone.

"I'm fine," Razor noticed Jade was going the other way. He quickly walked out of the garage and followed behind. "Where are you off to?"

Jade paused at the end of the heavily wooded area. "To hunt. I saw a lot of game out here."

"Fuck," Razor said under his breath. He knew there was no point in arguing with her. "Stay within shouting distance."

"Will do," Jade proceeded on.

Razor stared at her back until she disappeared within the trees. For a second, he pictured his daughter. He sighed. That was what he had to look forward to.

Clay walked behind him. "Should we head in?"

Razor turned around. He could see the confusion in Clay's eyes. "Yeah. I think I saw a way in through the garage."

The two men headed back into the garage. Cole, Zara, Keeper, and Jackson were in the far back corner—making sure not to be seen. The door that Razor mentioned was toward the front of the garage. Clay volunteered to test the door. He turned the handle and was surprised to find it unlocked. He slowly went inside, and Razor quickly followed.

It was a mudroom. It was empty, and a closed door was on the other side. Razor turned to look at the others.

"We'll be back soon. Listen out for anything suspicious. And please listen out for Jade."

"She'll be fine," Zara said. "But I'll call out to her from time to time."

"Thank you," Razor turned to Clay. "Let's get this over with."

Clay nodded and proceeded to the door on the other side of the room. Razor closed the door that led to the garage and quickly followed Clay.

Again, both men were surprised to find the door to be unlocked. Razor all but expected a trap to be inside. As they left the mudroom, the two men entered a big open room that housed the kitchen, living room, and dining room area. The space was huge, and it had large cathedral ceilings.

"Should we split up?" Clay whispered.

"No," Razor looked around. "I don't think we'll be able to hear if one of us gets in trouble."

Clay glanced around. "I think you may be right about that."

"We'll start on this floor, then proceed to the second floor. We'll save the basement for last."

"Sounds good," Clay began to go to the dining room area. "You take the kitchen, and we meet in the living room area."

Razor nodded and went further into the kitchen. He looked for anything suspicious and valuable. It wasn't much there. A few eating utensils. A plate and bowl here and there. But nothing out of the ordinary. And nothing that was of use.

Razor looked over to see that Clay was looking over the area dissatisfied. Both men slowly made their way to the middle of the room. There wasn't anything in the living room either. Clay thought he found something under the couch, but upon further investigation, it was only a stuffed rabbit. A children's toy. He tossed it aside casually. Razor stared at it for a moment.

"Do you see yourself having kids?" Razor suddenly asked.

Clay scoffed. "Come on, man, I gotta have sex to do that."

Razor chuckled. "I guess so."

Clay frowned for a second. "You're not thinking about it, are you?"

"Nah."

"Well, shit, the way Helena's been coming at you, you two might just end up with one."

"That's what I fear," Razor headed further into the house. He and Helena haven't actually used protection. They never have.

"A baby would be the worst thing for you and Jade," Clay paused once they got to the foyer. "Helena would adjust nicely."

"I think you're spot on with that," Razor laughed. He never knew how preceptive Clay was.

There was a study and a half bath across the foyer. Razor took the study while Clay went into the bathroom.

"All clear," Clay announced a few moments later.

"Same," Razor sighed as he left out the study.

"I don't think we're going to find anything here."

"I think you're right."

The two men proceed upstairs.

"So, are you going to warn me to stay clear of Jade," Clay stated as they entered the first bedroom.

"Would you listen to me if I told you to?" Razor opened the closet door and walked inside.

Clay didn't say anything for a moment. When Razor walked back out, it looked like Clay was really pondering the question.

"Probably not," he finally said.

Razor looked under the bed. "Then I'm not going to warn you."

Clay shrugged.

The two men were silent as they finished clearing the floor. There was no one there. And there was nothing of value. The men finally headed down to the basement. Like the rest of the house, the basement was huge. There was a bar, a bathroom, a bedroom, and a family room. The men began clearing the area.

"I do like her," Clay finally said. "In case you were wondering. But I'm not being so tacky that I'm taking this moment to hit on her."

"Never said that."

"But I'm sure you were thinking it."

Razor sighed. This really wasn't a conversation he wanted to be having. But he figured he should get it over with. "I honestly don't know what to think of it. All I know is that *I'm* still grieving over David's death...and so is Jade."

"You don't think I feel like shit right now? David was a great dude. He's always had my back when I needed him. But I can't help how I feel."

"That's something you have to deal with on your own," the basement was all clear, so Razor started heading back up. "My approval won't change the guilt you feel."

Clay didn't say anything else. He just followed Razor back upstairs silently.

**

The others were able to find good supplies at the other locations. The group's spirits were lifted when Jade returned from hunting with plenty of rabbits and squirrels. It'd been a while since they all had any meat. So, that night the group ate great. Razor appreciated that moment.

Jade was still a little standoffish to everyone—choosing to be alone. Razor could tell Clay was having difficulty giving Jade her space. But he still respected her decision and hung around Reagan for the night.

Razor knew that Jade didn't trust herself to be around him, and he hated that she avoided him like that. Yes, her reaction to him telling her Junior was a spy was alarming, but Razor still loved her. And he couldn't take her avoiding him like this.

He watched as she made her way down the basement. He waited a few minutes before excusing himself from Helena and Cole's conversation and made his way to the basement.

Jade was in the bedroom, lying across the bed, when Razor found her. She was lying on her stomach. Her face scrunched up as she stared out the patio doors leading to the wooded backyard.

"That's not ideal," she said as Razor sat on the edge of the bed.

Razor looked at the patio. "Yeah, someone might have to serve as lookout in here."

Jade sighed and rolled over onto her back. "I was really hoping to sleep in here alone tonight."

"Sorry, I don't think that's possible in this room."

Jade sighed again and closed her eyes.

"So, how long is this going to go on for?"

Jade didn't say anything.

"I can't take you avoiding me like this."

"I thought you'd love it."

"I hate it."

"The idea of hurting you...that's what I hate," tears fell from Jade's closed eyes.

"Like I'll ever let that happen," Razor smirked.

Jade chuckled a little. She opened her eyes. They were still glossy from her tears. She stared at him momentarily, and then a fresh new batch came streaming down. "You love me too much. You'd let me kill you if you thought it'd make me better."

Razor sighed. The Willer sisters did have a strange hold on him. If he thought it'd really make her better, Razor would give pause to the idea of Jade hurting him. Jade had him there, and they both knew it. He needed a way to convince her that it wouldn't happen because it drove him crazy not to have her nearby.

There was no use in arguing with her. Instead, he spread his arms, and Jade didn't hesitate to climb inside them. Razor held her tight as she cried on his shoulder—every now and then kissing her forehead. He didn't murmur comforting words like, "It's going to be all right," or "You'll get over this eventually," because he honestly didn't know. If Helena died, it would never be all right for Razor. The same could be said if he lost Jade. Razor would never be the same.

"I'll always be here for you, Jade," was the only thing Razor could promise her.

Jade responded by hugging him tighter—like she was afraid he might suddenly disappear.

Razor rested his head on top of hers. They sat there silently for what seemed like hours. Eventually, Helena found them. She didn't say anything. A question never left her lips. All she did was claim her spot on the other side of Razor. He instantly wrapped his arm around her and kissed her softly. Jade had dozed off at this point. But any movement he made, Jade responded by tightening her hold on him. Helena chuckled and kissed Razor again.

"Lay back, my love. I don't think you're going anywhere tonight."

Razor did as he was told. Both sisters immediately snuggled up to him. Razor sighed with relief and closed his eyes. He immediately fell into a deep slumber.

**

The following two days on the road were uneventful. That was the first bright side. The second bright side was that Jade was no longer avoiding him. No, she wasn't back to being herself, but she didn't go out of her way to evade him or Helena. Razor took that as a win.

Since leaving the mansion, the group has been taking it slow. It mostly had to do with the care of Jackson. Although Cole wanted to get off the road as soon as possible, he still insisted they take frequent breaks. That was why they only made it to Milton, Ontario, on their second day on the road.

Razor tried hard to fight off his annoyance. He wasn't sure if Cole insisted on the breaks because Jackson's situation was worsening, but he wished the doc would elaborate. They were nowhere near Toronto. According to a member he'd asked, the group still had 57.7 kilometers to go, about 36 miles. Razor was beyond frustrated. They needed a faster way to the Black Coats headquarters.

The previous night the group slept in the woods, which put Razor in an even worse mood. He barely got any sleep. And now they were taking yet another break.

Cole and Keeper were taking turns putting wet clothes on Jackson's body. Razor wondered if they were trying to fight off a fever.

"Deep breath," Jade instructed beside him.

Razor raised an eyebrow.

"I can feel the annoyance radiating off you."

Helena chuckled at his other side. "She's right. Everyone's been feeling it all morning."

"I'm sorry," he mumbled. Razor didn't realize his feelings were that obvious.

"It is concerning, though," Jade looked around. They were currently stopped on an open road. It used to be an intersection. "We're way too exposed out here."

"Just a little longer," Cole assured them apologetically. "I think there might be an infection somewhere."

Razor could see the concern written all over Cole's face. Something was seriously wrong, and they needed to get back to HQ asap. Razor was about to ask Cole how bad it was when the sound of speeding trucks filled the air. The group looked around in a panic. Jade had her bow and arrow ready but couldn't tell where they came from. None of them could.

"Two o'clock!" Reagan shouted.

The group all turned their attention that way. Razor tensed up as he pulled out his machete. Zara, Keeper, and Tatianna surrounded Cole and

Jackson. Clay took his place by Jade. The group stayed in a tight circle—ensuring no one could get to Cole and Jackson.

There were two pickup trucks. Both were filled with people—inside and on the bed. It didn't take much to figure out that these people were a part of the Radicals. The people on the bed quickly jumped off before the trucks could come to a complete stop.

"Well, this is just great," one of the members grumbled.

"Focus, everyone," Razor ordered. Now was not the time for the group to express dissatisfaction with their situation. This interaction was bound to happen at some point.

The Radicals expressed their delight in coming across the group by shouting obscenities.

Razor and the rest of the group stood strong and silent. They all waited for their enemies to get closer before they started their attack.

The Radicals didn't quiet down until the last person left the truck. It was a guy. He looked younger than the rest of the people there but had a strong command about him. Razor immediately knew who this was. The leader. Liam.

Liam stopped at the halfway point between his group and Razor. They were within hearing distance of one another. Liam smiled as he surveyed the group.

"Are you the group causing me so much hell?" he asked delightfully. He looked even more excited when his eyes fell on Blackwell. "Cole, is that you?"

Cole moved over a little so that he could get a better view. "How's it going, Liam?"

Liam laughed and shook his head. "I really shouldn't be surprised to find you with them. Our captive said you'd probably be out here."

"You mean *my captive*," Jade broke away from the group.

Razor cursed under his breath. He was hoping that Jade wouldn't do something rash.

Liam's eyes filled with glee as they landed on Jade. They lingered on her. Assessing how much of a threat she was to him. "You must be Jade. Our captive had much to say about you."

"The bastard's a traitor, and I'll like him back now!"

"A traitor, you say," Liam looked back at his group. They all smiled with anticipation. He turned his attention back to Jade. Fiery excitement filled his eyes. "Well, isn't that interesting?"

~20~

Nick

It was way too bright. At first, Nick couldn't figure out what was going on. All he knew was that he was moving too fast and way too dizzy. Nick could make out a silhouette of a child trying to fight off someone. Then, Nick realized his arms and legs were bound, and someone was dragging him.

"Let him go!" the child fought to no avail. The silhouette turned to him. "Nick, get up and do something!"

Raina's frustrated face came into clear view. The look made him think of Jade. His heart skipped a beat. She was fighting for him. Maybe she really cared, after all.

Nick needed to focus. Where was he? What was going on? The truck he was driving went off a steep slope and flipped over a few times. He remembered banging his head and blood running down his face, and that's all he could recall before he blacked out.

Nick glanced around. He couldn't get a good look at the guy who was dragging him by his feet. The guy's back was towards Nick. Raina kept trying to get the guy to let Nick go. Aiden and Levi walked beside Nick silently. Both boys didn't look at him, but the fear was apparent on their faces.

There were zip ties that bound Nick's hands and feet together. The assailant tied Nick's hands in front of him. Since they were still in the wooded area, it was unclear where Nick was being taken to. He slowly worked his fingers into his front pocket to retrieve his knife. The guy had no clue that Nick was awake. Raina, however, looked back to see that Nick was conscious and immediately came to his side.

"It took you long enough to wake," she complained.

"I'm touched," Nick whispered as he started cutting through the zip tie with the knife. "I didn't know you cared so much."

Raina frowned. "I don't. I just don't want to be dragged off to wherever they're taking you."

Nick smiled as he shook his head. How stupid and naïve was he? How could he ever think that she would care? From the moment he thought about it, Nick knew it was wishful thinking. To say that Raina cared about him was to say that Jade cared about him. And Nick knew they were nowhere near there yet.

Finally, the zip tie around his wrists freed, and Nick was now contemplating how to free his feet when the guy finally paused. Although his hands were no longer bound, Nick pretended they were, and he immediately closed his eyes. The guy stood still for a few seconds—eyes scowling at Nick.

"Cut the shit," the guy demanded after a few more seconds. "I know you're awake."

Nick continued to play possum.

The guy sighed. "Fine, have it your way then."

Nick waited for the moment when the guy continued on. He took a quick peek and saw that the guy's back was once again to him. Nick decided to strike quickly, but before lifting himself properly, the guy suddenly had a gun aimed at him. Nick froze immediately.

"I told you to cut the shit. You weren't fooling anybody."

Nick sighed and rolled his eyes.

"Since you've managed to undo your wrists, you might as well do your feet."

"Seriously?" Nick was surprised.

The guy sighed. "I'm really tired of getting caught between you and Chase's shit."

Nick took a good look at the guy. He didn't carry himself like any of the officers.

"I'm a soldier," he said, answering the unasked question. "Now, your feet, please. I don't have all day."

Nick swiftly cut the zip tie that bound his feet together. He looked back up at the soldier—awaiting more directions.

"Stand up. Let's get to walking," the soldier instructed. "It'll be much quicker this way."

"Where's the rest of your men?" Nick slowly walked ahead of the soldier, thinking of ways to disarm him.

"Probably dead. I don't really give a fuck. All I care about is getting out of here."

Nick paused and turned to look at the soldier. "You're not planning to kill me."

"I don't think I could even if I tried…and we both know that."

"Then what's with the gun?"

"To assure that you'd attempt to act right."

Nick laughed.

"There are two drivable vehicles up here. You can go your way, and I can go mine."

"I've never known a soldier to disobey orders."

"Trust me. We do it all the time. Especially lately," the soldier tightened his hold on the gun. "I've lost so many friends due to your petty ass fights with Chase. I'm over it, and I'm not losing my life over you assholes."

Nick laughed again. "So, what is my old friend Chase up to?"

The soldier didn't say anything.

"Oh, come on! You've already gone AWOL. Why stop now?"

The soldier glared at Nick for a few seconds, and there was conflict in his eyes. After a few more seconds, the soldier sighed in defeat. "Fine. Chase has assembled a crew to hunt you, Razor, Jade, and Blackwell down."

"The Senate approved that?"

"No, all of this is under the radar," the soldier paused momentarily. "I mean, they know about the claim of you being a traitor, but they don't know about the number of resources Chase is using right now. They would never approve of that."

"And I'm guessing they don't know about Blackwell being alive either."

"No, not yet."

Nick raised an eyebrow out of curiosity.

"A parting gift to one of the Senators I'm close with."

Nick chuckled. This guy really was tired of his and Chase's bullshit. How sad?

"There's a shoot-to-kill order out on Blackwell," the soldier continued. "And there's an order to capture, torture, and eventually kill you, Razor, and Jade."

"Of course, there is," Nick tried hard to suppress his anger. He really shouldn't have been too surprised that Chase was doing all this. Chase didn't want to lose his power and would do anything to keep it.

"That's all the information I know. Now, can we keep moving, please?"

"As you wish," Nick smiled. Well, at least he didn't have to torture the information out of anyone this time. Although, according to the soldier, his years of serving were torture enough.

The rest of the walk was a silent one. Nick wondered how long it'd be before backup arrived. He was hoping it'd at least be a few more hours. He really needed some kind of lead. So far, it's just been headache after endless headache. It was annoying. Nick just needed a small win.

The two men finally came up on the trucks. They weren't in the best shape but were drivable, just like the soldier said.

The soldier pointed to the truck closest to the road. "You can take that one."

Nick noticed that it was more beat up than the other.

"It has more gas," the guy said. "Where I'm going isn't as far as your destination."

"And where is that exactly?"

"Like I'd really tell you," the soldier smirked. "Get out of here, Nick. Or the next time I see you, I will kill you."

Nick laughed. "I'm sure you'll try."

The two men got in their respective vehicles and drove away. Nick had a full gas tank and maybe a few hours lead over the men hunting him down, and that was all he could ask for.

~21~

Jade

"This *is fun to him."* That's all Jade could think of as she looked the Radicals' leader, Liam, in the eyes. She had just told the group that Junior was a traitor, which seemed to bring a certain kind of delight that Jade couldn't comprehend. It was like music to his ears or something. Jade tried not to focus too much on his green eyes and how they reminded her of David. She tried not to focus on how appealing Liam looked. It was like he lived in a completely different world from them.

While all the men around her wore shaggy and rugged looks, Liam was well-groomed. His shoulder-length, blonde hair was slicked back into a ponytail. His beard was neatly cut and far from the Paul Bunyan look that Jade had grown accustomed to. Liam's clothes were crisp as if they'd never seen a speck of dust. As if they've never been worn twice. He wore just a simple pair of blue jeans and a light grey shirt that clung to his muscular frame, but his clothes screamed designer to Jade.

Surprisingly, Liam didn't seem that intimidating to her. As the leader of the Radicals, Jade was expecting someone who looked like Razor—or Bossman, even. Jade wasn't sure if it was his height or what. But she figured he was around 5'7...5'8 if you were really trying to stretch it. And staring down at someone just a few inches taller than her was very comforting.

"I would like my traitor back now, please," she demanded once again.

Liam smiled. "You're amusing. You and your little group have killed so many of my people, and you're seriously standing here demanding something from me."

"You started it," Jade pointed out.

Liam laughed and shook his head. "Incredible."

Jade was getting tired of all the back and forth. She was tired of traveling. She was tired of looking over her shoulder. She was tired of the group's fear and paranoia. Jade wanted nothing more than to retrieve Junior while wiping the smug look off Liam and the Radicals' faces. She just waited for him to make the first move.

There was no way he would leave without trying to make an example out of them. And then he will see. He would realize what she was capable of. He would witness how far she'd go and the lines she'd cross to get what she wanted. And at the very last second, Liam will realize in horror the terrible mistake he made when he defied her. Jade just needed to wait.

"I won't ask again."

"He's my traitor now."

"I can always just take him from you," the threat was clear in Jade's voice.

Liam looked around—amused. "I don't think I brought him with me."

"Funny. I'll just torture the information out of one of your people here," Jade looked around, trying to decide who her victim would be. "You'd be surprised how easily they fold. I don't think they last five minutes under our form of torture."

Jade glanced over at Razor as if she was confirming her statement. Really, she was looking over to see if the group was prepared for the fight she knew was going to pursue. Razor was tense as Helena stood beside him. He gave her a quick nod. They were all prepared. Weapons were out.

Jade looked back over at Liam. He was analyzing her every movement. "That's a little pathetic, don't you think?"

Liam laughed louder this time. "Well, they all can't be bad-asses like you and your little sis here," he watched as Jade tensed up. "Yeah, Junior told me about her too."

"Then you know what I'll do to you if you so much as think about hurting her," Jade warned. That was it. Liam was going to die a torturous death by her hands.

"You're going to regret mentioning my wife," Razor said in a callous tone.

"Oh, won't you two just relax," Liam sighed in annoyance. "I was just mentioning what I've been told. Speaking of folding, your guy has a real lax tongue."

"Not my guy," Jade clarified. "A traitor...*my traitor*."

"Did you know, Jade, that there's a hefty price on your head?" Liam looked past her. "You too, Razor. Courtesy of your so-called President," he paused for a moment. Closed his eyes. Sighed. Smiled. And then he looked Jade right in her eyes. "He made me an offer, Jade. And while I find you amusing. And very stunning. Seriously, Junior really failed to mention just how beautiful you are...unfortunately, it's an offer I'm more than happy to take him up on."

That was the secret order that the Radicals were waiting for. His people did not hesitate as they charged at Jade and the group. Jade kept her eyes on Liam. He stood completely still as his people rushed past him. Jade aimed her bow and fired at him. Someone quickly jumped into the line of fire and happily took the arrow for him. Liam smirked. Jade smiled. His death was going to be so satisfying to her.

Jade quickly turned her attention to the assailant who chose to target her. She swiftly pulled out her knife and immediately made contact with their throat.

Fighting ensued all around.

Liam stood rooted in his spot.

Once Jade killed her latest attacker, she made her way to Liam. His people left him completely exposed. A significant error on their part. Or so she thought.

Liam held no fear in his eyes. Just utter amusement. That's the only emotion he had expressed since he locked eyes with Jade.

It annoyed her.

As she got closer, his people quickly flocked toward him. All of them were coming for Jade. She didn't care, and she was even amused herself. They were so willing to die a terrible death just to protect their leader. If that were how they chose to go, Jade would happily grant them that wish. And she did.

Seven people fled to protect their leader. Only two were still breathing, and they both looked terrified of her. But Jade didn't care. They were in her way, and they needed to be removed. The two followers didn't even have time to move before Jade's knifes made the fatal blows.

Liam sighed as he watched them fall to the ground. "Pity," he said. "I really didn't want to hurt you."

"Well, that sucks," Jade smirked. "Because I really *want* to hurt you."

They both charged at one another. Jade was much quicker. And more lethal. Liam was bleeding from his face and abdomen when she slammed him to the ground. Both places where Jade's knife had made contact. They were shallow wounds. Liam managed to move out of the way just enough that they didn't cause severe damage. But he still wasn't quick enough. Jade had him pinned to the ground. Genuine fear entered his eyes momentarily as he realized he was about to die.

Jade didn't know whether to scream or laugh. She was pissed at how easily she was able to overpower him. Shouldn't he be more difficult to fight? Where was the challenge? It felt like she just wasted her time and energy. But she also found the situation hysterical. After fighting Bossman and the DCs, did Liam seriously think he could be a challenge to her?

Oh well. It sucks to be him.

Jade raised her knife to deliver the fatal blow when someone suddenly lifted her in the air from behind. The person's foot kicked Liam in the face—rendering him unconscious.

"Let's go," Razor said to someone as he carried Jade to one of the Radical's trucks.

Of course, it was him.

"Damnit, Razor! Let me go!" Why was he always stopping her from killing the people she really wanted?

She *needed* to kill Liam just like she *needed* to kill Junior. Just like she *needed* to kill Bossman. But Razor was there. Always there to stop her.

Damn him.

Razor ignored her as he threw her onto the bed of one of the trucks, and he hopped on himself and ensnared her in his grasp again. Helena, Keeper, Cole, and Jackson were also on the truck's bed. Zara, Tatianna, and Clay were inside the truck.

"Let's go!" Razor said again. The truck started moving.

Jade noticed that the others had taken the other trucks as well. The people Liam came with were dead. The only person left was him.

"We can't leave without Liam," Jade said. "We need to find out where he has Junior."

"None of that matters now, Jade," Razor tightened his hold on her. "We have much bigger problems now."

Jade cursed under her breath as they sped away.

~22~

Jade

Compared to the other buildings on University Ave. in downtown Toronto, the Black Coats' headquarters was a little underwhelming. Surrounding it was nothing but huge skyscrapers. Some buildings had nothing but glass windows going all the way up (those that weren't covered by vegetation). The Black Coats headquarters were about nine stories high, while the surrounding buildings were well above ten. The building appeared older than the rest, even though Jade couldn't be sure it was. But compared to how newer the other buildings looked (despite the apparent environmental damage), their building looked like it'd been there quite some time.

Although Jade understood Cole's reasoning for choosing this building to serve as the group's headquarters, she still wished he'd picked a better-looking one. The building was light brown, and the ground level was made of fancy glass, but the floors above were golden brownish brick. It was ugly. Jade wondered what kind of business this building housed. But because this building was so unappealing, it was hidden by the fancy skyscrapers surrounding it. Plus, it was on the corner, making evacuation easy and convenient. Jade knew that was why Cole picked it.

Even though the building served as the group's headquarters didn't mean that they didn't put the surrounding structures to use. The glass skyscraper building across from them housed a new members hub and a training facility. The building next door held the surplus of their supplies—mostly equipment and some weapons. That building looked very much like their headquarters, but it was taller.

Everyone was relieved once they finally made it. Razor released a huge sigh of relief once they made it through the back garage entrance. They were greeted by a group of members who had a medical background. There was already a proper gurney for Jackson. Cole immediately got him on there and began administering IVs and other drugs utterly foreign to Jade. Cole quickly began giving out commands that Jade didn't understand. The medical group promptly began to make their way further into the building, and Cole paused to look at the rest of them.

"Keeper, you come with me," Cole looked at Zara. "Get them all settled in."

"Copy that," Zara turned her attention to them as Cole, Keeper, and the rest of the medical group left in a different direction. "I'll give you all the tour and the breakdown of this place. And then we'll figure out housing."

Zara proceeded to the door on the far right. The group walked up the first two flights of stairs and entered the main floor. Jade had never seen so many people in one place. People were moving about, completing chores, and conversing with one another. It was like another world—a community. The scene made Jade think about the camp.

It broke her heart every time she thought about the camp. The many people who shared the space with her. Raina. Levi. David. It all felt like home. Something she hasn't felt in a long time. And that was all destroyed. It was all taken away—blown away by Bossman because Junior told him exactly where they were.

Junior.

They had to figure out where he was, so Jade could capture and torture him. He had to pay for what he'd done. Jade *needed* to kill him.

"So, we call this floor command central," Zara explained, bringing Jade back from her thoughts. "This is usually where all the information and action is."

Jade didn't notice it when they approached the building, but the big glass windows that made up most of the ground level were blacked out with sheets and blankets. Smart. No one from the outside could see what was happening in the building.

"I assume you have lookouts on the other floors," Razor said.

"Of course. There's a couple of lookouts on every floor above this one," Zara pointed to one of the large tables in the center of the room. "You'd find your daily chore schedules here, and it'll let you know what you're in charge of and what shift you're on to patrol or serve as lookout."

Jade was amazed at how long and how thick the list was. There were so many people. And so many things to do. Who kept track of it all? And who oversaw creating it every single day? That seemed like a very daunting task and something Jade wished that she'd never oversee.

"Well, Jade and I won't need assignments for a while," Razor announced.

Jade looked over at him, confused.

"What?" Helena asked, shocked.

Zara frowned. "I don't understand."

"You all heard what Liam said. Jade and I have a hit out on our heads, and we need to go out and investigate that."

"It doesn't need to be the two of you!" Helena said hysterically.

Zara looked around uneasily as her fellow members began to stare. "Look, let's table this for now. We'll continue once I get you all settled, and we actually rest for once."

Razor looked a little annoyed but agreed to it.

Jade was shocked. During the whole trip, it seemed like Razor wanted nothing more than to get here. They weren't even there for an hour, and Razor was ready to leave back out. It was confusing. However, Jade did agree with him. There was an official hit out on her, and by the President, nonetheless. She never really took the time to fully digest that. Her mind had been so preoccupied with capturing Junior that she didn't think about anything else.

Helena still looked upset, but the group continued. Jade really didn't pay that much attention to anything else. She knew none of it was going to apply to her. Razor would ensure they both got out there as soon as possible. That was just Razor. Once he set his mind on something, there was no changing it, especially when it came to their safety.

To Jade's surprise, they would be staying in some of the rooms at the actual headquarters. Initially, Jade had figured they'd be staying in the new members building. Although they weren't members, they were still new to the group. But apparently, that's what Cole wanted. Jade didn't fully pay attention until Zara suggested the group create their room assignments.

"Although the rooms are bigger here on the 8th floor, there are still only two rooms per suite," Zara informed. "So, keep that in mind."

"Helena, me, Jade, Clay, Reagan, and Danita will share a suite," Razor immediately said. "Is there a living room area in the suite?"

"It is. I'll show you which room you all will be in then."

There were nine rooms on the floor. Zara walked them down to the corner room. She opened the door and led them inside. Jade was impressed. The suite was very spacious. The living room area had a huge couch, which looked like it let out to a bed. There was a decent size loveseat and coffee table. A small kitchenette area was in the far-left corner. The bathroom was just to the right of it. One of the rooms had a queen size bed. The other room had two full-size beds.

"I'll take the living room," Jade quickly said. She still didn't trust herself to be around people like that, and a little isolation would be best, even though she knew that Clay would likely sleep out here with her.

"Cool, I guess Reagan and I will take the room with the two beds then," Danita proceeded to the second room.

Jade noted how she made no mention of Clay. She didn't know how to take that. Was her dependency on him that obvious? Of course, it was apparent. Jade was losing her mind. How could it not be obvious?

"Great," Zara said. "I'm going to show the others to their suites. Dinner is at 7 p.m. How about we reconvene on the top floor in the doc's suite then? We can discuss options about going back on the road."

"Sounds good," Razor said.

"My suite is on the top floor as well. Let me know if you need anything," Zara made her way out. "Get some rest."

Helena went into the bathroom and tested to see if there was any running water. There was.

"The pressure is low, but it's working," she said. "I suggest we all make it quick, though."

Jade waited to go last. Razor and Clay sat in the living room to discuss plans with Jade. She knew Razor wanted to talk with her while Helena was in the bathroom. It seemed like he planned on leaving her behind, and Jade knew Helena wouldn't be ok with that. So, it was going to be an argument that would pursue.

"Where are you trying to start?" Jade immediately asked Razor once Helena went into the bathroom.

"We need to figure out where the Radicals are hiding out."

"The members should know that, right?" Clay asked.

"They should be able to give us something," Razor sighed. "But if there's a hit out on us, then I'm sure there's a hit out on Cole too."

"More than likely," Jade said. "So, this is Bossman's way of ensuring we're caught."

Razor shook his head. "This is the last thing Nick would want. Nick hates politics and would never source anyone outside of the DC to get what he wants. This is Chase. And Chase is a whole lot more dangerous than Nick."

Jade frowned. She couldn't see how a former plastic surgeon could be more dangerous than Bossman.

"He'll do anything to remain in power," Razor said, reading her face. "Chase is dangerous when he feels threatened and desperate. His colleagues have been itching to find a reason to replace him, and you, me, and Cole are reason enough. And he'll do anything to eliminate that."

Jade's heart raced a little. She never thought about it like that. "So, why don't you include Helena in this?"

"It's too dangerous for her."

Jade snorted. "Really, Razor?"

"Trust me on this, Jade."

Something about his tone made her take him seriously. "Ok."

They could hear Helena finishing up in the bathroom. Razor stood up. "We'll finish more on this later."

Jade watched him as he went into his bedroom. Something was bothering him. Something more than the bounty on their heads. Let's face it, they've always been fugitives, and they've always been wanted people. A kill-on-sight order was something that followed them around constantly. So, why was it getting to Razor now? There had to be more to it.

Jade was the last to go into the bathroom. It was a nice shower. It was low pressure, and the water was cold, but it was nice to actually take a shower. The bathroom had already been stocked with soap, toothpaste, toothbrushes, lotion, and other amenities. The Black Coats were great at gathering supplies, apparently. Jade took the time to enjoy the luxuries.

By the time she came out of the bathroom, Clay had already pulled the bed from the couch. He gave her a shy smile.

"Sorry, I hope this is ok," he gestured toward the bed. "No one actually included me in their claimed space."

Jade smiled. "They all assumed you'd be bunking with me."

"I can sleep on the floor."

"Don't be ridiculous, Clay," Jade got into the bed and patted the space beside her. "Get in, and let's get some rest."

"So, this Liam guy seems to be a real character," Clay got into the bed and sighed as he rested on his back.

Jade turned to lie on her back. She stared at the ceiling. "They all are."

"I guess that's true," he looked at her and smirked. "You seem to attract the crazies."

"That says more about me than I care to know," Jade sighed and closed her eyes. "David wasn't crazy, though."

"No, he was just crazy about you."

Tears fell down Jade's eyes as she thought about David. Guilt washed over her. She was sharing a bed with someone else because people assumed they were together. This was her fault. Jade got so dependent on others that she needed Clay around just to keep her sane—or what passed as sane for her. And now she feared hurting him. Of driving him away. How would she survive, then?

"It's all right, Jade," Clay said after a few minutes passed. "I know exactly how you feel."

Jade didn't say anything. She just continued to shed silent tears. Eventually, Clay pulled her to him. She snuggled up to his chest, and he kissed the top of her head. And they both fell asleep.

**

Cole looked clean and exhausted when they got up to his room for dinner. So did Keeper. Jade wondered how it went with Jackson. She waited to ask her question. Right now, she was stunned by the size of Cole's room. If you could really call it that. It was more like a penthouse suite, and it basically took up the entire floor, except for the tiny room next door that Zara occupied.

The group and some Black Coat members could all fit comfortably in the open space that served as the kitchen, dining, and living room area.

"Eat up, everyone," Cole announced in a tired voice. "I believe it's meatless spaghetti tonight," he looked at Zara for confirmation. She nodded.

Jade got into the line that quickly formed. Tatianna was standing in front of her, looking a little annoyed.

"Hey, Tatianna," Jade said in a low tone. "Did Keeper get any rest yet?"

"No, when I woke up, he wasn't in our room," she shook her head.

"This journey has been exhausting, and he's been pushing himself to the limit on the road."

Jade understood why Tatianna was so annoyed. Between taking care of, and protecting Jackson, while trying not to be killed by the Radicals was taking its toll on Keeper. It was taking its toll on everyone.

"Don't worry about that. After dinner, we'll make sure he gets some rest," Jade reassured her. "Even if we have to beat him unconscious."

Tatianna laughed. "I like that idea."

"We'll get him right," Jade gave Tatianna a quick wink.

"Thanks, Jade," Tatianna was at the front of the line, and she proceeded to pile her plate with spaghetti.

Jade quickly got her plate, and then Razor waved her over to the table he was eating at. There was a seat available right next to him. Helena, Tatianna, Keeper, Cole, Zara, Clay, and Reagan were sitting there. Jade preferred to sit at the adjacent table with Yoko and Calvin. But there was a lot of information they needed to dissect. Jade sighed and proceeded to the seat that was next to Razor.

"I know we all would love to rest right now," Razor stated as soon as she sat down. He was already done with his food. "But there's something we really need to address."

Cole sighed. "The bounty on your heads is quite concerning. And I'm sure there's a bounty out on me too."

"Assume that it is," Razor said. "We need to figure out what Liam knows."

"Yes, I know," the exhaustion was evident in Cole's voice.

Jade finished chewing the spaghetti she had in her mouth. "How's Jackson doing?"

"Better, thanks for asking," he gave her a weak smile. "There was an infection. Luckily, we've got the medicine to help fight that. So, his fever has gone down quite a bit."

"That's great," Jade shoved another forkful of spaghetti in her mouth.

"Hopefully, he'll wake soon."

"Yes, that's what we're all hoping," Razor said in a rush tone. "I'm sorry. I don't mean to be insensitive, but we really need to focus on the problem at hand."

"I don't know exactly where the Radicals' headquarters are, but they mostly hang out in the Chorley Park area," Cole admitted. "It's a little over five kilometers from here."

"Is that a far journey from here?" Razor asked.

"Not at all," Zara answered. "That's a little over three miles. Most of your time is spent ensuring you're discreet on the journey there. When we have to walk that area, it takes us about half a day."

"Give or take," Cole confirmed.

"So, we should expect about two days to go into that area and find someone to get information from," Razor concluded. He didn't seem happy about it.

"No," Cole sighed. "This isn't the type of information some random Radical member would know."

"Then who would know it?" Jade knew that this whole thing wouldn't be easy, but she still found herself annoyed with another obstacle.

"That'd be either Fallen or Crimson," Zara said.

"What kind of names are those?"

Zara just laughed and shrugged.

"What do they look like?" Razor pressed.

"Well, Fallen is a blonde woman, and Crimson is a ginger man," Zara said matter-of-factly.

"So, that's how he got that nickname," Jade chuckled.

"Not sure," Zara shrugged.

"That doesn't give us much to go on," Razor complained.

Cole sighed. "We know, but that's really the only way to describe them, and they don't really stand out or look unique."

"Obviously, I or someone else will have to come with you," Zara stated. "But either one of them will know more about President Chase's actions."

Razor nodded. Jade finished the rest of her food.

"Well, let's start coming up with a plan," Razor finally said.

~23~

Razor

If Razor had it his way, he and Jade would already be on the road. But under Cole's heavy advisement, they took a couple of days to rest and prepare for the trip. Of course, Razor objected to it at first.

"You all haven't had a good night's rest since you've gotten to Canada," Cole stated. "You need time to recuperate."

Razor would've probably objected more, but he saw how much Jade slept and thought giving her time to rest was best. Maybe then she'd feel a little more stable. That was one Willer sister that was under control. Now, he just needed to get a handle on the other one. Helena was insistent on not being left behind. But Razor felt like she needed to stay back and rest. It felt like he was losing control of both sisters and desperately wanted to get a handle on it.

Helena was grieving David's death through sex, and Razor wanted to make sure she could deal with that feeling another way. Plus, being apart was a definite way he could deny her because it was clear that he couldn't say no to her regarding sex. And then he would be able to focus all his attention on Jade and the problem at hand—the bounty that Chase put out on their heads.

There was no mention of Helena, but Razor was sure it was implied. Especially if she was there when the Radicals came to collect, Razor needed to handle this situation as fast as he could. It was probably best if he took the time to rest, but Razor wanted to create a crew to go out on the road with him.

He took Clay, Reagan, Yoko, and Calvin from their group. Razor included Yoko and Calvin because he recalled Jade complaining that she hadn't been able to spend time with them since the night a group of Radicals almost killed her and Calvin. He thought that'd cheer her up a little. Plus, he was leaving behind Tatianna, so Helena would have someone to talk to and vent to. He needed to keep both sisters happy. Or try, at least.

The news about Tatianna staying behind had no impact on Helena. She was still adamant about coming.

"Please, Helena," Razor begged one night. He was sitting on the edge of the bed, trying to unwind from the day. "Just sit this one out."

"I don't understand why you're so hell-bent on me not going," she crossed her arms and frowned at him. Helena was currently standing in her underwear. She was changing into her pjs when the subject was brought up once again.

Razor sighed and looked away. He'd cave and give her what she wanted if he stared too long.

"Did I do something wrong?" she asked when he said nothing.

"No," Razor stood and walked over to her.

Helena sounded so sad. And the look on her face verified that. Razor needed her to understand that he wasn't trying to punish her in any way. He uncrossed her arms and took her hands in his. He looked her in the eyes, kissed each hand, and kissed her forehead. She had her eyes closed when he pulled away. Razor waited until she opened them before he spoke. He wanted to look into her beautiful eyes while he explained his reasoning.

"I won't be able to focus if you're there," he finally admitted.

Helena frowned.

"I know, I know," he interrupted before she spoke. "It's usually the other way around. But since that night on the Detroit River, I realized I couldn't focus on you and Jade. Choosing between the two of you is difficult. If I focus on you, Jade falls apart. If I focus on Jade, I'm leaving you vulnerable. My stress level is going berserk."

"I'm sorry," she finally said. She wrapped her arms around his waist, and Razor pulled her close. Helena nestled her head against his chest. "I know we can be a lot."

Razor chuckled. "That's an understatement."

Helena pulled back enough so she could look him in the eyes. "I'll stay behind and help Cole with Jackson or something."

Razor sighed with relief. "Thank you."

"Why don't you properly thank me," Helena smiled and guided him toward the bed.

Razor sighed again. He feared that she would suggest this. And although he told himself that he would say no if put in this position, Razor didn't hesitate to follow her to the bed and give her what she wanted.

Helena was his ultimate weakness.

**

The next day, Razor discovered who was coming out with them from the Black Coats. He was really hoping that Zara would be among them, but of course, she was staying behind to protect Cole. Razor was conflicted. Zara staying behind made him feel better about leaving Helena, but he preferred to have her out with him. Especially since he was leaving Helena and Tatianna behind, they were strong fighters. Jade and Reagan were excellent fighters, and Yoko could hold her own, but Razor would've felt more confident if he had another superb fighter like Zara.

Zara informed him that the third in command, Brice, would join them.

"Brice knows the areas Fallen and Crimson like to hang out," Zara explained. "He's also had a few run-ins with them, so he's aware of their fighting skills."

"That's something," Jade yawned as she sat on the pull-out. Zara had come early in the morning to let them know who would accompany them.

"Yeah, but I'd take that with a grain of salt," Zara smirked. "Especially when it comes to Fallen."

"Why's that?" Razor asked.

Zara looked over at Jade when she responded. "Fallen thinks Brice is hot."

"So, in other words, she won't be as gentle with me," Jade laughed.

"I wouldn't bet on it."

"So, is Brice the only person from the Black Coats who's coming with us?" Razor was expecting her to give them more names.

Zara just shrugged. "Brice has his go-to people. He might use them, and he might not."

Razor was instantly annoyed.

"This is just a scout mission," Zara quickly informed him. "There's no need for you to do anything just yet."

"Like hell it is," Razor was pissed now. "I've been saying this whole time that we need to capture one of them to get intel!"

"And Cole and I think there's a better way of doing that."

"Why are you telling us this now?" Jade came to Razor's defense.

"You can't bring them back here," Zara said like it was obvious. "We need to have another secure place first."

"I'm not a fucking amateur," Razor growled. "I've already thought about that."

"So, you have a location in mind then," Zara challenged.

She had him there. Razor knew they'd need another location to perform their interrogation, but he didn't have an exact place in mind yet. Honestly, he hoped the Black Coats would provide that for them. Didn't they do interrogations?

"I do," Jade said. There was conviction in her voice.

Zara raised an eyebrow.

"It's a place not too far from here, so if there's trouble, you all will only be a few minutes away," Jade explained. "But it's not too close where it can be linked back to you."

"And where is this place?"

"It's on Richmond," Jade frowned momentarily as she tried to recall the place. "I believe the building is called the Sheraton Centre. One member mentioned that you don't use that place for anything."

"That's true," Zara confirmed.

"It's perfect," Jade went on. "There was some construction going on over there at some point, so that area is taped off, and there's a lot of black drapes and white sheets covering the place up. So, no one can see what's happening there, and it'll confuse our captive."

The place sounded promising to Razor. He was thankful that Jade had the foresight to have a location in mind.

"Is the building cleared?" he asked.

"Yeah, we check on the buildings near us once a month," Zara said. "The latest check was last week."

"Then we're all set," Razor said, satisfied.

"Ok, then, this is no longer a scout mission," Zara headed toward the door. "But that doesn't mean Brice will bring some of his people along."

Razor cursed under his breath. He'd just have to make do with the people he had.

"I think we'll have more than enough people," Jade stated once Zara left out of their suite.

"Yeah, well, I'm glad you're confident," Razor sat at the edge of her bed. Clay and Reagan had gone to get supplies and weapons for the trip. Helena was helping Cole and Keeper in the hospital wing. And Danita had taken a shift as a lookout on one of the floors below. Razor was allowing Jade to sleep as much as she wanted. He was on his way to sleep before Zara came.

"What's wrong?" she asked.

"I'm just not sure how this will play out."

"We never know how it plays out," Jade yawned and reclined back on her pillow. "But we keep going."

"Yeah, I guess."

Jade nudged him with her foot. "Stop being such a downer."

Razor smirked. "That's rich, coming from you."

Jade rolled her eyes. "Oh, Razor, you're such a worrywart."

Razor chuckled as he remembered Helena calling him that too.

"So, what do we do once we get this information from Fallen or Crimson?"

"Depends on the information," Razor admitted. "But the plan was always to return to the States and finish what we started."

"Well, that's something," Jade frowned for a second. "And what does this mean for Bossman?"

"Honestly," Razor shifted on the bed to get a better look at her. "I think he's in the same position we're in."

Jade's frown deepened.

"If Chase was willing to go to this extreme, then I bet he's done it with Nick, too," Razor explained. "The last time Chase did something like this, he and Nick fought each other, and I'm willing to bet it's the same this time."

"So, finding him will be harder then," Jade sounded disappointed.

"Not exactly," Razor had been thinking about this a lot, which was why he was so grumpy. "He knows that Cole is alive, and he's probably trying to make his way here too."

"Well, that's interesting," Jade smirked. It seemed like she enjoyed that idea, and it terrified Razor.

"Trust me, Jade, it's not," he got up, not wishing to argue with her. "I'm going to bed. Try not to cause any trouble while I'm sleeping."

Jade sighed as she rolled onto her side, her eyes following him. "I won't, *Dad*."

Razor ignored her comment as he went into his room. He closed the door behind him. He tried not to think about the glee in Jade's eyes when he mentioned that Nick might be close. He couldn't think about the issues that could occur if they crossed paths with Nick. Razor quickly laid down and closed his eyes. He'd worry about that another time.

**

If Razor had to describe Brice in two words, it'd be "pretty boy." He understood why Zara mentioned that Fallen found him attractive. Their interactions haven't been severe as Razor and Jade's will be. Upon meeting with Brice, Razor could tell things never came difficult for him. With his good looks, he was sure people just offered things to Brice. Plus, he had good charisma.

Before talking to him, Jade and Razor had watched Brice from afar. People just naturally flocked to him. Members went out of their way to say hello to him, especially the women. They all but tripped over each other to get his attention.

Jade looked on, a little disgusted. "This is what we have to work with?"

"Zara speaks highly of him," there was a little doubt in Razor's tone. He wasn't so sure about this guy.

But Razor had to respect that Brice gave each member his undivided attention. Whenever they called on him or mentioned that they had a problem, Brice would go out of his way to ensure it was handled. Razor understood why Cole made Brice his number three.

After half a day of staking Brice out, Razor and Jade finally approached him. Razor was a little leery about including Jade. But since she's been well rested, she didn't seem *that* out of it. Plus, it was better to get any craziness out of the way in the beginning. At least Brice would know what he'd be getting into early on.

When Razor and Jade approached him, Brice was in command central going over assignment details. Brice quickly finished his conversation to give them his full attention.

"You must be Razor," he smiled and paused when he looked at Jade. "I'm sorry. Which sister are you?"

"Jade," she sounded a little annoyed.

"Oh, that's right," he chuckled. "Helena is the one with the short hair."

"Zara tells us that you'd be going with us," Razor fought off his annoyance at how Brice greeted Jade.

"That's right. I'll give you the little tour of Fallen and Crimson's hangout."

"Will there be anyone else joining us?"

Brice set his clipboard on the assignment table. "I'm afraid not," he gestured them toward a secluded room in the far back corner.

Razor and Jade followed him. They didn't speak until they were in the room and the door was shut. It looked like it was a manager's office. A desk and a chair were behind it, and two folding chairs sat in front. Razor and Jade took a seat on the folding chairs.

"Why won't there be anyone else?" Razor demanded.

Brice sat in the chair that was behind the desk. He quickly propped his feet on the desk. "Because I'm not subjecting my people to unnecessary risk."

"Unnecessary risk," Jade was beyond annoyed with him, and Razor was behind her.

"There's a hit out on your leader, and we're trying to gather more intel on that," Razor tried to keep his composure. "How is that an unnecessary risk?"

"I'm well aware of the situation. And that's why I would prefer to keep my people here. Where they can protect their leader."

"Given your knowledge of the two, who do you think would be easier to capture?" Jade pressed on.

Razor knew what she was doing. There was no point in arguing with Brice when he clearly had his mind made up. The best thing to do was to devise a plan before they went on the road. Razor swallowed his annoyance and decided to move on as well.

"I would say Fallen."

"Because she has a thing for you," Jade's tone made it clear that she saw that as a weakness for Brice. She looked over at Razor. "I think Crimson will be our best bet."

"I agree," Razor quickly said.

Brice looked shocked at both of them. "I just told you Fallen would be more ideal."

"And I'm willing to bet Crimson knows more," Jade countered.

Brice was about to say something else, but Razor cut him off. "You don't think Liam knows that you're Fallen's weakness? If it's clear to the members here, then it's clear to them too."

Brice sighed and got up from his seat. He paced back and forth behind the desk. After a while, he ran his fingers through his hair and looked at them. A hint of fear was in his eyes.

"Crimson is vicious," he finally admitted.

"We've dealt with worse," Jade folded her arms and glared at him.

Brice looked away, unable to withstand her judgment.

"Still want to go without your people?" Razor challenged.

"If you've dealt with worse, then why do I need my people," there was anger in Brice's tone.

"Then I'll be the bait," Jade looked over at Razor.

"You are hard to resist."

Jade smirked and looked over at Brice. "We'll focus on Crimson's hangout. I'll walk out by myself and lure him back to an ambush."

"He'll kill you where you stand," Brice said.

"I'm sure he'll give it his all," Jade's voice had no hint of fear. She stood and looked down at Razor. "I have to meet Helena. She's insistent on rebraiding my hair."

Razor laughed. Helena did threaten him if he'd kept Jade from getting her hair done. "Have fun."

Jade rolled her eyes and walked out of the office. She slammed the door behind her.

Brice stared at the closed door in awe. After a few seconds, he shook his head in disbelief. "She's a piece of work."

"Watch what you say about my sister."

"She's seriously not afraid?"

"She's dealt with worse."

"You don't know what Crimson is like!"

"And you don't know what we've been through," Razor tried hard not to let his anger blind him. "What she's been through. Trust me when I say she can handle herself. Don't underestimate her."

"Then let's get this over with," Brice sounded like he was ready to be through with them.

"Finally, something we can agree on," Razor stood up. "We leave tomorrow morning."

"Perfect."

Razor ignored the sarcasm in Brice's tone. He quickly left out of the office. Honestly, he'd rather have Brice draw him a map of the places where Crimson hangs out. But none of them knew what he looked like. So, they were stuck with Brice. They needed to make this journey quick. Or else Razor might end up killing him.

**

The group met up in command central at 6 a.m. Jade's hair was freshly braided, and she looked well-rested. Helena stood by her sister's side, determined to see them off. Clay, Reagan, Yoko, and Calvin were down there, packing their bags with supplies. Cole and Zara had come down to wish everyone well. They were all just waiting on Brice. Razor tried to focus on Jade and Helena to hide his annoyance.

"He has some reservations about going out," Cole said to Razor as if reading his mind. "But he knows how important this is."

"Is he going to be a problem?"

Cole chuckled. "Oh no, my friend. Brice always worries about going out."

"Which is why he stays couped up here as much as he can," Zara grumbled.

"Well, that's just fantastic," irritation leaked through Razor's voice.

"Going out is a part of being a member," Zara stated as a matter of fact. "Brice knows that."

"He'll be fine on the road," Cole reassured.

"Is your bag packed, Razor?" Jade asked. He could tell that she was trying to distract him.

Razor followed her and Helena to the assignment table where supplies had been laid out. Jade started putting a few MRE packets in her bag.

"Don't worry about him," she said, gathering up a few bottles of water. She poured one of the bottles into her canteen. "This is going to be a short trip."

"You sound sure."

"That's because I've been doing some recon," Helena stated as she grabbed some MREs for Razor and packed them in his bag. "A few members told me there are only two places where Crimson hangs out. And they both aren't too far from here. Plus, they gave me this."

Razor unfolded the piece of paper that Helena gave to him. It was a sketch of an odd-looking man. He had a crooked nose, and his eyes looked too small for his face. He had a crew cut and a wild-looking beard. There was a long scar on the left side of his cheek. This guy must've been Crimson.

"A member drew what he looked like," Helena stated. "In case something happened to Brice."

"This is great, Helena," he kissed her on her forehead.

"They also drew me a map of the two places he might be," Jade strapped her knife holsters to her thighs and began loading her knives in them. "It's in the small pocket in front of my bag."

Razor unzipped the small pouch and retrieved the map. They both were right. The areas marked were very close by. Razor was impressed. And he was relieved that they didn't need to rely on Brice solely.

Jade put on her combat mask while Helena filled Razor's canteen with water. Razor began packing his bag with his weapons. He was more than ready to get out on the road. As everyone was packed up, Brice burst through the front doors. A member quickly followed behind him. The member went to the assignment table and began packing a bag for Brice.

"Sorry I'm late," Brice greeted them. "I took a small team out to scout ahead. And be glad that I did," Brice pulled something out of his back pocket. "These are posted up everywhere."

Brice handed the item to Razor. It was a light red piece of paper. Correction, two pieces of paper. They were folded up. Razor unfolded them.

Brice looked over at Jade. "I think your plan will work after all."

Razor stared at a wanted poster of him. It was his DC officer photo. That wasn't really concerning. What worried him was the wanted poster of Jade. It wasn't her original wanted poster. The poster with her wild curly hair and her infamous red scarf. No. This picture of her was much more current. On the poster, Jade had cornrows and her combat mask on. She looked ominous on that reddish background. How did they get this recent picture of her so quickly?

Jade walked over and took a look. She stared in disbelief. After a while, she looked at him. "Well, hell."

~24~

Nick

Nick's hands were covered in blood. He cursed as he tried to catch his breath. Five minutes. Nick hadn't been across the Canadian border for five minutes before the so-called rebel group, the Radicals, attacked him. It was just a small group, but he honestly didn't think they'd attack so soon.

"Shit," Raina looked down at the dead bodies in shock. "Why did they attack?"

"It's the way of the world," Nick wiped his hands on the front of his pants. He looked at the blonde woman who was unconscious. Nick knew she was higher up in the Radical group.

"I hate this world," Aiden groaned. He and Levi decided to stay in the car as Nick fought off his attackers.

Nick sighed as he looked for something to tie the blonde woman up. "I know, son."

There wasn't anything in plain sight, so Nick decided to try his luck in the truck. Raina stood near the front of the car. She still looked disgusted by the violent scene in front of her. Nick went to the trunk of the car and tried his luck there. It was a success. Nick found a piece of rope. He went over to the blonde woman. He tied her up and put her in the truck. Nick quickly sped off before any more members of the Radicals came his way.

It wasn't clear where Nick was going to take her. He just knew he needed somewhere secluded to get information out of her. He was unfamiliar with the area, so Nick just found a small, hidden place. There was a small gas station that looked promising. Nick focused on the little garage first. He made sure it was all clear before he looked into the small convenience store area of the gas station. It was empty as well. But there were a few things he thought would be helpful to his torture tactics.

The small garage is where Nick decided to perform his torture on the blonde woman. He tied her to the end of a workstation in the back. Nick laid out knives, pliers, a hammer, and a screwdriver. It was all he could find, but the material would make do.

Nick waited patiently for the woman to regain consciousness. Then he would find out what was really going on here. It was common knowledge to every upper-class government official that Canada wasn't the promised land everyone made it out to be. There was no promised land. Sure, how other countries and governments handled healthcare was different and more humane than what they did in the States, but every country still had difficulties. There were still marauders, rapists, and murderers out there.

Evil people doing evil things exist in every country. Just because they handled the health care system differently didn't mean it was a safe haven.

Of course, Nick wasn't supposed to know any of this. Although he was the former Commander of the DC task force, he still wasn't an "upper-class government official." Knowing the truth about Canada and other countries was classified information. However, Nick always had his ways of extracting information from people, whether through torture or other methods.

The blonde woman groaned as she came to. She tried to move her arms but couldn't. They were tied tightly to the leg of a workbench. The woman looked around frantically. Her eyes met Nick's. He was standing calmly in the middle of the room. Her eyes were blue. So unlike Jade's. God, he wished he was staring into her eyes instead of the woman before him.

"Sucks to be you," he sighed in disappointment.

"Fuck you," she spat. "Where am I?!"

Nick didn't respond. Instead, he swiftly stabbed the woman in the leg. She screamed out in pain. Raina jumped at the sound. She was the only one who ventured into the garage with him. Aiden and Levi were insistent on staying outside. Levi mentioned that they would be lookouts, but Nick knew the truth. They were afraid. They were afraid to be in the same space as Nick. And they definitely didn't want to see Nick torture someone. Raina made herself look. She forced herself to watch. And with each passing moment, her hatred and disgust for him grew.

The woman shook her injured leg. As if to try to get the knife out of it. Her screams got louder every time she moved.

"Shut it!" Nick went over and smacked her.

The woman cried, but she did stop screaming. After a moment, she breathed deeply—trying to endure the pain.

"What do you want?" she groaned.

"Information."

"About what?"

"Everything."

"Everything is broad," she sighed. "I need you to be a little more specific."

"Fine," Nick paced. "Who do you work for? What are you doing here? What are your current missions?"

"I'm with the Radicals," she glared at him. As if she wished she could snap his neck where he stood. Nick found it humorous. "But I'm guessing you already knew that."

"I did," Nick laughed a little. "You're higher up in the group. Your name is ridiculous, and I can't seem to remember it."

"It's Fallen, you asshole!"

"Right. What were your parents thinking?" Nick shook his head and smiled as her glare intensified. "Well, allow me to introduce myself. I'm Bossman."

All the color drained from Fallen's face. Genuine fear seeped in as she realized her fate. Nick loved that look. The realization that his captives know they're in. It filled Nick with such glee that sometimes it was indescribable.

Fallen began to look around the room, trying to come up with an escape route. She couldn't find a visible one. She sighed in defeat.

"We attack newcomers who cross the border and take their supplies. If they're good fighters, we offer them the opportunity to join us."

"And those who decline?"

"We kill," she said flatly.

Nick chuckled. "I guess you don't get many people who turn you down."

Fallen shrugged. "Those who we cannot kill generally join our opposing group."

"Another rebel group?" Nick was delighted by this news. Canada sounded more intriguing.

"They call themselves the Black Coats. This quack of a doctor name Blackwell leads them."

"Dr. Cole Blackwell!" Nick shouted with glee. Fallen jumped at the sudden loudness of his voice. "Glad to hear my old friend is doing so well here."

"Friend," Fallen frowned.

"Where can I locate him?"

"I don't know," she spat.

Nick smiled. "Wrong answer," he quickly tossed another knife at her.

This time it went into her right shoulder. She screamed out in pain. Nick screamed out in happiness. Oh, how he loved inflicting pain. The ones who endured the pain in silence bored him. But the ones who screamed and made all kinds of noises were the ones that got him off. That made him excited. That made him happy to give in to those urges he had denied himself years ago.

"I swear!" she screamed. "I swear I don't know the exact location. They're good at keeping that hidden."

Nick believed her, of course. They could never get an exact location when Blackwell led the Black Deficit, so why should it be any different now? Nick had to give it to the doc—he was crafty. Blackwell knew how to navigate through this chaotic world while being stealthy and seen at the same time. If only they had similar views, who knows? Both men might've ended up friends.

"I believe you," he finally said. "But surely, your leader must have a theory."

"Downtown Toronto. That's as far as we could narrow it."

Nick didn't like that answer but knew Fallen was telling him the truth. He sighed. This was way too easy. She was at the top; she should've at least put up more of a fight. Fallen was so unlike Jade. Jade would've fought. She would've put up more of a resistance. She would've endured the pain. She would've figured out how to escape by now. They would've been fighting. And Jade would've been giving him more love scars.

Oh, how he missed the wounds she'd given him. The pain. The hatred of when she gave them to him. The love and admiration he'd feel towards them when it was all said and done. Nick would give anything to feel the blade of Jade's knife once again. He desperately needed to find her.

"What are your current missions?" he asked. Nick knew that Chase put a hit out on Razor, Jade, and Blackwell. He just wondered if this group had been informed of that.

"There's only one mission at the moment," Fallen said. "To capture and deliver persons named Razor, Jade, and Dr. Blackwell to your President. That's where Liam is putting all his manpower."

Nick sighed. "So disappointing," he kneeled in front of her. Blue eyes. So very different from the ones he longed for. "I already know all of this."

Fallen frowned at his words. "I don't understand."

"I am much smarter than you, Fallen," Nick stood and began pacing. "Much smarter than your group. You're all running around pretending to play bandits. But in reality, you're all just stupid little children who are way over your heads."

Nick looked over at her to see her glaring back at him. The hatred was there. Nick laughed. It was clear that no one had ever talked about this group so harshly. But it was the truth. The Radicals were nothing but children to him—children who were experiencing, for the first-time non-adult supervision. Of course, they were going to run amuck.

"It really sucks to be you, Fallen," Nick sighed. "You are such a disappointment."

"Fuck..." Fallen couldn't get her next word out. Another one of Nick's knives found its way to her skull.

Nick looked down at Fallen's body as it slowly slumped over. He sighed again. "Very disappointing." This time, it was Raina's eyes that were glaring at him.

"What did I do now?" he asked her as he collected his things.

"You're a real asshole."

"I'm well aware of that, my dear."

"Killing her wasn't necessary."

"It was," Nick kneeled beside Fallen's dead body and rummaged through her pockets. "She was weak, and the weak have no place in this world."

"You made that clear when you killed Levi and me!" there was fire behind Raina's eyes. "Do you need to keep doing that to others?"

"She was going to hurt Jade," he explained to her.

"Jade would've been able to handle herself."

"By killing her!" Nick found a knife in Fallen's pocket. Why didn't she attempt to retrieve it at some point? So weak. So unlike Jade. He stood and kicked the corpse out of frustration.

Raina was appalled by his action. "You made her that way!"

"No, I believe you did," Nick spat at her. This child shouldn't be getting to him this much, but she was, and she was clawing her way under his skin. "If I remember correctly, you were the reason she killed that DC officer. She had a taste of blood, Raina. And once you get a taste of it, there's no going back. *You* did that!"

Raina looked furious. She cocked her hand back as if she was about to punch him. But she was too far away actually to land a hit. That and she was a figment of his mind. But she still proceeded with her punch anyway. Nick was about to laugh when something actually hit him. Something hard. Hard enough that he felt himself tilting over. Nick landed hard on his side. He hit the ground so hard that the side of his head started bleeding.

Raina looked shocked as she looked around. "Oh, crap."

Junior stomped into view with a smug look on his face. A few other men followed him. Nick tried to stand up, but one of the men kicked him in the abdomen, causing Nick to fall back to the ground.

"Talking to yourself there, Nicky," Junior said humorously.

"Fuck you, traitor," Nick was pissed. Of course, Junior betrayed him. That's what he did. Junior was the type of person who aligned themselves with the winning team. Nick's ship was sinking. So, it was only natural that Junior would jump ship with Chase.

"Funny, Jade does the same thing," Junior said. There was curiosity in his tone.

Nick's heart leapt at the mention of Jade's name. "How did she take it about you being a traitor?"

Junior smirked. He raised his hand. His palm had an ugly scar. "Well, of course, she tried to kill me. Still hunting me down, how I hear it."

Nick chuckled. That was so like Jade.

"He fucking killed Fallen," one of the men said.

"She was weak," Nick rolled onto his back. There was no use in fighting. They were taking him to their leader. The exact place Nick wanted to be. This was going to be quicker than he thought. "The weak have no place in the world. Didn't you Canadians get the memo?"

"Now, now, Nicky," Junior stood above him. "Let's not get my new friends here all riled up."

Before Nick could say anything else, the bottom of Junior's boot quickly appeared. Then darkness.

When Nick came to, he was tied to a chair. He chuckled as he began to rotate his head around, getting the cricks out of his neck in the process.

"And where was my lookout," Nick mumbled to himself. "Oh, that's right, they were hidden outside...and dead children."

"Sorry, Dad," Aiden said from somewhere Nick couldn't see.

"Don't worry about it, son."

The sound of footsteps filled the warehouse that Nick sat in the middle of. It was completely empty—eerie looking. The type of place meant to intimidate any captive who ended up there. It did nothing for Nick, however.

A short, muscular, blonde-haired man stepped into his view. He looked angry at Nick. He glanced back at Junior as he got closer to Nick. Junior gave him a short nod.

"So," the guy folded his arms and glared at Nick. "This is the guy who killed my number two."

"And another person on the President's most wanted list," Junior informed him. "Trust me. You hit the jackpot with him."

Nick looked at the guy closer. Rage and jealousy instantly filled him as he stared at the long, fresh-looking scar across his face. He had met her. This pathetic-looking man, who was Liam, met *his* Jade. And she gave him a love scar. This was unacceptable.

Nick wanted to kill this man. And judging by the scar on Liam's face, so did Jade. They were so alike. They were meant to be together. Jade was nearby. And that brought joy to him.

"So, Liam," Nick began to laugh. "I see you've met *my* sweet, sweet Jade."

~25~

Jade

For the first time since the night on the river, Jade felt like herself again. Well, somewhat like herself again. Those days of resting really did help her ease her mind a little. The group made frequent stops on the road at different safe house points. It was tedious, but Jade understood the cautiousness. The area was very active. And it was imperative that they wouldn't be seen.

Brice wasn't lying when he said the area was covered with Jade and Razor's wanted posters. Almost every building was plastered with Jade and Razor's faces. It was amazing that they could accumulate so much paper to post around the town.

During the breaks at the safe house points, Jade couldn't stop looking at the new wanted poster of her. It was unbelievable how detailed it was. And it was unbelievable that they took the time to create a new picture of her. It was something about the image that was a little off-putting. Something that she couldn't put her finger on. Jade stared at her eyes in the picture. They frightened her. They looked deranged. *She* looked deranged.

Is that how they saw her?

Is that how she looked now?

The woman in this new poster bothered her. She looked so unlike herself. Is that what she was resulting to? Becoming? No wonder people were looking at her like she was crazy. That's what she was becoming. And Jade wasn't sure if she was ok with that.

"Enjoying the view," Clay sat beside her at the latest safe house. "You've been staring at that picture at every stop."

"I look so unhinged," she whispered. "So unlike myself."

"That's Junior just trying to get to you."

Jade shook her head. The thought did cross her mind for a brief moment, but she couldn't accept that explanation. *No.* This was how she looked to others. This was what she was becoming. No wonder Raina's ghost didn't want to be around her. Jade wasn't the same anymore. She wasn't the same person that Raina loved. Jade had to be that person again. But how? She felt so far gone at this point.

"This is me," she finally said.

"You know what I see when I look at that picture?" Clay asked. "I see a woman who's fighting to survive. There's nothing wrong with that, Jade."

"The Queen in battle!" Calvin boomed from across the room. He smiled as he held up his copy of Jade's wanted poster. He looked so proud at that moment.

Jade smiled a little. "The Queen's always in battle," she sighed at the thought.

They were always in a battle. It was exhausting. It was days like this that Jade wished she could quit. Just drop off the face of the earth. Lay low. Hide somewhere and live off the land. Find a little peace and solace in this chaotic world. But the people Jade lost always came back to mind. And the fire to continue to fight burned on.

Clay smiled at her. "See, it looks like some of us love that new poster of you."

"You do look badass," Yoko chuckled as she glanced at the picture Calvin was holding.

"Thanks, I guess," Jade sighed. She decided not to dwell on it too much longer. There was no point. The posters were out there. And she looked how she looked.

Jade pulled out her canteen and took a sip of her water. She wanted to be sure that she stayed hydrated. She needed to be physically prepared should any random attack occur.

"All right," Brice stood in the center of the room. "We just have one more safe point before we get to Crimson's hangout. So, we should go over the plan now."

"Agreed," Razor said.

Brice turned to Jade. "Did you have some sort of strategy in mind?"

"I do," Jade put her canteen away. "I'll walk into his hangout under the guise of looking for Junior. I'll demand that he tells me where my traitor is, and I'll make it a point of not being aware of who Crimson really is. And I'll get him to follow me back to the ambush point."

"Which is where exactly?" Razor stood. Jade could tell he was annoyed about not having that information yet.

"It'll be one kilometer from the hangout," Brice paused. "That's a little over half a mile."

"That's manageable," Jade said.

"We'll have a vehicle ready for us," Brice looked over at Razor. "I assume you'll be able to incapacitate him."

Razor rolled his eyes in response.

"If you have vehicles available," Reagan sounded annoyed. "Why didn't we use them on the way here?"

"They'll be too noticeable. We're only using them on the way to the interrogation spot because I don't want to risk Crimson waking while we transport him there on foot."

"And I'll imagine it'll be more difficult carrying an unconscious man, too," Jade didn't think about that when she was developing her plan. It looked like it was worth bringing Brice along after all.

"Correct," Brice pulled out a pocket watch and glanced around at everyone. "Time to move out."

The group gathered all their things. Calvin stomped toward Jade, his sword and picture of her in his hand.

"The knight will stand beside the Queen," he announced.

"I would love that, my knight," Jade smiled. She hadn't hung out with Calvin since they were attacked in the woods. Jade's mind got the better of her then, and she was determined not to let that happen again.

They all filed out of the building and resumed their roles during their journey on the road. Reagan and Brice scouted ahead. Yoko, Calvin, and Jade secured the middle while Clay and Razor brought up the rear. The group was silent throughout the journey except for Calvin and his counting. But even he whispered that.

"35, 36, 37, 38, 39."

Jade clenched her knives as she looked around. Buildings still surrounded them, but they weren't skyscrapers. These buildings were more like neighborhood stores and restaurants. They were very quaint. It looked like someplace that Jade's parents would drag her and Helena to. She pictured them all sitting on one of the small patios, eating lunch. All of them laughing and enjoying each other's company. Jade would give anything to have that moment. A moment when they were a family again. She pushed the thought out of her head and focused on the mission.

It was surprising that they hadn't come across anyone during this whole journey. Sure, Brice led them through alleyways and secluded parking structures, but Jade thought they'd come across somebody by now. Maybe travelers knew not to be seen in this area. That made her wonder what the Radicals would do if they saw someone on the streets. It had to be dreadful. Why else would it be no man's land around here?

"76, 77, 78, 79, 80," Calvin was on his fifth round of counting to a hundred.

Brice stopped when they got to a tight alleyway. There was indeed a van that was parked and awaiting them. It looked run down, but it was usable. Brice paused as he looked around. He glanced over the team as if trying to decide who goes where.

"All right," he finally said to everyone. "Reagan and I will serve as lookout on the patio up here," he pointed to the stairway on the building they were currently behind. It looked like it used to be a convenience store. "Clay and Razor will be lookouts to the east and Yoko and Calvin to the west."

"And where exactly am I supposed to be going?" Jade asked. Brice still didn't elaborate on where the hangout was.

"You'll take the east exit of this alleyway and go south straight down," he quickly explained. "Trust me. You won't miss it. Crimson will come out to greet you before you get too close."

"Ok, I really hope so," Jade was a little leery about not having exact details on the location. But she had to believe Brice on this.

"Trust me," Brice said confidently. "He'll be there."

"All right then," Jade looked around at everyone. "I'll be coming in hot, so be ready."

"Don't worry, Jade," Razor assured her. "We'll be prepared."

Jade nodded and headed out in the direction Brice had shown her. She immediately pulled out her bow and an arrow once she exited the street alone.

Jade wouldn't lie to herself; she was a little nervous about her confrontation with Crimson. Brice's fear of him did concern her a bit. She was going in this all alone. Crimson might have a lot more people than Jade could handle. Whether Warrior Jade showed up or not. She had to come up with a tactic. But it was hard to devise a tactic for an opponent you've never seen before. Jade would have to wing it like she's always done.

The streets were still quiet, and no soul besides Jade was in sight. She didn't know how Brice could be so sure about her running across anyone the further she traveled. Then she hit a street that was littered with different stores and businesses. There still weren't any people in sight, but the number of storefronts overwhelmed Jade.

This place had to be busy before the world turned chaotic. Jade could picture the vast amount of people this little street brought in. There were plenty of check-cashing places, nail shops, restaurants, shoe stores, and even a China shop. This was another place Jade could imagine her parents dragging her and Helena to.

Nothing could indicate it, but Jade had to be closer to Crimson's hangout spot. There was just this intense feeling in her gut. So, Jade strolled—assessing her surroundings.

Nobody was in sight, but Jade could feel potential lookouts. Their eyes felt like they were on her. Jade needed a place to hide momentarily and gather herself and her thoughts. She walked to the end of the block and took refuge in a small alleyway behind a jewelry store at the corner.

Jade hid underneath a stairwell and focused on her breathing. She wasn't having an asthma attack or anything. She was just thinking ahead. Jade closed her eyes as she inhaled the medicated mist of the breathing treatment her mask was giving her. After her treatment, Jade decided to move on. Something told her that instead of returning to the block of businesses, she should turn right out of the alleyway and try her luck down the block of brownstones.

The brownstones looked very beautiful on the outside. Jade found the ones covered with vines to be the most beautiful. Again, this seemed like a sight her parents would drag her to if they had been on vacation here. Jade wasn't even halfway down the block when a guy walked out of a brownstone with a red door. He casually leaned against the railing on the front porch. He watched as Jade stopped in the middle of the street.

Jade allowed there to be three brownstones in between her and the mystery man. It was hard to tell if this person was Crimson or not. But either way, Jade was going to be cautious. She held on tightly to her bow.

"Hello there," the mystery man greeted. "I'm afraid to inform you, but you're trespassing."

Jade glanced around. "I don't see any signs posted."

The guy shrugged. "Nevertheless, you've been given a warning, and if you go any further, there will be consequences."

"I'm looking for someone."

"Look somewhere else."

"He's a traitor," Jade continued. "And I'm going to look *everywhere* for him. Trespassing or not."

The man chuckled as he walked down the porch. He opened the small gate that led out to the sidewalk. Jade's grip on her bow got tighter. She squinted to get a better look at him. It seemed like he had red hair, but Jade couldn't be sure. The sun could be playing tricks on her. Plus, Brice was convinced that Crimson would try to kill Jade on sight. This might be someone else. Perhaps Crimson's number two or something.

"So, is this traitor worth you dying?" he stopped at the brownstone next door to the one he had just left.

"He got people I loved dearly killed," Jade looked at the man harder. His hair definitely appeared red. And if she wasn't mistaken, there was a scar on the left side of his cheek. Just like in the sketch. "So, it's worth the risk."

The guy tilted his head slightly as if trying to decipher something by looking at her. "Out on the Detroit River."

Jade responded by drawing back her bow and arrow. This *had* to be Crimson.

The guy chuckled. "You're definitely Jade. You're an extremely wanted woman."

"Crimson, I presume," Jade immediately ditched her plan of pretending she didn't know who he was. Her gut encouraged her to show her cards. Something told her that he'd appreciate that.

"Ah," he smiled. "Someone's been doing their homework."

"Funny, I was told you'd try to kill me on sight. I didn't know you were so chatty."

"What can I say? You intrigue me."

Jade rolled her eyes. What was it with men always saying this to her? What was so intriguing about her? She was just like every other person on this planet. She was just fighting to survive. That's it. There was nothing unique or intriguing about that. But that's what she constantly heard.

What were they expecting? Her to be cowering in fear? To be shaking in her boots? She wasn't going to do that. Is that what made her so fascinating? That couldn't be it. There were so many other women who were more badass than her. Like Helena. Zara. Tatianna. Reagan. In Jade's eyes, they were way more intriguing than her.

"You're looking for Junior, is that correct?"

"Where is he?"

Crimson shrugged. "Liam thought it was wise to give him free rein."

"Stupid."

"I agree," he looked over Jade intently. "You fucked him up good. I wanted to finish him off when we came across him."

"And."

Crimson shrugged again. "I just thought you should know we had that in common before I killed you."

"Noted."

"You're not very talkative," he chuckled.

"Not to those who wish to kill me," Jade noticed the few people slowly leaving the alleyway she had just left. And those who were coming out of the alley that was behind Crimson.

"That's good to know," his smile grew as Jade noticed the people. "It was nice meeting you, Jade. And I am honored that you'll be dying by my hands."

Jade smirked as she shot off the first arrow. It whizzed past Crimson. He jumped out of the way as the arrow found its mark on the man's chest standing just behind him. Jade spun around and fired two more arrows at the assailants close to her. Then she took off running toward the block of businesses.

"Don't let her get away!" Crimson shouted.

Jade sprinted back toward the ambush spot. Her combat mask went into overdrive as she pushed herself to run faster. Jade did a quick glance behind her and counted five assailants. And that number included Crimson. All she needed to do was take out the four remaining people, and then she'd be ok. Crimson lagged behind them. Jade wasn't sure if it was because they provided him with cover or if he was just a slow runner. But either way, Jade was confident that she could outrun him.

She quickly ducked into the first alleyway she mapped out along the way. Jade was positive that Crimson would have people with him. So, she noted every alleyway and parking garage she could use for cover along the way.

Jade pressed up against a wall and retrieved her knife. She'd sheathed her bow during her run. Not having it in her hand made her run quicker. Jade could hear the heavy footsteps of her attackers. She waited for the first two people to run past before quickly pulling the next person into the alleyway. Jade immediately slit their throat and ran her knife into the next person's gut as they entered the alleyway.

Crimson was yelling for his people to come back as Jade hopped over the fence that was in the back of the alley. Crimson didn't notice her take cover behind a dumpster.

"Move your asses!" he yelled. "She went over the fence!"

Jade heard two people hop over the fence. Crimson was still on the other side of it. Jade could feel it in her gut. He would linger behind and let his people be on the brutal end of Jade's wrath. Pathetic. What kind of leader was he?

The first person ran past, and Jade slit the back of their ankle. The person screamed as they fell to the ground. The next assailant went for Jade's waist as she got to her feet. Jade tripped over the first person, and she and the new assailant fell to the ground. Jade on her back. And the assailant on top of her. Jade shoved her knife into the person's side. She twisted it, pulled it out, and pushed the person off her. Their blood splattered across her chest. Jade looked down at it—disgusted.

Crimson was making his way over the fence.

Jade quickly got back to her feet and took off sprinting again. She returned to the main street that led her to the ambush spot. Jade deviated through different alleyways and parking garages along the way. When she finally glanced back, her heart dropped. Crimson was nowhere in sight. *Shit.* It looked like she did too good of a job losing him.

She appeared only a few blocks away from the ambush sight. Jade contemplated turning back, but she didn't know where exactly she lost Crimson. It could've been several places. She really didn't think it'd be this easy to lose someone like him. Not someone who was this high up in the group. It was a bit disappointing.

"Nice try, Jade," Crimson stood before her. She hadn't noticed where he came from.

Shouldn't the others have attacked by now?

"I'm not sure what you mean," Jade said casually. Did he come across the others? Did he suspect an ambush on the way here?

"Did you really think you could outrun me?" he glanced around. "I know this place better than you do. This is my domain."

"Seriously," Jade sighed. "Can we just get on with this already?"

Crimson chuckled. "I have never seen someone so ready to die."

Jade pretended not to notice Razor sneaking up on Crimson. She sighed again. "And I have never seen someone so afraid of it."

Crimson frowned as he was about to say something else, but Razor's arm made its way around his throat. Crimson fought hard against him. He thrashed around, trying his best to get out of Razor's hold. But he was no match for Razor. Usually, no one was. Crimson slumped against Razor. Razor immediately dropped him from his hold, allowing Crimson to fall to the ground. The van quickly pulled up, and Clay and Razor loaded Crimson into the back.

Jade watched as they bounded him with zip ties and blindfolded him. Clay gestured for Jade to get inside the van.

"It took you long enough," Jade complained as they entered.

"Sorry," Razor slammed the door shut. "Our cover was blown."

"What?" Jade looked around in a panic.

"A random group of the Radicals came across us," Brice stated as he sped off. "But we've dealt with them."

"I hope this doesn't ruin the plan."

"Let's hope not," Razor said.

**

Jade couldn't help but stare as Crimson swung by his ankles—blood dripping from his face as he swayed back and forth. It was clear that he was on the verge of passing out. Razor hung back, cracking his knuckles and preparing for another round of interrogations. Jade had meant to ask him, but she wondered why Razor preferred having his victims hang this way. Was it more intimidating? Did it make the victims' tongue looser? It looked uncomfortable. Jade knew she didn't want to be in that position.

To her surprise, Crimson was smiling. Even with an eye swollen shut. Bruises covering his face. And his lip busted. Crimson seemed to be having a good time—that worried and excited Jade.

Crimson smiled as he looked in her direction. "Oh, Jade, you know not what you do."

Razor responded by punching him in the stomach. Crimson groaned from the pain for a second and returned his attention to Jade.

"My people will find me," Crimson warned Jade. It was hard to take the warning seriously as Crimson said it with struggled breath.

"Stop fucking talking to her!" Razor responded once again by punching Crimson.

Again, Crimson moaned from the pain. But after a few seconds, he began to laugh. The others started to get noticeably uneasy—Brice in particular.

"I told you we wouldn't get anything out of him," Brice mumbled.

Jade ignored him. "What's President Dooms up to?"

It was time for them to take control of this situation. Ever since he gained consciousness, Crimson has been prolonging this situation. He was saying things to get under their skin. He seemed to bother Razor and Brice. Crimson had a knack for pissing Razor off. And in the process, he appeared to frighten Brice to no end.

Crimson kept laughing for a few more seconds before stopping abruptly. "Isn't it obvious? He's tying up loose ends."

"*I'm* a loose end," Jade couldn't see how.

Yes, she was fighting back against the DC, but so were many other people. The only thing that made her unique was Bossman's obsession with her. And maybe the fact that she was Razor's sister-in-law. But still, Jade didn't see how either of those scenarios made her a loose end.

Crimson shrugged with indifference. "Apparently so."

"It's all about keeping his leadership," Razor said quietly as he approached her. "If there's anything or anyone who goes against his agenda, Chase will view you as a threat and try to take care of it by any means."

"All to save face," Jade scoffed.

"People will do anything for power, Jade."

Jade shook her head in disbelief. The number of lives lost on both sides is all in the name of someone who didn't give a shit about them. It was sad. Heartbreaking. And enraging. All for power. Jade was trying to live her life in this crazy world. And so was everyone else. But one person's greed destroyed their lives, and they were forever changed.

Brice looked around—still terrified. "We really should start heading out."

"Anything else we should ask him?" Jade whispered to Razor. She was trying to hide her annoyance for Brice.

Razor cracked his knuckles. "I don't think he will give us anything else."

Jade nodded. "Should we kill him?"

"That is the question," Razor sighed and looked around.

"If we do that, we're inevitably starting a war," Brice warned.

"Look around, Brice," Jade looked at him in disbelief. "We're already in one."

"Let him hang," Razor concluded.

"All right," Jade would've preferred just to kill him. But leaving Crimson to hang by his ankles was basically doing the same thing. And Jade was ok with that.

"You're going to regret taking me," Crimson stated in parting words.

They ignored his comment. Razor called everyone out of their lookout spots. They all gathered around at the gate by the entrance. Once again, Calvin requested to stand by his Queen. Jade wanted nothing more. Brice glanced back at Crimson one last time before opening the gate.

Jade, Calvin, and Yoko walked out first.

"1, 2, 3, 4, 5," Calvin began counting.

"I'm not sure we got enough information from him," Yoko stated.

"10, 11, 12, 13, 14, 15."

"We got all we're going to get," Jade assured her. "Trust me, we learned enough."

"I guess so," Yoko paused. "I don't know. I guess I was hoping for something more."

Jade sighed. "We all were."

The two women turned their attention back to Calvin. He was a few steps ahead of them, watching his surroundings as he counted.

"34, 35, 36, 37."

Jade turned around to see where the others were at. Reagan and Clay were just behind them. Razor and Brice were bringing up the rear. For a quick second, Jade locked eyes with Clay. He smiled at her. Jade smiled back.

Then Clay's eyes widened in horror.

Yoko screamed.

Jade turned around to see Calvin falling onto his back—blood and brain matter spewing out of what used to be the back of his head.

Jade screamed at the top of her lungs as she blacked out.

~26~

Jade

Out of everything she's been through, Jade could clearly say she'd never had trouble gaining control of herself as she did now. Jade and Warrior Jade were having a power struggle, and Jade was losing. Here's what she could make out of their current situation.

One: Calvin lay dead on the ground, blood pouring from his head. Yoko kneeled beside him, screaming and crying.

Two: Warrior Jade and Reagan began firing off shots at snipers. Reagan with her rifle. Warrior Jade with her bow and arrows.

Three: Razor, Clay, and Brice shouting incoherent commands.

Four: Warrior Jade was now out of arrows. But she knew the ones responsible for Calvin's death were still alive. Unacceptable. There's running. Warrior Jade pulled out her knives as she met her attackers a block away from Calvin's dead body.

Five: So much screaming. So much blood. Lifeless bodies lay at her feet.

Six: Warrior Jade was running again. Back to the interrogation spot. Back to where he was hanging. This was all his fault.

Seven: Razor, Clay, and Brice shouting incoherently.

Eight: Crimson's terrified face as Warrior Jade rushed back into the place, Calvin's sword in her hand (when did she even pick up his sword?).

Nine: Crimson's head dropped to the ground. His headless body was still swinging as blood poured out of the spot where his head used to be.

Ten: Brice looked horrified as he whispered, "I told you he wasn't the one we should've gone after."

~27~

Razor

If there was ever an ounce of hope that Jade would be her usual self again, that just went out the window when Calvin fell to the ground. The only word that he could describe her at the moment was catatonic. Once she killed Crimson, she screamed at the top of her lungs and dropped to the ground—frozen. Brice and Reagan had to return to HQ to get help moving her, Yoko, and Calvin's dead body.

Helena was in hysterics when she saw the state her sister was in. That, and she was still trying to process Calvin's death. It wasn't until she saw his body that she cried too.

It had all gone so very wrong.

Razor knew they weren't entirely clear when they left the

interrogation spot. Still, he didn't realize they were *that* vulnerable. There was always a possibility that Crimson could've had people following him. But Razor ensured that no one wasn't before they captured Crimson and before he began his interrogation. Clearly, it wasn't enough. And Calvin paid for that with his life.

It was all still unbelievable.

Calvin couldn't *really* be dead. There was just no way. He was a giant. And he always seemed so invincible.

When they all returned to HQ, Cole immediately suggested that they have a service honoring Calvin. It seemed like he offered it to help calm Yoko down some. She was so distraught. And rightfully so. It was always just the two of them. Yoko and Calvin. There was no telling how long she and Calvin had been together before they came along.

Still, Razor couldn't get over the fact that they would have a funeral. An actual funeral. No one performed those anymore. No one had the money, resources, or time. Even the rich found it unnecessary. But this would help them all find closure. And it was needed for Yoko. And for Jade.

They all needed a couple of days to prepare for the ceremony. Razor spent most of his time serving as a lookout on multiple shifts. Cole and Zara assured him that his number of shifts wasn't necessary. But Razor needed them. He needed a chance to redeem himself. Because he felt nothing but guilt and responsibility for Calvin's death, Razor should've been more cautious. He should've had the group making rounds across the area more frequently. Razor should've taken Brice's fear of Crimson more seriously.

Razor did none of these things. And for that reason, Calvin lost his life.

Of course, Helena tried to convince him otherwise.

"There was no way you could've avoided it," she said one night while he was on his shift. She visited him after helping Cole and Keeper in the medical wing. "All of this shit is unavoidable."

"I should've been more cautious, Helena."

She sighed. She wore a look of defeat. Dealing with Jade and Yoko mourning and Razor blaming himself for Calvin's death was all too much for Helena. She was spreading herself thin, trying to comfort everyone else while dealing with her feelings.

Helena didn't say anything else to him. She just kissed him goodnight and told him that she loved him.

When Razor was finally done working as a lookout, he went up to his room. He found Jade lying on the pullout, eyes open, tears streaming down her face. Since they returned from their mission, Jade hadn't left her spot. She'd lay there every day, not moving a muscle. Clay tried to get her out, to no avail. Surprisingly, Helena did nothing. The only move she made was to join her sister in bed from time to time. Yoko would come in to lay with Jade as well. The two women would cuddle together, cry, and try to comfort one another.

But at least Yoko was up and moving around. Jade was like a zombie, and she barely even spoke. The only noise she made was the whimpers from her cries.

Razor didn't know what to say to her. It felt like all he'd been doing was apologizing to her lately. Saying I'm sorry was no longer enough. He needed to remedy the situation. Somehow. Some way. He was going to do that. And Jade would become her old self again.

The first time Jade spoke to any of them was the day of Calvin's funeral. Everyone was getting dressed and preparing to go down except for Jade.

"I don't want to go," she explained.

"Jade," Helena sat on the edge of the pullout. "Don't you want to at least say goodbye to him?"

Jade shook her head. "I don't want to remember him that way. I want my last memory to be him smiling and demanding that he stand by his Queen. Seeing him lying dead like that...it'll tarnish that memory."

"I think you'll regret not going, Jade," Razor intervened. Helena looked over at him and shook her head. Razor frowned at her reaction.

Helena smiled and kissed her sister's forehead. "I'll say goodbye to him for the both of us."

"Thank you, Helena."

It wasn't until they were gathered in command central that Helena explained herself.

"It's best if we don't fight her on this, Razor," she said. "We did that when she lost David, Raina, and Levi. That only made things worse. Let her feel how she feels. She'll pull herself out of it...she always does."

Razor nodded. He knew Helena was right, but he just hated seeing Jade that way. It broke his heart. Seeing someone he loved broken to pieces really upset him. But Razor decided to let go of the matter...for now.

Helena guided them to the rows of chairs up front. Razor, Helena, Clay, Reagan, Yoko, Danita, Tatianna, and Keeper sat in the front. Everyone took turns consoling Yoko when they weren't crying themselves. Clay, of course, was anxious. He kept looking around, hoping to see Jade. Razor tried hard to fight off his annoyance.

"There's nothing you can do to help her at the moment," he whispered to him. "Be here for Yoko now. She needs all of us."

"Right," Clay cleared his voice in embarrassment. "Sorry."

Clay went over to Yoko and immediately offered his shoulder for her to cry on. She graciously accepted.

Cole started the ceremony. He encouraged everyone to be there for one another. The time they all lived in was dangerous, and the show of care and humanity was more important now than ever. He urged everyone to love each other and express their feelings to those around them. He then prompted those who knew Calvin the best to give a few words. Of course, Yoko was the first to get up to give her speech.

It took her a moment to speak. "I would say that Calvin and I have been traveling together for about five years. It's hard marking dates and times nowadays. But if I had to guess, I would say it's at least been that long."

Yoko stopped for a moment to wipe the fresh tears that had fallen from her eyes. Helena blew her nose. And Tatianna let out an audible cry.

"When I first met Calvin, he was protecting me," Yoko cleared her throat. "He was protecting me from a horrible fate—this giant. At first, he could appear so scary. But in time, you realize that he was a gentle giant. Protecting those he cared for."

Again, Yoko stopped to collect herself. She was on the verge of breaking down. Razor could see it on her face, and he could read it from her body language. There was a battle going on inside her. She was determined not to break down and give in. She was determined to remain strong. Razor admired her for that.

"Many people we've met on the road encouraged me to abandon him. They viewed him as a liability. He was only going to weigh me down in the end. But unlike them, I didn't consider him being on the spectrum as a liability. I actually found his mindset refreshing. It was so innocent compared to others out there. I wouldn't be here today if it weren't for Calvin. He protected me right to the end."

Yoko looked over at the closed, makeshift casket Calvin was in. She kissed her hand and placed it on top of the lid. Fresh tears ran down her face.

"I'm going to miss you so much, my gentle giant," Yoko cried. "Although she didn't have the strength to make it here today, Jade will miss you too. We both love you so much. My giant. Her knight."

Yoko stood beside Calvin's casket a few seconds longer. This time she cried even harder—allowing herself to succumb to her emotions. Razor stood and walked over to comfort her. She cried in his arms for a moment. He tried his best to give her many words of encouragement. But none of them felt like it was enough. He finally escorted her back to her seat, where Helena was waiting with open arms.

Razor paused as he looked back at Calvin's casket. "He was the only man I truly feared when I first met him," Razor cleared his throat, pushing back his emotions. "It's hard to believe he's gone because he always seemed invincible. Thank you for always being there for us, big guy. You will truly be missed. Rest peacefully, Calvin."

"Rest peacefully," they all said in unison.

The ceremony lasted a few minutes longer, with everyone else in the group saying their goodbyes. Cole closed it out by reminding everyone to be good to one another. Then Razor, Cole, Clay, Keeper, and a few more Black Coat members carried the casket to the designated area where Calvin was to be cremated.

Yoko could be heard crying the whole way. Once they set the casket down, she kissed the top of the coffin and said goodbye one last time. Then Helena and Tatianna helped escort Yoko back to her room.

Overall, it was nice that they all got a chance for closure. But it really did bring the morale of the group down. Redemption was needed for all of them. And Razor knew where to start.

The Radicals.

They needed to be defeated. Then they could return their wrath to Chase, Nick, and the DC task force. Anyone who was making their life miserable needed to be dealt with. Razor was going to see to it all.

**

Razor allowed a few days to pass before bringing the issue up to Cole. He waited until after dinner. He'd found Cole, Helena, Keeper, Zara, and Brice in the medical wing. Keeper and Helena were helping Cole with his rounds. And it looked like Zara and Brice were reporting the end-of-day information to him. They all stopped what they were doing when Razor walked in.

Brice wore a look of guilt. He'd been wearing that look since they returned from their mission, and it was more prominent whenever he crossed paths with anyone who was on the mission.

"How's Jade?" Brice asked immediately. He asked this whenever he came across someone from the group. Razor was sure he'd already posed the question to Helena and Keeper. Maybe he expected Razor to have a different answer.

"The same," Razor tried not to sound annoyed. But he recalled him freezing up out there whenever he looked at Brice. They were under attack and had a man down. And Brice stood frozen, looking like he was going to shit himself. If it weren't for Jade losing control, none of them would be here.

Brice knew that. That's why he kept asking about Jade's well-being.

"What can I do for you, my friend?" Cole greeted him.

"We need to discuss how you want to deal with the Radicals."

"Of course," Cole sighed.

"We know from Jade that Liam has allowed Junior to roam freely," Razor informed them. She relayed that information to him before they got to the interrogation spot. "That's not really ideal."

"No, it most certainly is not."

"And with you, me, and Jade having a hit out on our heads, we must move swiftly."

"I guess you'll want to take them out," Zara suggested.

"If we can," Razor admitted. "There's no telling how big the group is. But we must take out Liam and Junior. There's no question about that."

"What about Fallen?" Zara asked. "She's Liam's number two."

"Word from the current patrol group is that she's dead."

Zara and Brice looked at each other, shocked.

"They have to be mistaken," Brice said. It sounded like he was in pain.

"They're pretty sure. They said they overheard it from some Radicals they were tailing."

"Well, I guess we no longer have to worry about her," Zara was still in disbelief.

"She's not an easy person to get to," Cole frowned. "Did they overhear who might've done this?"

"Someone vicious," Razor gave Cole a knowing look. When he heard about Fallen's death, Razor knew Nick had made his way over and was trying to gather intel. Razor didn't know how to feel about that. Now that they all were wanted, Razor wasn't sure what his encounter with Nick would be like.

"Well, we both knew it was only a matter of time," Cole said casually.

"So, how should we proceed?" Zara asked. He could tell she was trying to stay focused, but the news of Fallen's death still shocked her.

"The patrol members mentioned that the Radicals said they captured her killer."

"We just need to find out where they're holding him," Helena whispered. Razor could see the conflict on her face. The news that Nick was close by wasn't comforting to her. Jade was vulnerable, and the information about Nick would surely push her over the edge.

"That'll be ideal," Razor admitted. "But finding Junior or Liam would be a top priority."

"Agreed," Cole said. He had walked over to Jackson's bed to check his vitals. "Zara, Brice, I want you to gather a team to scout for any Radicals. I want them to tail them. They need to report what they see, where the Radicals are going, whom they are meeting with, and how many are generally in the area. Is there anything I missed, Razor?"

"No, that'll do."

"Copy that," Zara said. She and Brice were about to walk out of the wing.

"No, no, no, no," they heard someone grumble.

Razor looked over at Jackson's bed, completely shocked.

"No, no, no, no, no," Jackson groaned. His eyes snapped open. He looked around at everyone around him, and his eyes landed on Razor. So many questions were behind them.

~28~

Jade

All hope was lost. There was no need to carry on. There was no longer any motivation to. What little piece of Jade had left (a part of her she didn't know existed) was gone forever. Everything happened so fast that it all felt unreal. Surely, her eyes had to be deceiving her. There was no way that Calvin could be dead. Not her giant knight. It all had to be another nightmare. A waking nightmare. But this was reality. Calvin was actually lying in the middle of the street in a pool of his blood. The back of his head was missing.

Reagan had found the sniper and took them out. But Jade had already lost it—going after any adversary in her path.

Once they returned to HQ, she couldn't find the strength to get out of bed or do anything. All she could do was cry. Calvin was gone. He was really gone. No one was invincible. His death was just a huge reminder of that. Images of Calvin's death flooded her mind. Jade could've sworn she saw a hint of a smile on his face. Counting his steps always made him happy. At least, it was a quick death. He didn't feel any pain. That was one bright side to it.

Jade's admiration for Yoko grew throughout this whole ordeal. At least *she* could find the strength to get out of bed and move about. Yoko did cry a lot. But that didn't matter because she was still getting out there. On the other hand, *Jade* couldn't find the strength to move an inch. Let alone could she find the courage to go to Calvin's funeral. It was a nice gesture for Cole to go out of the way to do that. But Jade didn't want to say goodbye to him during a sad ceremony. She wanted to say goodbye to him in her own way, in her own time. And she stood by that decision. Jade was grateful that the others understood her choice, especially Yoko.

A couple of days after the service, Raina visited Jade. Jade was crying when she felt a small body snuggle up to her. She instantly knew that it was Raina. Clay took to sleeping on the floor or giving Jade some space. And Helena and Yoko were out. It felt like forever since Raina had visited her.

"Don't worry, Jade," Raina assured her when Jade turned to face her. "I'll look after him."

Jade smiled through fresh tears. Raina looked so grown. It was as if she matured during her time away from Jade. "I know you will, my little munchkin."

Jade clenched onto Raina as she cried harder. Raina consoled her as best she could, whispering encouraging words. This world was breaking Jade. And she wasn't sure how more broken she could get.

When Jade finally woke up, she found herself cradling Calvin's sheathed sword. Then she recalled a conversation that she swore was a vivid dream. Yoko had come in and sat on the edge of the bed. She smiled at Jade with tear-filled eyes.

"I've brought the Queen a present," she informed her.

Jade frowned, wondering what she was talking about.

Yoko revealed the weapon. "A Queen should wield her fallen knight's sword into battle."

Jade sat up. She was intrigued by her gift. "You don't want it?"

"No, I think he would've wanted you to have it," she said. "Plus, I have many of his belongings that I'm keeping."

There were no words for her to say. "Thank you so much, Yoko," Jade clenched the sword.

"You're welcome."

Jade didn't remember falling back to sleep. And she didn't recall Yoko leaving. But when she woke up with Calvin's sword beside her, Jade decided she had spent enough time grieving him. It was now time to avenge him. Liam and Junior would pay for Calvin's death.

When she entered command central, Jade could see nothing but the look of satisfaction on Razor's face. She knew that he was worried about her. Not that she could blame him. Jade could feel that she was one slip-up away from the point of no return, which wasn't very comforting.

Jade greeted everyone with a nod. Razor immediately walked over to her.

"I'm glad you're up," he stated. "We need to talk."

"Great," Jade said sarcastically. The last thing she was in the mood for was talking. But Jade was sure some events and things had transpired while she was out that she needed to be caught up on.

"Take watch with me," Razor said as he walked toward the stairway.

Jade silently followed him. They didn't say anything to each other until they occupied one of the lookout rooms on the fourth floor.

"So, how are you feeling?" Razor was looking at her intently, trying to figure out just how bad she was.

"I'm taking it one day at a time," Jade sighed. "I believe there are some things you want to tell me."

Razor sighed. There was so much conflict behind his eyes. He hesitated to tell her the news. It must've been bad. Jade dreaded the words, and how much more she could take wasn't clear. But she was definitely on edge.

Razor turned his gaze to the window—assessing the outside. Jade proceeded to do the same. She was in no rush to hear the news. A few more minutes of silence went by, and finally, Razor sighed and turned his attention back to Jade.

"There's evidence that Nick is nearby," there was dread in his voice.

Jade froze. She dared not move for fear that she didn't hear him correctly.

"According to some members here, he killed Fallen and then was captured by Junior," Razor went on.

Burning rage coursed through her body. "That bastard Junior has him."

"The members believe that Junior took him to Liam."

"Well, that all works out great," a plan quickly formed in Jade's mind. "I can kill all three of them in one swoop."

"You have to be smart about this, Jade."

"I am, Razor!" Jade had to stop herself and take deep breaths. "These three bastards have killed everyone I loved. They *need* to pay."

"I understand that, Jade. But let's not be stupid and get yourself killed in the process."

Jade took a deep breath. Razor was right. She needed to be smart about how she proceeded. Emotions couldn't cloud her judgment. Not now. The situation was just way too critical.

"Ok," she finally said. "How should we do this?"

"Locate Nick," Razor said. "I'm sure he'll have more intel on Liam and Junior. And probably Chase too."

"Ok," Jade couldn't fight the nerves in her stomach. "Ok."

"One last thing," Razor paused, waiting for Jade to look at him. "Jackson's awake."

"Seriously?" Jade didn't have any hope for him.

"Yeah, I'm waiting until he feels a little better before I ask him what happened on the river that night."

Jade nodded. There were so many questions that needed to be answered, and it was unclear if she was going to like them or not.

"You're strong enough to hear it," David encouraged as he appeared beside her.

"I wouldn't be so sure," she whispered. It'd been a while since he visited her. She was glad that he was there now. "I'm barely holding on as it is."

"You'll adapt, Jade," he smiled at her. "Give yourself a little more credit."

But that was the problem. For Jade, it seemed like she was struggling to adapt to the things that were being thrown at her.

Jade looked over at him and smiled weakly. "And I think you're giving me too much."

"I know the woman I fell in love with," David smiled as he caressed her cheek. Jade sighed. "You always know how to be prepared."

Those words stayed in her head.

The rest of the lookout shift went by in a blur. Jade couldn't even recall them having a conversation after all of that. She wasn't sure if Razor had asked her something else. Jade's mind was too far gone even to remember. All she could think about was how she needed to prepare.

It wasn't until their shift was over and they were back at command central that Jade could comprehend what was happening around her. She began looking around the area, hoping to spot the person she was looking for.

"What's wrong?" Razor demanded.

"I'm looking for Zara."

"Why?"

"Because I need her to train me to fight with a sword."

~29~

Nick

Blood trickled down Nick's wrist as he hung by them. The pain from the weight of his body finally subsided. It actually receded a long time ago. But despite the position that he was in, Nick wasn't worried about his situation. Their form of "torture" wasn't nothing that Nick hadn't endured before. The only annoyance was him hanging by the wrist most of the time. But again, it wasn't anything he couldn't deal with.

The real reason he was here was to get intel on the group's leadership. Nick was sure that Chase would use this group in his fight, and Nick needed to know what he, Razor, and Jade would be up against. According to what he'd witnessed, the Radicals weren't anything to worry about. However, they could be a nuisance from time to time. And that was why they needed to be handled sooner rather than later.

Nick was giving it until the end of the day before he made his escape. The next person he, for sure, needed to take out was Liam's other number two, Crimson. Seriously, what was up with these ridiculous names? Junior was also on top of the hit list. Without anyone else to depend on, Liam would go down quickly. From Nick's observation, Liam relied heavily on others. Take that away, and people like him will break. Nick's seen it countless times.

From the sunlight peeking through the windows in the warehouse, it had to be noon, and this was usually when someone came to torture Nick. But no one was there. Instead, Nick heard some yelling and commotion going on just outside. Something must've happened. And by the sounds of it, it wasn't anything good.

The door burst open, and Liam, Junior, and other Radical members rushed inside. From what Nick could make out, they were carrying a dead body. It looked like it was missing a head. Nick saw Junior carrying something wrapped in a sheet when he looked closer. It appeared to be the missing head.

"Who the fuck could've done this?!" Liam demanded.

"We're not sure, sir," one of the Radicals admitted.

"Some members recalled hearing commotion serval blocks from here a few days ago," Junior reported.

"And no one checked it out?!"

"We did, sir. When we got there, nothing indicated that anything happened."

"Not until we began searching inside some of the buildings," another member responded.

"Why was Crimson in that area in the first place?" Liam asked. "That's not even his hang-out area."

Nick laughed at this. Well, that was one less person he had to kill.

"You find this funny!" Liam shouted as he made his way to Nick. Junior and two other members followed.

"I do," Nick smiled. "Your leadership is taking a real hit."

"Fuck you!"

"Let me guess. He was found hanging upside down," Nick was enjoying this moment.

The two members looked nervously at each other. They didn't say a word. Nick took this as confirmation. He laughed even louder.

"You know who did this," Liam gritted.

"I can narrow it down to two people," Nick looked over at Junior. "And so can Junior."

"Names," Liam demanded.

"Jesus, are you seriously this stupid?"

Liam didn't respond. He just glared at Nick.

"Razor or Jade," Junior finally said.

"My guess would be my sweet, sweet Jade," Nick was delighted by the idea that she would do something that cruel. She was finally free. It was nice to know that performing that vicious act actually worked. Jade was becoming the woman he wanted her to be.

Liam looked at Junior. "I don't care what you do. Find her and Razor and bring them both to me! I want to see the life drain from her eyes."

Nick laughed hard at this. Liam was absurd with his statement. There was no chance that scenario would happen. What would certainly occur was that Jade would watch the life drain out of Liam and Junior's eyes.

"I do not appreciate your reaction to this situation," Liam glared.

"Oh no, are you expecting sympathy from me?"

Liam looked over at Junior. Junior responded by punching Nick in the face. Nick continued to laugh. Liam grew angry. He responded by punching Nick in the face himself. This only made Nick laugh even harder. It all was a huge joke to him. He couldn't control himself. It was funny to see that they couldn't handle this situation. They were in over their heads here.

Once he was able to compose himself, Nick looked at Liam. "If you go after Jade, you'll be signing your death certificate. Trust me."

"I'm not you, Nick."

"No," Nick chuckled. "No, you're not."

Then Nick slipped out of his bondage. His blood provided enough slip. Plus, it helped that he was able to dislocate his wrists. Liam yelled out of shock. With his wrists dislocated, he elbowed one Radical in the throat. Nick quickly relocated one wrist and jabbed another member in the eye. Then he twisted his other wrist back into its socket.

"Kill him!" Liam demanded as he took refuge behind Junior.

Of course, many were hesitant to attack him—even Junior. Nick smirked—such cowards. Nick went for the person closest to him. Some tried to take that opportunity to attack him, but Nick tore through them all the same. By the time he was done with them, Liam and Junior were running out the door.

Nick chuckled—such cowards. He didn't even bother to go after them. Instead, he gathered up his weapons and picked over the supplies of those he killed. Once he was done, he began making his way to the door.

"We're going to see Jade?" Levi asked.

They had been absent this whole time.

"Looks that way, kiddo."

"She's not gonna want to see you," Levi warned.

"Yeah, Dad, she hates you."

"Well, I don't think she'll have a choice in the matter," Nick looked around for Raina, but she was missing.

"There's never a choice with you."

Nick looked over at Levi. He didn't look healthy. Images of Nick shoving a machete through him came rushing to his mind, and Nick had to look away from him.

"You're right," Nick admitted. "But this time, it's different. Now, let's go."

Nick walked out of the warehouse as the two ghost boys followed.

~30~

Jade

"Don't think about the weight of it," Zara instructed. "Focus on your stance. Stand firm."

Jade tried to focus on Zara's instructions, but Calvin's sword had a heavy weight that Jade couldn't grasp. She focused on making sure her feet were planted firmly. She scrunched her toes inside her boots—as if that would secure her even further. Jade was determined. She was *going* to get this. She *needed* to get this. *This* was how she'd avenge Calvin. By wielding his sword—effortlessly. Beautifully. Fear would be stricken into anyone who was on the end of it. But right now, she needed to get the hang of it.

Zara narrowed her eyes at Jade before she unsheathed her swords and began attacking. As always, Jade was a blundering mess. She could never match Zara's speed. Zara was a natural with the sword. It was as if they were an addition to herself. Zara tried to drill that into Jade's head on numerous occasions.

"It is an extension of your arm," Zara encouraged. "Move that way."

Jade was barely blocking Zara's attacks. One time she got cut with one of Zara's swords.

"Do you have to use actual swords?" Helena complained as she stitched Jade's shoulder.

"We don't have time," Zara stated. "This is the best way she'll learn."

"She won't be able to do anything if her limbs go missing!" Helena was in a grumpy mood lately. And, of course, Jade's fighting sessions weren't making it easier on her.

Zara looked uneasy for a moment. As if she, too, were afraid of Helena and her mood. "I apologize. I'll try to be more mindful of my movements."

Jade didn't even bother to tell Helena to relax a little. She was also afraid of pissing Helena off. No one was sure where the irritation was coming from with Helena. But no one wanted to be on the brutal end of it. Even Razor was walking around on eggshells. Eventually, Jade just chalked it up to Helena dealing with Calvin's death. She figured Helena was at the anger stage of grief. Jade couldn't fault her there. She was there herself.

"You must move faster!" Zara demanded as she continued her attack on Jade.

Jade tried to move faster. Her blade was barely blocking Zara's. Technically, Jade would've been dead already. While she focused on one of Zara's swords, the other mimed fatal blows that both women acknowledged. But instead of starting over, Zara insisted they continue until Jade could block both. She still couldn't.

For most of the day, the sound of blades crashing into one another filled the building. Everyone was used to the two women grunting and Zara shouting out commands. By the time Jade got ready for bed each night, her body would be screaming in agony. Her whole body would be sore. But it would all pay off. Eventually, she'd be able to move as swiftly as Zara with her sword. There was no doubt about that.

During her training, Jade barely spoke to anyone who wasn't Zara. For some reason, she felt all her attention needed to be focused on that. It was as if anything else would've hindered her from improving. Surprisingly, everyone was giving her space. Even Razor and Helena. Jade figured that they all were preoccupied with Jackson being awake. She was stunned by the news. And she was very leery of interacting with him.

Looking at Jackson brought too many bad memories of that fatal night. Memories that Jade couldn't afford to cloud her mind with at the moment. She needed to focus on getting better at fighting with a sword. That's all she could allow in her head.

When she wasn't training, Jade was working on strengthening her arms. She desperately needed to with that sword. She'd do multiple reps of push-ups and go down to the fitness room to lift weights. It still amazed her the various luxuries the Black Coats had been able to accumulate. Oddly enough, Jackson would always have his physical therapy whenever she went. Jade tried countless times to go down at different times of the day, but it never failed. Jackson would be there.

Whenever she came across him, Jade nodded and proceeded with her training. Jackson would do the same. Jade did her best to focus on her training, but she could feel Jackson's eyes on her occasionally. And when resting between sets, her eyes would drift over to Jackson. Luckily for her, those moments were when he was focused on taking steps.

Learning to walk and move his body correctly had to be hard for him.

Not to mention that he was probably grieving the death of his twin, Beverly. That had to be difficult. Coming to and learning that he had survived this traumatic incident, but his sister didn't. Jade pitied Jackson. But she couldn't bring herself to communicate with him. Not yet.

It was strange seeing Jackson as skin and bones. Well, not literally, but this new Jackson was shocking compared to how he was when Jade first met him. He looked so frail—weak. It was to be expected, but it was still jarring. Jade had to give it to him; Jackson was determined to get back on his feet again. It seemed like he was in the gym more than she was.

"Still haven't talked to him yet?" Razor inquired one day.

Jade had just finished up another day of training. She was leaving the gym and preparing to shower quickly before dinner. Jade looked back to see Jackson taking quick strides before losing his balance. Keeper promptly rushed to his side, but Jackson shooed him away.

"No," Jade looked away from the scene. "He needs to focus on his recovery."

"I suppose you're right," Razor followed her to the stairway.

"Did you find out what's eating Helena?"

"I'd guess many things."

Jade paused on the steps. That was so unlike Razor. "You guess? You never guess. You're the intel man."

Razor sighed. "She won't tell me. And honestly, I'm tired of trying to get it out of her."

Jade nodded and continued up the stairs. She and Helena could be very stubborn at times.

"Anyway, I've been putting all my time into finding out where Nick is."

"That information still hasn't turned up."

"No. Clay, Reagan, and Brice have been looking everywhere."

A tinge of guilt hit Jade as she opened the door that led to their floor.

Clay, Reagan, and Brice had been on the road for a week. She knew she should be with them, but she was putting all her focus into training.

"I'm sorry I'm not out there with them," she said as she reached their suite.

"There's nothing to apologize for," Razor reassured her. "You need to prepare."

Jade nodded as she went inside. Razor's words didn't help subside the guilt she was feeling. Clay and Reagan were always there for her. She should be there for them now. They most certainly shouldn't be out there with Brice alone. The guy was known for freezing up when things went chaotic. Jade should be there to help. But she needed to prepare.

When she got into their suite, Jade quickly went to go shower. She noticed that Razor went into his room. Jade moved swiftly as she showered. She could hear Razor and Helena having a heated discussion as she dressed.

"Everyone is noticing it, Helena."

"I don't give a damn what they notice!"

"I'm begging you, just tell me what's going on."

"Nothing is going on, Razor. I'm fine."

Jade heard footsteps retreating. A few seconds later, someone was banging on the bathroom door. Jade jumped. She didn't realize that she'd stopped getting dressed.

"Damnit, Jade! How much longer are you going to be in there?!"

Jade began to move faster. "Sorry! Give me a minute."

She rushed to get dressed and left out the bathroom. When she got out, Helena was leaning against the opposite wall—arms folded. Jade could feel the irritation radiating off her sister. Helena didn't say anything to Jade. She just brushed past her and slammed the bathroom door shut. Jade was a little stunned by Helena's behavior.

"I'm trying to get to the bottom of it," Razor said. He was standing at the suite door. "Let's leave her alone for now."

"Ok."

Razor opened the door and gestured for Jade to follow. Jade did. They walked silently to the mess hall. Jade's brain drifted off to Helena and her behavior. Helena was known to have irritation moments, but lately, she's been living in them. Jade wasn't used to that. And clearly, neither was Razor. Jade would need to talk to her sister sometime soon. There was no getting around it.

Razor and Jade ate their dinner silently. Helena joined them after a few minutes. She mostly talked to Tatianna, and it didn't seem they were discussing anything serious. From what Jade heard, it was nothing but small talk. But Tatianna appeared to be the only one who wasn't on the wrong end of Helena's attitude. Jade wasn't sure how to feel about that.

Keeper came to sit between Jade and Razor. He sighed as he sat down.

"How's it going?" Jade asked.

"It's going," Keeper took a sip of water before eating.

"I see you've been helping Jackson with his physical therapy."

"Yeah. Between that and making my rounds with Cole, I'm exhausted."

"I'm sure you've learned so much more working under Cole," Jade reflected on how Keeper was the unconventional doctor in their group.

"Yeah, ya can say that."

"Jackson should be permanently on his feet soon," Razor stated.

Keeper sighed. "If he keeps going the way he's going."

"It sounds like you don't approve," Jade pointed out.

"I don't agree with rushing," Keeper said between bites. "Especially when hate is a fueling factor."

"I think hating Bossman is a justifiable reaction."

"I'm not talking about Bossman. I'm talking about hating ya own father."

Jade paused at that. She never did consider how Jackson would feel about finding out that his father was alive this whole time. As she recalled her last conversation with Jackson, he mentioned how he was angry that his father left him and Beverly to deal with leading the Black Deficit. Knowing he's been alive and well the whole time would feel like a severe betrayal.

"He has a right to that feeling," Razor said.

"I'll just be glad when his recovery is over, and I don't have to be in the middle of it."

Jade nodded. She understood Keeper's feelings. No one wants to be in the middle of a family dispute, especially with something as heavy as this. Jade looked at Helena to see that she was still conversing with Tatianna. Keeper followed her gaze.

"Tatianna doesn't know what's eating Helena either," Keeper answered Jade's unasked question.

"It's starting to bother me," Jade admitted.

"Zara mentioned that she overheard Helena crying in the bathroom the other day."

Razor paused at this. A look of frustration covered his face.

"She's not telling us anything," aggravation seeped through Jade's tone.

Keeper shrugged as he finished the last bit of his food. "Maybe it has to do with Calvin."

Jade sighed. "Maybe."

They all finished the rest of their food in silence. Once they were done, they all left the mess hall and went to their respective areas. Razor and Jade had lookout duty, and Keeper had more rounds to make in the medic wing. But as they walked through control central, Clay, Reagan, and Brice came in.

**

"It's worse than we thought," Brice informed them, panicked.

Reagan rolled her eyes. "He's being a little dramatic."

"There were dead bodies throughout that warehouse!" Brice paced back and forth in Cole's living room.

Jade, Razor, Helena, Tatianna, and Keeper sat on the couch. Cole and Zara were seated in two armchairs across from them. Clay and Reagan were leaning against the mantle on the fireplace. Brice continued pacing while Jackson hovered in the entryway of the living room. He wasn't sure if he should enter or not.

"Was that the place they were keeping Nick or not?" Razor was beyond annoyed with Brice.

"It looks that way," Clay said. He looked over at Reagan, and she nodded. "It definitely seemed like his handiwork."

"Our guess is he got the information he needed from them and killed them when he was done," Reagan informed them.

Brice stopped pacing. "How can you all be so nonchalant about this?! He was their prisoner!"

"Enough, Brice!" Zara was annoyed and disappointed. "If you have no more information, you may leave."

"Clay and Reagan can inform you of the rest," the insult was clear in Brice's tone.

"Visit the medic wing if you have trouble sleeping," Cole stated as a goodbye.

Brice didn't say anything else. He stormed out of the room and slammed the door behind him. No one spoke until he was gone.

"It looks like he might be trying to find the headquarters," Reagan stated.

"Is he a threat to Cole?" Zara demanded.

"I don't think so," Clay said.

"No, he needs Cole," Razor stood. "He needs us all. Nick is trying to get to us before Chase's people do. We're all on the same side of the shit coin right now."

"Great," Jade mumbled.

"It's actually a bright side," Razor looked at her. "That's one less enemy we have to worry about. Right now, we can focus on Junior and Liam. They have to deal with *Nick and us*. They'll fall soon."

"That's something," Jade wasn't sure if that was a good thing. But it was something.

Zara sighed. "All we can do now is increase our patrol and lookout."

"I agree," Razor stated. "Thanks, Clay and Reagan, for doing this."

"It was no trouble at all," Clay stated, his eyes meeting Jade's. Jade swiftly looked away. She felt embarrassed for some reason.

Everyone said their goodbyes and went to their respective places. Zara asked Jade to stay back for a minute. Cole excused himself to his bedroom. And Jackson disappeared somewhere in between the debriefing.

"With this news, I'm assuming you'll want to increase your training," Zara stated.

"You assumed right."

"Fair warning then, I will no longer be holding back on you."

A part of Jade was deeply frightened by Zara's threat. But she appreciated it. This was the push that Jade needed to get herself together and master her training with the sword.

~31~

Jade

Zara wasn't lying when she told Jade she'd no longer be holding back with Jade's training. Actually, Jade was surprised that Zara was holding back at all. This full-force Zara was something fierce and terrifying. Jade could no longer match her speed, and she tried. And trust, Jade tried *hard*. But Zara's speed was something else.

The stakes for Jade's slowness increased. Now, if Zara landed three fatal blows in a row, it resulted in a small cut somewhere on Jade's body. Although Jade hated it when it happened, she approved. It motivated Jade to be better. However, she ensured she went to Keeper to attend to her cuts instead of Helena. There was no need to sic an angry Helena on Zara.

Jade began adding cardio to her workout regimen, with the stakes now higher with training. She needed to match or beat Zara's speed. So, she ran laps around the gym and then worked on her arms. And, of course, Jackson was always there when she was. Honestly, Jade was starting to find it very annoying. It seemed like he was doing it on purpose. Like Jackson knew she was avoiding him, and he was trying to make that difficult.

"Why don't you talk to him?" Clay probed one night.

Since returning from the road, Jade's been asking for his company at night. Whether she did it out of guilt or genuinely craved his company was unclear. The part of her still loyal to David wanted it to be the former. But Jade knew it was primarily her selfishness kicking in, so it was the latter.

"I can't distract myself by reliving that night."

Clay shifted as he placed an arm behind his head. Jade looked over at him. He was staring at the ceiling—a slight frown forming.

"Maybe that's exactly what you need," he finally said.

"What?" Jade sat up, and it hurt her to do it. Her body was extremely sore.

It took Clay a moment to look at her. "It might add more fuel to the fire...you know, for training."

Jade hadn't thought about that. She thought that Calvin's death would be fuel enough. But it was looking like that wasn't the case. Maybe she needed her mind to go there. Perhaps she needed the pain to push her and keep her moving sharply. It was a grotesque idea but one that could work.

"You might be right," she sighed. Jade looked over a Clay to see that he was watching her. It was a minute before he diverted his eyes back to the ceiling.

"Besides, his presence is starting to annoy you. You don't perform well when you're annoyed."

Jade was a little stunned that Clay appeared to know her so well. Any irritation or annoyance did affect Jade's fighting. It was surprising that Clay noticed that. He seemed to be more observant than she thought.

"I'll try talking to him tomorrow and see if that'll change anything," Jade wasn't optimistic that it'll work, but she thought it was worth giving it a shot.

"Sounds good," Clay yawned.

Jade looked over at him and smiled. He looked so tired, but Jade found that appealing for some reason. Since Calvin's death, Jade had kept her distance from Clay, and Clay had given that to her. But tonight, she didn't want space. Tonight, she wanted to be held and made to feel like she was safe. Plus, if she was about to rip open barely healed wounds, then the least Jade could do was be held.

Jade scooted over to Clay and laid her head on his chest. Clay instantly wrapped his arms around her. This time he held her tight—as if he missed holding her. The notion made Jade feel sad. She didn't want to know she had the power and the ability to hurt Clay because that was the last thing she'd ever wanted to do.

Clay kissed the top of her head. "Night, Jade."

Jade closed her eyes, taking in his affection. "Goodnight, Clay."

**

After another failed training session, Jade trudged to the gym to work out. As usual, Jackson was down there doing his physical therapy. This time he was there with a random member instead of Keeper. Jade watched their session out of the corner of her eye. It appeared Jackson was giving them a hard time. A few minutes went by before Jade made her way over to them.

"Umm," Jade cleared her throat. "I can take over from here...if that's ok."

The member didn't say anything. They were all too happy to hand over the reins to Jade.

Jackson was frowning as he sat on the ground. Sweat slid down his forehead as he was breathing heavily. They were working on his legs today. The member quickly walked out of the gym. Jade sighed as she sat down in front of him.

"How's it going?" she asked.

"Took you long enough to speak to me," Jackson was clearly grumpy.

Jade sighed again as she leaned back on her hands. She didn't say anything. Instead, she shrugged.

Jackson didn't say anything else for a while. Instead, he looked over at Jade from the corner of his eye. An awkward silence hung in the air between them. At first, Jade was okay with the quiet and was determined to sit in it. But as seconds turned into minutes, Jade started to get uncomfortable.

"So," she said, finally giving in. "Do you want to start?"

"No."

"Ok."

"Why won't you ask me what happened that night?" Jackson seemed annoyed with her.

"Because I imagined you were tired of telling it."

"Bullshit."

Jade sighed. She really didn't sell that lie. "I didn't want to relive that night."

"I can't say that I blame you there."

"Are you tired of retelling it?"

"I haven't told it yet."

"What?" Jade was caught by surprise by that confession.

"Everyone said that I should tell you first. And I thought they were right."

"Oh," Jade didn't know where to go from there instead of going in. "So, what happened?"

Jackson sighed as he reclined back. He put his hands behind his head and closed his eyes. "They were on us before we even got started. David, Raina, and Sarah were captured first. Beverly, Rosalind, and I tried to devise a rescue plan, but we were still worried about what to do with Levi."

Jackson paused momentarily as if he was afraid to go on with the story. A few seconds went by before he cleared his throat. "Before we could even move, DC officers were on us. Rosalind and Levi were captured next. We thought it was best if she watched over him. But again, we couldn't do anything before Beverly, and I were captured by DC officers."

Jade closed her eyes, trying to block out the images of it all. They never stood a chance. Junior gave up all the details. Rage was flowing through her veins. *He needed to be killed.* And Jade was going to be the one to do it. She felt it in her gut. And her gut reaction was all she needed.

"After that, everything happened so fast it was all a blur," Jackson continued. "We were tied, gagged, and thrown onto a boat. The next thing I remember, David's body was hitting the water. As soon as the shots started ringing out, I knew we were done for. I went to elbow the officer behind me, but I wasn't quick enough...I saw...I saw..."

Jackson couldn't finish his sentence. His voice broke off. Jade didn't say anything, and she didn't want to push. She knew the following events and didn't need Jackson to say it. But apparently, it was something he needed to do. He cleared his throat, took a deep breath, and attempted to start again.

"I saw... Beverly's body...hit the water...before I heard the shot behind me."

"I'm so sorry, Jackson," Jade truly was sympathetic towards him. She couldn't imagine seeing Helena die right before her eyes. Jackson was living Jade's worst nightmare.

"I'm sorry, Jade. I promised you that I would keep Raina and Levi safe, and they were endangered as soon as you handed them off to me."

"There's no need for an apology," the rage in Jade intensified. "There was a traitor in our midst. We were doomed either way."

"Junior, yeah, I heard," there was a fire in Jackson's voice. He felt the same rage Jade did.

"Don't worry. We'll get him."

"There's no doubt there," he stared off momentarily and then sighed. "Besides, I need it to take my mind off other things."

"About your dad being alive."

Jackson shook his head. "I get why Razor did it, but the anger I still hold for them won't go away...they could've given us a hint. Beverly died for nothing, and we could've played all this smarter."

Jade sighed. "There's a lot of things we all could've done differently. But I won't tell you that you shouldn't be angry."

Jackson didn't say anything else, and it seemed like he said everything he needed. But after a few minutes of silence, he looked back at Jade.

"I'm sorry to hear about Calvin too."

"No more apologies and sympathies, Jackson," Jade glanced around the gym. Anger fueling her. "We're going to avenge them. And we'll make those responsible wish they've never crossed us."

Jackson smirked at that notion. He rose to his feet, and Jade followed. They began making their way out of the gym when the alarms started blaring. Jade had never heard that sound before, so she froze.

"What the hell is that?"

"Intruders," Jackson looked over at her wide-eyed. "It must be the Radicals."

~32~

Razor

As he sat on the edge of the bed, Razor couldn't recall a more frustrating time than this one. Helena was sitting on the other side with her head down. They just had a shouting match, one of their first. They've had disagreements before but never raised their voices at one another. Well, Helena never raised her voice at him. Razor never thought to raise his voice at Helena. Never had. Never will. The shouting match that occurred was utterly one-sided—Helena yelling at him.

Once again, Razor inquired about what was bothering Helena. Again, she told him nothing. When he mentioned that she was lying to him, the shouting began, and Razor was caught entirely off guard. Apart from telling her that he was spying on her when she was with Vicky and her crew, Helena never yelled at him. And even then, it wasn't as vicious as it was now.

Razor stood in front of her, frozen. He didn't know what to say or do. The anger behind Helena's eyes concerned him. Something was clearly wrong. And Razor couldn't figure out what it was. After all this time, he never thought he'd fear that his marriage would be in jeopardy. But that's what he was feeling now.

Razor said nothing while Helena shouted at him. Once she was done, she cried and sat on the bed. Razor joined her, but he did nothing to comfort her. He was too afraid to. He just sat there in silence. But he wasn't going to leave her alone. Razor would never leave her alone unless Helena asked him to. And he always hoped that she would never ask.

"I'm sorry," she sniffled. They had been sitting in silence for a long time.

"I love you, Helena," Razor assured her. "I just want to help."

"I know, Razor," Helena paused. "It's just...I fucked up...*bad*. And I don't think this is something you can fix."

Anger rose in him as an absurd thought went into his brain. But he had to ask. "Is there someone else?"

At that, Helena laughed. Razor closed his eyes and took in the sweet sound of her laughter. It had been so long since he heard it.

"Absolutely not. I only have eyes for you."

"Then tell me what it is. Whatever it is, Helena, we'll get through it."

Helena sighed. She turned to face him, and Razor motioned for her to move closer. She got up from the other side of the bed and walked over to him. Instead of sitting next to him, Helena sat on his lap. Razor wrapped his arms around her and kissed Helena on her forehead.

"Ok," she sighed. "The thing is—"

The alarms began blaring throughout the building. Helena looked over at him with concern.

"What is that?"

"The intruder alarm," Razor stood while Helena was still in his arms, and he gently planted her feet on the ground.

"Where's Jade?" she was beginning to panic.

Razor began gathering his weapons. "I'm not sure. Let's check command central first."

Helena nodded as she collected her weapons too.

As they were about to head out of the suite, Danita and Reagan rushed in. They went into their room to gather the weapons they'd had there.

"What's going on down there?" Razor demanded.

"No idea," Danita said.

"They believe a perimeter was breached," Reagan added.

"We need to find Jade," Helena panicked.

"Clay mentioned she was going to the gym."

"I'll go there," Razor said. "You three get to command central and verify what's happening."

Although he didn't want to, Razor watched as Helena left with Danita and Reagan. He wanted to know what was going on with her, but as the alarm kept blaring, Razor knew that a more pressing matter needed to be addressed.

Razor headed toward the staircase that led to the gym. The echo of the alarm blared through the stairwell. A few members rushed down the flight of stairs toward the command center's floor. The gym was in the basement. As the stairs cleared, Razor frowned as he approached the basement floor. In between the alarms, Razor could've sworn that he heard some fighting.

As he reached the bottom of the landing of the gym floor, Razor saw Jackson sitting breathlessly on the steps as Jade was fighting off an intruder. As Razor went to intervene, another intruder came through, and Razor headed them off.

It didn't take long for Razor and Jade to overpower the intruders. They kept them alive and apprehended them.

"We were on our way to command central," Jade explained.

Razor helped Jackson to his feet. "I figured that...let's go."

"What do we do with them?" Jade gestured to the intruders they had arrested.

"We need somewhere to stash them."

Jade dragged one of the intruders to the gym, and Razor followed with the other intruder. Jade led them to the corner of the gym by the weight area, and they hid the intruders and returned to the stairwell.

Jackson stood when they came back and slowly walked up the stairs.

"We've been breached," Jade said as she followed Jackson. "That is not a good sign."

"I wonder how they found us," Razor guessed that one of the members might have been trailed, but he couldn't be sure about that theory.

"Someone must've been followed," Jackson voiced his theory as he held the door open for them.

Jade quickly went through the doorway. As Razor entered command central, there was total chaos. Many members were gathering up weapons, and people were shouting out commands. Jade was heading toward Zara and Brice—who were giving out orders.

"Two intruders invaded the basement," Jade stated.

"They're tied up and hidden out of view," Razor added as he approached them. "What's the status?"

Brice looked uneasy. "We don't know yet."

"Well, we can interrogate the two we have and see what's going on," Razor suggested.

Brice looked like he was going to pass out from the suggestion. Zara rolled her eyes at Brice's reaction. Razor was a little annoyed himself.

"Do it," Zara said. "We need to know what's happening."

**

The intruders glared at Razor through swollen eyes. Their faces were bloody. Various limbs were broken. Razor's knuckles were sore. But Razor got what he needed out of them. They were scouts. According to them, Liam sent them to gather information on the Black Coat's headquarters. The plan was to coordinate a surprise attack. Razor wasn't happy about the news. The intruders went mum when asked how they knew where they were located.

Razor cracked his knuckles. "I'm less nice when I have to ask the same question twice."

The captives looked at him with defiance. They weren't willing to give up any more details. However, they've already given him enough information.

"All right," he sighed as he stood up and approached the youngest of the two. "Suit yourself."

Razor broke one of their fingers. The young guy cried out in pain. The older one glared at Razor with so much hatred in his eyes. Razor stared back as he broke the young guy's next finger. The next thing he knew, the older guy screamed out in pain. Razor stood back, trying to register what had just happened.

Jade's knife was in the guy's hand. Jade stomped over to him—a frown prominent on her face.

"What the hell?!" Razor didn't see her enter the room. They'd decided he'd do the interrogation on his own.

"Answer the question!" Jade demanded—ignoring Razor's surprise.

The guy continued to groan in pain. When he still didn't answer, Jade wiggled the knife. The guy yelled out some more.

"How did you know where we were?" Jade asked.

The guy continued to wither in pain. The younger one looked on with agony as Jade pulled out another knife.

"Make me ask again, and this is going somewhere that'll cause you even more pain," her knife hovered over his crouch.

"Give us what we want," Razor demanded. He knew that Jade wasn't bluffing, and he really didn't want to see a knife go into a guy's penis today.

The older guy still hesitated, but the younger one caved first.

"It was the new guy!" he rushed. "Junior. He had a theory about what area the headquarters might be located in."

Razor growled while Jade looked like she was ready to snap someone's neck.

Fucking Junior.

~33~

Nick

The building that Nick was hiding in seemed to be a building that the Black Coats used for storage. Nick wanted to play nicely, so he made sure that he avoided anyone who was around. This place wasn't as heavily guarded as their headquarters seemed to be. Nick could only find the headquarters' location off a hunch. Before he killed Fallen, she told him that the group narrowed the Black Coat's headquarters to the downtown area. And during his time being "tortured," Nick overheard the street that Junior thought it might be on—University Ave.

Nick explored the area for days. He spent most of the time trying to think like Blackwell. There were obvious buildings that he ruled out as contenders. The high, flashy buildings were immediately cut. Those buildings were clear choices for looters. No self-respecting person would choose a flashy building to set up their operation. Not a person with enemies, anyway.

After ruling out the obvious choices, Nick spent the rest of his time focusing on rundown buildings. Buildings that would get overlooked intrigued him, and it took him longer to rule those out. He would stake out the potential locations for a day or so and move on to the next contender when it was clear that site wasn't it.

This went on longer than Nick wanted, but he kept going because he *needed* to find them. He *needed* to find Jade. Then Nick came across a building on the corner of University Ave. and Adelaide. There were two ugly brown buildings nestled in between two flashy ones. It was the perfect location—for Nick, anyway. The problem was that he couldn't figure out which was the headquarters. That was what made this plan ingenious. Pick the wrong one, and Blackwell and his group would be quickly alerted. Nick was a little bit jealous. He wished he'd come up with a similar plan with his headquarters.

A fancy-looking building was on the opposite corner of University Ave. and King Street, and Nick set up there. It was apparent that the building was being used, so Nick didn't need to clear it. However, the building wasn't visited frequently and became Nick's perfect hideout. He realized he was in the right area on the first day there. Although they were very discreet moving about, it was clear that the Black Coats operated in the area. Still, Nick couldn't narrow down which building they were working in, and it wasn't like they were walking out of the front door.

The first day was uneventful. It was the second day in his hideout when Nick saw some real action. During the morning, Nick stayed inside the building and surveyed the little activity around the area. By noon, Nick was looking to change things up a bit. He decided to go outside and get closer to the suspecting buildings. Nick hid on the steps leading into the basement of a parking structure on the corner of University Ave. and Pearl Street. All was quiet for a while there. But Nick wasn't deterred. He knew that getting closer was a good idea.

By late afternoon, Nick finally saw some action. At first, he thought his eyes were deceiving him. Two Radical members were probing around the two ugly brown buildings. After a few minutes, they focused more on the shorter building. Nick moved up a step when he saw them decide between the two. Nick had a hunch that they may have been operating out of the shorter one, but he wasn't sure.

The two Radical members went around the back and disappeared from Nick's view. It was eerily silent for a moment. Then, not even five minutes later, alarms began blaring. Nick looked around the street. No one came along. After a few minutes of the alarm going off, it fell silent again. The two Radical members never came back into view. Nick wasn't sure if they got away or not. He needed to wait it out, and he needed a better view.

It was risky, but Nick moved down to the alleyway directly across from the headquarters building. Fortunately for him, a few broken-down cars cluttered the alleyway, providing Nick with an excellent cover.

"What do you think?" Raina asked.

"Well, look who finally decided to show up," Nick hadn't seen her since he got captured.

Raina didn't say anything. She just rolled her eyes.

"I believe an apology is in order."

"You're shitting me, right?" Raina looked at Nick like he was insane.

"Such foul language for a girl your age," Nick chuckled.

"Are you seriously demanding an apology from me right now?!"

"Seeing how I was caught because you distracted me, yes. An apology is in order."

Raina glared at him. Nick was sure that if she could kill him, she would. He laughed again. It took a moment for Raina to respond.

"You'll get your apology when I'm *alive*."

Nick laughed harder at that. "To answer your question, I will finally reunite with Jade."

"She doesn't want to see you."

"I believe that was mentioned more than once."

"And yet you pursue."

"I'm never one to give up so easily."

Raina didn't say anything else. Instead, she looked across the street silently. Levi and Aiden appeared behind her. They huddled up to her closely. Nick sighed at how cowardly they appeared. It was no use telling them to be brave. These boys were never going to be brave in this crazy world. It was the reason why they were no longer here. At least Raina showed promise. But Nick couldn't bring her back. What's done was done.

It was well into the night before any more activity occurred. There was a disturbance coming from the alleyway across the street. The two Radical members came back into view—beaten and tied up. They were followed closely by a black woman who appeared to have tattoos on the side of her head. Then, Razor and Jade came into view. They seemed to be having an intense conversation.

Nick's heart began skipping beats as Jade came into clear view. She looked angry. She looked determined. It was clear that someone (if not more) would lose their life tonight. Nick loved that look. Jade was becoming the very woman he dreamed of her being.

"Let's go," Nick chuckled. He knew who was about to get her wrath.

Liam would soon be a dead man, and Nick was excited to see it.

~34~

Razor

As they got the prisoners to their feet for export, Razor couldn't fight off the anxiety feeling. They agreed to lead them to the hideout where Liam and Junior resided. Although Jade's torture tactics were intense, Razor couldn't help but feel that the men gave up the information too quickly. Or maybe he was just being a little paranoid. But he couldn't shake the nagging feeling he had as they prepared to head out.

They decided to have Zara go with them. Since it was more of a recon mission, they didn't think it was necessary to bring anyone else. And in all honesty, Razor didn't want anyone else going. Jade and Zara were enough. Razor certainly didn't want Helena going out with them, not after their last conversation. It was better if she stayed back—back with Cole.

As Jade and Zara prepared the prisoners for transport, Razor resumed his conversation with Helena. She finally told him what was bothering her, and ever since, Razor has been trying his best to avoid reflecting on that conversation. Helena was right. They had fucked up—bad. Razor wasn't sure how they'd get out of this one. Something in him told him that he couldn't. This was something they'd have to ride out and adjust to. But he questioned if that could even be done.

"Second thoughts?" Jade asked as they walked out of HQ. It was her idea to have the captives show them Liam's hideout. Razor wasn't opposed to the plan. But he didn't voice that he was all for it either.

"No," he sighed. "This is the only way we'll know for sure where they are."

Jade nodded.

"It's crucial that we're careful...now more than ever," bits of Razor and Helena's conversation came to mind as he said this.

Jade frowned at him. Razor could see the questions forming in her mind, but she didn't say anything. After a few seconds, she nodded again.

Zara was closely following the two Radical members as they led the way. Jade closed in on the middle while Razor took the rear. This business with the Radicals could all be over soon. Razor needed it all to be over soon. He needed to reevaluate the drawing board. There were new things that needed to be put into perspective. And the perspective was tremendous—*crucial*. It was life-changing, even.

"You sure there's nothing you wanna share?" Jade asked as she slowed down a little.

"Nothing," Razor just wanted to shut his brain off and focus on the mission.

Jade shrugged and quickly resumed her pace.

Razor watched as Jade walked ahead of him—Calvin's sword slinging across her back. *Calvin.* A person he thought was invincible. But he wasn't. None of them were. Any given day could be their last. It was not a world where one could find much hope. It wasn't a world where one could grow in. However, that was what they were trying to do. Grow. *Survive.* But they were all hanging on by a thread. All of them. Especially Jade. Razor wasn't so sure that he was doing any better than her. Particularly now.

The future was feeling really bleak to him, and he couldn't get out of his head. Razor needed to—desperately. He needed to focus on their current mission. But all he could think about was his conversation with Helena and what that meant for their future. All of their future. Razor hadn't found the courage to tell Jade yet and wasn't sure when he should inform her. There was too much going on, but Razor knew he should inform her—soon. Jade was already teetering on the edge of sanity. Razor wasn't sure which way she would go with this news.

Razor sighed as he tried again to remove those thoughts from his head.

The whole group was silent for a while. It was quiet out, but that was to be expected. It was the dead of night. Razor didn't think they'd run into anyone else out there...but still. This was a chaotic world, and people did deadly things in a hectic world like this. As they continued moving, Razor couldn't shake this feeling. He had a feeling that they were being followed.

Razor allowed a few more minutes to go by, hoping that the feeling would go away soon, but it didn't. In fact, as time moved on, the suspicion only grew. It seemed that Jade had the same feeling because she stopped walking a few times to look around.

"Let's get off this road for a minute," Razor suggested.

Jade nodded.

"Is there another way to their place?" Zara asked the captives.

"It is," the youngest one answered. "But it'll take longer."

"We just need to detour for a little bit," Razor didn't want to be out longer than they had to. "Then we'll come back to the road."

"You feel it, too," Jade said.

Razor nodded. "Just to be safe."

The Radical members led them to the wooded area on the side of the road. Razor stayed behind for a moment. He wanted to see if the potential follower would strike if they saw that he was alone. Minutes passed, and no one did anything. No one revealed themselves.

Razor sighed as he moved on to follow the group. This all needed to be done. Razor was so ready for everything to be over and done. He never thought it could happen, but the fighting started to get to him, and he was tired of it. He longed for a moment of peace. They needed that. The road to vengeance was bloody, and Razor needed to deviate them from that path.

Jade would never go for it. Razor knew that. Her mind was too focused on revenge. Plus, after everything that's happened with Calvin, there was no turning back for her. Razor knew that, but still, he had to try. Recent events gave him no choice. At this rate, there'd be no future for any of them.

They detoured for about three miles. The nagging feeling of them being followed didn't go away. However, Razor figured if the person hadn't attacked by now, they likely wouldn't.

"How much longer?" annoyance coated Jade's tone.

The young Radical looked back at her—wearily. "4.8 kilometers."

Jade sighed and rolled her eyes. Razor could tell that she wasn't trying to convert that into miles. It was about three more miles. If Razor's math was correct. It wasn't exactly a subject he thrived at in school.

"Should we try back for the main road?" Zara asked.

Razor pondered that question. What was the most thoughtful way to handle this situation? They couldn't just walk up to the front door. That would be stupid. It'll also be the quickest way for them to die. Razor looked over at the captives.

"Is there another entrance to the hideout?"

"No," the older guy answered. "It's only one way in and out."

The smirk on the guy's face was a little unnerving. The younger guy looked uneasy. Razor couldn't tell whether the older captive was telling the truth. There was no choice. They had to move on.

"This road," Razor began. "Will it lead us to the front or the back?"

The older guy went silent. The younger guy spoke up. "The back."

"Let's stick to this path, then."

"Sounds good," Zara continued on the path.

Everyone fell silent—left to their thoughts as they watched their surroundings. Razor sighed. His thoughts were the exact place he didn't want to be. Plus, the feeling of them being followed hadn't gone away; it was one annoyance after another. After about 20 minutes, Razor stopped again and looked around to see if the person would finally reveal themselves.

No success.

"This is getting ridiculous," Jade unsheathed her sword and held it to the older guy's neck. "Do you have another person out here tailing us?!"

"No," the guy gritted. There was clear hatred for Jade behind his eyes.

"Lie to us, and I'll take off your head."

"It was just us," the younger Radical piped up. "I swear."

"That's enough, Jade," Razor said. "If it were one of them, they'd attack us already."

"Yeah," Zara added. "I don't think they'd let us get this far."

Jade removed her sword away from the guy's neck and slung it back on her back.

Razor looked around again. "This is someone else...we should keep moving."

Zara and Jade nodded and moved on ahead. Razor lingered to see if he could spot anything. Once he was sure it was all clear, he moved ahead.

Razor focused on how the Radical members were moving as they got closer. There was definitely some leeriness there. It could've been nerves, but Razor felt it was something else. Naturally, Razor slowed down a little.

"Slow up," he ordered to the others.

Jade turned around with a frown. The older Radical member sped up a bit, and Zara went after him as he let out a whistle. Zara immediately tackled him to the ground and covered his mouth.

"What the hell was that?" Jade looked around, her knives out.

"I'm not sure."

Jade approached the younger guy and held a knife to his throat. "What was that?"

Whistles rang out through the area surrounding them. Razor took out his machete as he glanced around. Jade pulled on the guy's hair as her knife pressed harder against his throat. Razor could see droplets of blood running down.

"Please," the young guy pleaded. "I didn't do anything."

"Tell us what that was!" Razor demanded. More whistles rang out in response.

Zara took out her sword and tightened her hold on the older Radical member. He struggled to laugh as Zara's hold went to his throat.

"It's reinforcements," the young guy said. The older guy made a noise of disapproval. "It's members who patrol the area."

"Shit," Razor mumbled. As he turned around to look behind him, the first attacker came. What was supposed to be a recon mission turned into a furious battle.

~35~

Jade

Jade's heart raced as the first attacker charged at Razor. Seconds later, the attacker was lying on the ground, bleeding from his stomach. That was one down, but they had so many more to go. Although Jade was furious about the intrusion at HQ, she wasn't expecting it to go down like this. A fight was always a possibility, but she didn't anticipate it when they left out. Plus, Razor was acting strangely when they left HQ, which was a little unsettling. That's why she was so afraid when the assailant came for Razor first. Razor didn't seem like his usual ruthless self.

It wasn't clear what weapons Jade should use first, but since her knives were already out, she decided to utilize those. One knife found its way to an attacker's chest while the other went to another's neck. Then Jade pulled out her sword. It was time to give it a try—for Calvin. More assailants seemed to flock to her once her sword came out, and Jade was more than happy to show them how she moved with it. She was flawless. None of them stood a chance.

Sure, compared to Zara, Jade was an amateur. Still, as the two women fought off Radical members in the heavily wooded area, you couldn't tell the difference.

Both of their captives lay on the ground. The younger one was curled up on the ground, while the older one found the courage to rise to his feet as Zara's back was to him. Jade fought her way over to them. It looked like the guy was about to attack Zara. Jade couldn't let that happen. This predicament they were in was all because of him. He needed to pay.

Jade swung her sword as hard as she could. She wanted a clean cut, but it wasn't strong enough. The guy's head hung to the side—touching his shoulder. His face wore a look of shock as the life slowly drained from his eyes. The scene was a little horrifying. Zara looked back—stunned. She still didn't realize the guy even attempted to attack her.

"You monster!" the young captive cried out.

The insult didn't bother Jade. She just moved on to the next Radical member. It seemed never-ending. There were a lot of them patrolling the area. Or were they expecting them? The latter seemed more likely. Liam, or Junior, had to realize that the scouts would get captured and tortured. They had to know that they were coming.

"Don't let them corner us!" Razor commanded as he fought off two people.

Jade nodded as she moved on to the next. Zara did the same thing. They needed a higher view to get a good idea of how many people they were dealing with. Jade fought off a few more people before scouting for a tree to climb. After killing more people than she anticipated, Jade found a perfect tree to get a higher view.

"I'm going up," Jade told Zara.

Zara nodded as she continued to fight.

As Jade settled onto the branch that gave her the perfect view, her heart instantly dropped. There was a stream of Radical members that were converging on the area. This was all a trap. It had to be. Those scouts were meant to get caught. They were meant to be tortured and made to lead them here. How could they have been so stupid? Jade heard Junior's name, and all she could see was red. She wanted nothing but revenge, and she failed to see the big picture.

Jade immediately retrieved her bow and an arrow. She began firing off shots—trying to take out as many as possible from afar.

"How's it looking?!" Razor demanded.

"Fucked!" Jade released another arrow. "This was all a ruse!"

"Shit!" Razor was coming to the same realization as she did. "How many?"

"Too many to count!" Jade definitely didn't have enough arrows or knives for them. This was going to be a tiresome fight.

"Get down from there," Razor had made his way closer to her.

Jade continued to shoot off more arrows. "I haven't run out yet. Besides, we must find a way to get out of this."

"It's no use. Reserve your arrows."

Jade looked down at Razor, confused. What did he mean? They *had* to get out of this. If they get captured, they'll be killed for sure. At least, Zara would. Jade and Razor might stay alive a little longer.

"Zara, get out of here!" Razor demanded.

"What? I can keep fighting!" Zara sliced and diced her way over to them.

Jade quickly climbed down the tree and met them.

"Go back to HQ," Razor said as he slashed a Radical member with his machete. "Let them know what happened, and tell them that Jade and I were captured."

Jade looked over at him in alarm as the reality of their situation sunk in. They weren't going to make it out of this. They were going to get caught. They were defeated. There was no telling if she was going to see Helena again. Or Clay. Or Reagan. Or Keeper. It was overwhelming. Tears fell from her eyes as she furiously fought off attacker after attacker.

"Go, Zara!" Jade demanded.

Zara looked over at her with sadness in her eyes. She nodded. "I'll be back soon."

Jade and Razor fought strong as Zara ran off. They kept the Radicals fixated on them. They were top priorities.

"We don't give up until we're forced to," Razor encouraged. But there was uncertainty in his tone. This wasn't something that he wanted. It certainly wasn't something they expected. And he was going to be away from Helena. That had to be killing him.

"Go," Jade said. It'd be better if she were caught by herself. It would devastate Helena if they both were captured. "Get back to Helena."

"No way," he said. But Jade could tell that there was longing in his voice. There was no way that he was going to abandon her. Jade knew that he wouldn't be able to live with himself.

Jade fought harder. She couldn't accept this. She needed to get Razor back to Helena. They couldn't be apart. They *needed* each other. So, Jade fought.

When the Radicals kept coming—Jade fought.

When there were opponents who gave her a hard time—Jade fought.

When the situation increasingly grew overwhelming—Jade fought.

She would keep fighting. Despite the odds. Despite how tired she was. Despite how bloody up she got. Jade would keep fighting to get Razor back to her sister.

Then, there was a moment. A moment where multiple Radical members were taken down at once. Then more. And then even more. Someone else was fighting. Did Zara come back? She couldn't have gotten reinforcements that quickly. Was this someone else? It had to be. But who?

The unexpected person pushed Jade even further, but it wasn't enough. First, Razor was knocked out. Jade panicked. She definitely didn't think that he'd be taken out first. Terrified, Jade kept going. But then, she got hit from behind. She fought against the darkness that threatened to creep up on her. Jade struggled to fight more. The mystery attacker was still going and taking out more Radicals. Jade was able to kill a few more of them before she was hit from behind again.

It was much more challenging for Jade to fight against the darkness this time. She was able to kill one more person before she was hit one last time.

Then, darkness.

~36~

Nick

It wasn't until the second time Razor stopped and waited to see who was following them that Nick noticed some disturbance from afar. At first, Nick thought it might've been a wild animal or something, but once he could check it out, he saw that a massive group of Radical members were on their way. This didn't seem like a coincidence. If he had to guess, it appeared to be planned. That was something he didn't consider. Nick didn't think Liam was intelligent enough to plan a trap like this.

No. This had to be Junior. This seemed like something he would do. Junior's traveled and fought with Jade and Razor. By now, he had to know how they'd think and react to certain situations.

Shit.

Why didn't he think about this? Nick was so excited to see Jade kill Liam that he thought of nothing else. He couldn't let the group see him, or they'd give away his position. Or worse, they'd capture him. Nick needed a way to signal Razor and Jade about the unexpected group. But again, it had to be a way where he didn't also reveal his position. Nick pondered for a moment. Sadly, it wasn't for too long because someone spotted him.

The person was quickly killed before they could alert the others. The three of them couldn't get captured, not now. Nick wasn't sure what they'd do to the other woman with Jade and Razor. But if he had to take a wild guess, they'd probably kill her. At least he knew that they'd keep the three of them alive. Of course, there would be endless amounts of torture, but at least they'd live for a while.

A couple more Radicals, who'd scouted out ahead of the group, spotted Nick crouched behind a nearby bush. Nick reacted swiftly. He killed the two men and dragged their bodies behind the bush with him. Nick rifled through their pockets and took their weapons and whatever else he found helpful. It was going to be a long fight. The sheer number of the group showed that.

Just as Nick was about to ambush a small group coming his way, a whistle rang through the air. The group responded by whistling the same tune. *Shit.* That was a signal. The group began running in the direction the whistle came from. The small group near him turned to join their comrades, but Nick quickly jumped from the bush to confront them. Luckily the bigger group didn't notice his appearance.

Once he was done with the small group, Nick slowly made his way to the larger one. Nick took care of the stragglers as he went to where Jade and Razor were. It wasn't long before arrows started flying in his direction. Nick couldn't stop the smile from creeping on his face as he ducked for cover. These arrows were Jade's, and she knew the group was there.

A few people tried to dodge the arrows, but most found their marks. The few lucky ones, Nick finished off. The group wasn't expecting a long-range attack, so they still didn't notice Nick's presence. Nick took advantage of the distraction and dwindled the numbers even more. They had to succeed at this. If all of them were caught now, there would be no telling how they'd get out of it. Or if they'd get out of it.

Jade hated him.

Nick was sure that if she saw him now, she'll likely try to kill him. Even if they were captured, Jade would do her best to end his life. Not that he could blame her. After what he did. How could she not?

Razor, however, would see the benefit of them all momentarily working together. Nick was sure Razor could eventually convince her of that fact. But time wouldn't be on their side in that situation, and Jade would have to see that fact immediately.

Nick continued to fight some of the Radicals while trying to keep a low profile. Then he saw the woman who was with Jade and Razor. She was retreating—most likely going to get reinforcements. It was vital that she didn't get caught. So, Nick revealed himself. He made sure that all eyes were on him. Once his presence was known, those who weren't running to attack Jade and Razor rushed to Nick.

It was a bloody interaction. Nick couldn't recall whom he came in contact with, but he knew he was merciless. He gave them a horrific death. A death that would terrify the others. And he did. Some of the Radical members who were nearby slowly backed away. Now, it was Nick chasing after them. The plan was going wonderfully. No one noticed that the woman with Jade and Razor retreated.

"Oh no!" Raina shouted. She was looking up ahead. "They're gonna get her!"

"What?" Nick barely dodged an attack. He cursed under his breath. Raina showing up was unexpected. The children had left him alone while he tailed Jade and Razor.

"The bad people! They have Jade and Razor surrounded."

"Shit," there were just too many of them out here. Nick thought he could even the odds if he took most of them out beforehand. But it seemed like he wasn't making a dent in their numbers.

This was no good. They were going to get caught—it was almost inevitable. Then Nick spotted something hanging off his latest victim's belt loop. It was small, but it looked like an explosive. Nick wasn't sure what amount of damage it could do, but he shrugged and threw it at a group heading toward Jade and Razor. Nick immediately took cover.

There was a small blast. It wasn't too major, but enough people were harmed by it. Nick went back to attacking those who were sidetracked by the explosion. And that's when she came into view—Jade. She was there fighting ferociously with a sword. She upgraded her weaponry, and she looked like a natural with it. Nick couldn't help but smile at that. The woman was vicious in her attacks. He hated to be on the other end of that sword.

Then, to his horrific surprise, he saw Razor go down. An attacker managed to knock him out from behind. Nick could see the shock on Jade's face. She fought harder, and so did Nick. This wasn't good. It was looking like they were going to get caught after all.

"What are you gonna do, Nick?" Raina asked. She was panicking as she looked for a way to escape.

"Nothing I can do, sweetheart."

Raina frowned. "Don't call me that."

Nick laughed as he sliced someone's throat. He turned to see how Jade was doing. She was still fighting strong, but someone attacked her from behind. Nick's heart dropped. This was the end. But Jade kept pushing. It was clear that she was woozy and fighting unconsciousness. But she wasn't ready to give up just yet. Nick watched as she killed three more people in her weakened state. He was in awe. So, Nick fought harder.

Then Jade was hit again. He could see her wobbling and struggling to stay on her feet. Still, she wasn't ready to go down just yet. Jade slashed at another person, their midsection tearing open as they dropped to the ground. Annoyed by her stubbornness, the attacker hit Jade again. This time, Jade fell to the ground—unconscious.

Fuck.

Nick fought some more, but now he was getting swarmed. Everyone who was left fixated on him. It was over. They were getting captured. Nick memorized the layout of the area. He could forget, trying to avoid getting caught. Right now, he needed to come up with an escape plan.

A plan formed as he continued to fight. It wasn't anything solid, but it was something. And it gave Nick a little bit of hope. How many people he had killed since Jade went down wasn't clear, but unfortunately, it was Nick's turn. He took out five people before it happened.

Darkness.

~37~

Jade

The sounds of thudding and Razor grunting not too far away made Jade's stomach clench. She struggled to fight back the tears knowing that Razor was being tortured. He was getting hurt, and she could do nothing about it. Right now, she was hanging by her ankles from the ceiling, and it looked like she was in a room at a warehouse. How long she'd been out or how far they moved her from Liam's apparent hideout wasn't clear.

Jade had eventually awakened by the sounds of punching and groaning. At first, she couldn't make out what was going on. But then she noticed that she was hanging upside down. Her hands were tied, but luckily, they were tied in front of her. If she needed to defend herself, she could at least attempt to do that. The punching and groaning continued as Jade tried to recollect herself. Then after a few minutes, Jade realized that the groans were coming from Razor.

Her heart dropped. And then it seemed to have stopped beating for a few seconds. Jade needed to react—quickly. She squirmed around, trying to find a weak point in her bondage, but it was useless. The rope that was tied around her ankles was pretty tight. So, Jade focused on the rope wrapped around her wrists instead. Her wrists burned with every movement, but Jade fought through the pain. She needed to get out of this. She needed to help Razor.

They were so stupid. How could they not see that the break-in at HQ was all a ploy? Wanted posters of Jade and Razor were plastered all over the place. How could they not think that the Radicals wouldn't try to lure them into a trap? And they fell for it so quickly. Jade's obsession with getting revenge clouded her judgment. Now, her mistake put Razor in jeopardy. Why didn't Razor fight her on this more? Why did he go along with her plan?

No.

There was no time to reflect on where they went wrong now. Now was the time for Jade to figure out an escape plan. Jade worked ferociously at the rope around her wrists—her flesh bleeding as the bondage dug deeper.

"Oh no," Raina looked sad as she appeared before Jade. "This doesn't look good."

Jade hadn't seen Raina since Calvin's death. During that time, Raina hadn't said that much to her. She only comforted Jade.

"Don't worry," Jade grunted. "We'll get out of this."

Razor's beating seemed to intensify as time went on. The hits got louder. The commotion increased. And Razor's groans held more pain.

This was bad.

This was *all* bad.

Jade fought through the panic. "We have to get out of this," she cried. The tears ran awkwardly down her face.

Raina nodded. "Focus, Jade. You'll get out of this if you keep your focus. You *have to* help Razor."

Jade nodded as she focused on loosing up the rope. She tuned out Razor's beating. If she didn't, she would've continued to panic, which she couldn't afford to do now. The bleeding from her wrists grew, but they provided excellent lubrication against the rope. If she could free her hands, they could find a way out.

Suddenly, a noise came from the area in front of her. Jade paused. The door to the room was to her left, and no one had entered yet. Was there someone else here? Someone who was instructed to watch her? No. That couldn't be it. The person would've stopped her attempted escape already.

Someone was there—someone she couldn't see clearly.

Raina turned to look and froze. She turned back to Jade, a weird look on her face. "Whatever you do, remain focused."

Jade frowned at her phrasing. She didn't understand what was going on...

...then he spoke.

"Don't let me stop you, my sweet, sweet Jade."

Jade stopped. No. It couldn't be him. How could it be? Wait, the mystery fighter. That was him? Jade squinted as she tried to get a better look. After a few seconds, his silhouette came into view. There he was...

...Bossman.

He was tied up to a chair and looked like he had been beaten himself. His right eye was swollen, and his lip was busted and bleeding. His cheekbone looked deformed. Jade wondered if it was broken. Despite all of that, he still smiled at her. The man who killed Raina, Levi, and David dared to look at her with a big goofy smile.

It enraged Jade.

"You...*bastard*," Jade gritted.

"Don't get distracted now. It sounds like they're almost done with him," Bossman said, ignoring Jade's insult.

Jade fought through her rage as she realized that he was right. It was quiet, and she could hear someone giving commands, but she couldn't make it out clearly. Jade needed to focus. She continued to work on her wrists.

"Just so you know," Jade struggled. "I'm going to kill you when I get out of this."

Bossman chuckled. "Let's get out of here first. Then you're free to take off my head."

Jade wasn't expecting such a defeating response. How badly did these people torture him? She expected something like, "You could never kill me," or, "I'll like to see you try." But nothing that equated to "ok." Now she was really dreading seeing Razor.

"Who decorated your face?" she didn't want to continue talking to him, but she needed the distraction.

"Junior," Bossman sighed. "He really is a huge dick."

"I figured you'd love him."

"No one loves a rat. He was just useful for the time being."

"And now the President finds him useful," Jade fought off the nerves that settled in her stomach. All she could think about was ways Junior was going to torture her.

"Chase finds anyone useful if they're against me."

"What the hell does he want with me anyway?" she could never understand that part. Surely it wasn't because she was a debtor.

"Appearances, my love," Bossman smiled. "You're thought to be a potential leader to the bigwigs."

"I'm not your fucking love!" Jade was infuriated. She could feel herself shaking. Raina rushed to her side—a look of worry on her face.

"You have to stay focused, Jade."

Jade closed her eyes and took some deep breaths. "You're right. You're right. I need to get us out of here."

It was silent for a moment.

"You were talking to Raina," Bossman stated after a while. It wasn't a question. It was a statement. As if he knew exactly what she was going through.

"Don't you *dare* say her name."

"Why not? She *is* haunting me."

Jade didn't say anything. She was trying to process what he was saying. Raina was haunting him? Did that mean he actually felt remorseful for killing her and Levi? No. That couldn't be it. That would mean he was human, and Jade couldn't accept that. She wouldn't.

"Levi haunts me too," he continued. "Along with my son. But Raina's the one who harasses me the most. She's braver than the two of them."

"I didn't know a monster like you could breed," Jade was determined to hurt him somehow.

"He's what turned me into a monster," Bossman paused. "Or I should say his death did."

Jade focused on her wrists. She wasn't going to allow Bossman's words to distract her. She and Razor needed to make their escape.

"I tried to be good for him," Bossman carried on. It was like he was determined to make her understand him. "But I procreated with a stupid woman who made foolish decisions, and in the end, my son got killed. I failed him as a father...as a man. From then on, I was determined never to fail as a man again."

"So, that's why Raina and Levi had to die," Jade didn't care about his sob story. "Why David had to die?!"

"I don't give a damn about killing your boyfriend," he said nonchalantly. "He was breaking the law, and the penalty was death."

"Oh, fuck you!" Jade spat.

"But the children," he went on as if she didn't speak. "I truly regret that. It makes me no different than the man who murdered my son."

Jade paused at that. She found the nerve to look at him. A look of remorse covered his face. He truly meant what he said. This just angered Jade even more. She wanted him to be pure evil. She needed him to be it. Then there'd be no room for regret when she finally killed him. He couldn't be human. Jade wouldn't allow it. He would forever be a heartless monster in her eyes.

"I'm no leader," she returned to working on her wrist. "The bigwigs are stupid to think otherwise."

Bossman chuckled at that. "You'd be surprised."

"And that's justification for putting a hit out on me," Jade was so tired of the stupid government.

"For Chase to save face, yes."

"What an asshole."

Bossman laughed again. "He's a coward. And cowards can do some dangerous things."

"Trust me, I know. We're talking about the man who gave you free rein in governing medical care."

Bossman suppressed another laugh as the door to the room finally opened. Jade's heart stopped. Razor was dragged in and thrown to the ground right beside Jade. His legs and wrists were bonded together, and it looked like he barely had any life in him. Jade wanted to reach out and touch him but was hanging too far up. The Radical member stepped back as Junior walked in. Jade's heart went into overdrive—she was so furious.

Besides Bossman, she never wanted to kill someone so badly.

Junior smirked as he kneeled before her so their faces were at the same level. "It's so nice to see you hanging, Jade."

Jade smiled as she cocked her head back and headbutted Junior with everything she had. Junior fell over. Bossman's laughter boomed throughout the room.

"Fuck!" blood poured from Junior nose. He wiped it with shock.

"Fuck you! You rat!" Jade knew she should be playing this differently, but her rage just took over.

Bossman continued to laugh as Junior recollected himself. He looked embarrassed. The Radical member stepped away from them. Jade could tell that the member thought a little less of Junior.

After a few seconds, Junior rose to his feet. He glared over at Bossman, who was still laughing. Junior looked down at Jade and then quickly punched her in the gut. Jade was expecting retaliation, so she braced herself. The wind was knocked out of her, but she wouldn't give Junior the satisfaction of making a sound.

"I have some special things planned for you, Jade," Junior said smugly.

Jade glared at him. She wasn't going to say a thing. And when the torture began, she would stay silent too. Jade wouldn't give Junior any satisfaction that he was getting to her.

"You're gonna regret that later," Junior threatened. He and the Radical member stomped off.

"I told you he's a dick," Bossman said once the door closed.

"Razor," Jade grunted. "Are you ok?"

Razor remained silent.

"I know the beating didn't bother you *that* much," Bossman said, surprised.

"No," Razor mumbled. He shifted a little. "We need to get out of here."

Jade went back to trying to get out of her restraints. "I'm working on it."

"You can't be too reckless, Jade," Razor warned.

Bossman chuckled. "Reckless is all she knows how to be, my friend."

"Shut it," Jade strained as the rope dug deeper into her wrist. "Don't worry, Razor. I'll get us out of this, and I'm going to get you back to Helena."

To Jade's utter surprise, Razor broke down crying. Just how badly was he beaten? Jade paused for a moment and assessed his injuries. Nothing appeared life-threatening. His face was bloody, but Jade couldn't see anything that was too alarming.

"I fucked up, Jade."

"Did you give them information on Cole?"

Razor shook his head. "Nothing as trivial as that."

Jade hung still—waiting for Razor to continue. It took him a few seconds to carry on.

"Helena's pregnant."

All the blood seemed to have left Jade's body. Helena was pregnant. Her little sister was going to bring new life into this chaotic world. Jade moved franticly. She had to get the rope off her wrists. They *needed* to get back to Helena. Her sister needed her now more than ever. And Helena needed Razor by her side.

"We're gonna get out of this. We're gonna get out of this," she kept whispering. The blood flowed from her wrists even more.

The three of them stayed quiet for a while. After a few minutes, Jade looked at Bossman and saw that he was also working on loosening his restraints. Razor lay still for a moment, but after some time, he also worked on his restraints.

Finally, one of Jade's wrists slipped through the ropes slightly.

Unfortunately, the door opened, and Junior entered with two Radical members. Jade immediately stopped moving. She didn't want them to see her progress in getting out of her bondage. A plan was quickly forming in her mind. It'd probably be better if she made her escape from the torture room. Something told her that they wouldn't have her so secured in there.

One of the members lifted her while the other removed the rope around her ankles from the hook in the ceiling.

"Be careful with her," Junior warned. "She's crafty."

"Oh, don't forget about us, my sweet Jade, when you make your escape."

Junior looked over at Bossman. "She won't be able to move once I'm done with her."

"That's where I went wrong," Bossman sighed. "Underestimating her."

Junior glared at him as they started to leave out. "Like I'm going to take advice from you."

As they carried Jade away, she couldn't help but smile a little. They were going to get out of this. Her gut was telling her so. But the best part is that she still had the opportunity to kill Junior. And that excited her.

~38~

Jade

The blood that filled Jade's mouth kept her focused and alert. The bloody mouth didn't have anything to do with Junior. He kept most of his hits concentrated on her abdomen area. That seemed to be his favorite spot. The bloody mouth was due to Jade biting her lip, ensuring no noises escaped her. When he first began, Junior tried to be creative. They had her hanging from her ankles, and Junior used chains and bats to beat her. Jade had to admit that the time Helena tortured her was worse than this. Jade wasn't sure if Junior was holding back or if he was that bad at torturing people.

After Jade remained silent and unbothered by those tactics, Junior decided to resort to his fists.

"I gotta admit," Junior said as he cracked his knuckles. "I don't like the idea of hitting a woman, but you're something different, Jade."

Jade sighed. She didn't understand the point of all of this. Why the torture? Junior wasn't asking any questions or trying to gain any information. So, what was it all for? Show? Why take the time to torture all three of them? It seemed like a lot of work. The only thing that Jade could conclude was that all of this was made to stroke Junior's ego. He wanted to appear more important than he was.

Ego would be the very thing that would get him killed.

Junior went a few minutes of punching Jade's midsection. Jade frowned as she bit down on her lip. She was still working on releasing her wrists from the rope during this time. Jade would've freed herself if it weren't for the torture. Once Junior was done with his assault, he stepped back and cradled his hands. The torture was getting to him. It was tiring him out.

That was when Jade could no longer remain silent. She began to laugh, and her laugh got louder as time passed.

"It looks like she finally broke," one of the Radical members said, amused.

Junior scowled at her as he flexed his hands. "She's nowhere near close to being broken."

"Is that all you got?" Jade teased. "I really was expecting more."

"Watch your mouth," Junior warned.

"Not everyone can be Razor," Jade sighed. "Or Bossman, for that matter."

"Bring it in, now!" Junior instructed the members. One of the members left out.

Jade continued her laughing. She knew it would be a weapon but didn't care because her left wrist finally got loose from the rope. Luckily for her,

her left wrist was shielded by her right, so no one could tell she freed it.

The member came back into the room with Calvin's sword. At first, Jade was enraged, but she became delighted as a few seconds passed.

"Oh, great, you brought in the weapon I'm going to kill you all with."

Junior roared with laughter. "Let's not be too cocky there, Jade," he took the sword and swung it back and forth like a golf club. "I'm not allowed to kill you just yet, but this will surely wipe that smug smile off your face."

"Sorry, the smile is here to stay."

"Let's see if it will after a few slices."

As Junior walked closer to her, Jade swung her body into him. She slipped her left hand out of the rope and grabbed his left thigh. She pulled him closer and bit down on his groin. Junior screamed as he tried to free himself, but Jade had a tight hold. The two members tried to approach them, but Junior swung the sword so wildly that they couldn't get any closer to intervene.

Junior accidentally cut the rope from Jade's ankles during all of the commotion. She kept her hold on him as the lower half of her body dropped to the ground. Junior dropped the sword and began punching Jade. Most of his blows were to her head, and she endured the pain by biting down even harder. Junior screamed again, and his punches were less severe. With her right hand, Jade grabbed the sword. One of the members rushed toward her, but Jade thrust the sword into his gut.

Jade finally released Junior from her hold. She spat out all the blood in her mouth and rose to her feet. Junior fell over in pain—nursing his wound. Seeing what she'd done to the two men, the last Radical member backed away, but Jade still slashed him with her sword. No one was going to leave out of this place alive.

Junior's groans filled the room as Jade caught her breath. She began to wipe her mouth. It was covered with blood. Junior tried to keep the pressure on his injury. He looked up at her with pure hatred.

"You psychotic bitch!"

"And I told you," Jade smiled at him as she drew her sword back. "I'm going to kill you!"

Satisfaction coursed through her as she pierced her blade into Junior's midsection. He grunted—his eyes wide with shock. Then Jade pulled the sword out and slashed his neck. Junior slumped over—the life slowly draining out of his eyes.

Jade sighed—sweet, sweet relief. Since she learned he was a traitor, Jade envisioned this moment. She yearned for it, and finally, she got it.

After a few minutes, Jade focused on the new task—getting their weapons and escaping. It wasn't clear if Junior was in charge here. There was still Liam to deal with. But they needed to leave. They needed to get back to Helena. What her poor sister must be going through right now? Jade couldn't even imagine.

With her sword clutched in her hand, Jade slowly opened the door. She peeked around the hall, and there was no one in sight. Jade gradually made her way down the corridor. There was no activity around, but she felt she was not alone. Certainly, Junior's screams must've alarmed someone. But the warehouse was big, so she'd might not come across someone for a while. Jade had to think quickly. Where were their weapons? When Junior sent out that member, he swiftly returned with Calvin's sword. That meant that their weapons had to be nearby. There had to be a room that was close.

Jade went left at the end of the hallway. There was a room at the end of it. Jade crouched down against the wall and listened for any activity. It was silent. The room door was closed. Jade pressed her ear against it to see if she could hear anything. Again, silence. She took a deep breath as she reached for the handle. The door was unlocked. Jade opened it cautiously. There was no one inside. However, their weapons were there. Jade was thrilled. But she was also very skeptical about the emptiness of the area. She quickly grabbed all their weapons and returned to the room where Razor and Bossman were being held.

Although she hated admitting it, Jade couldn't kill Bossman yet. As much as she wanted to, it wasn't the smart play right now. Unfortunately, she would need his help getting Razor back to Helena, which was a priority. Her niece or nephew would need both parents, and Jade would ensure they had that—no matter what.

Restraining herself around Bossman would be hard, however. Jade knew that. But it's what she would do. Her family was growing, and she would do anything to protect that.

When she returned to the room Razor and Bossman were in, they immediately looked at her. Razor looked apprehensive, while Bossman looked amused. Jade went to untie Razor first.

"Are you ok?" he was staring at her face.

"It's a mixture of my blood and his," Jade knew she was still a bloody mess.

Razor nodded as Jade undid his ropes and handed him his weapons.

"I love the sounds you caused in the other room, my sweet Jade," Bossman said, delighted. "I told him not to underestimate you."

"Shut it," Jade reluctantly went to untie Bossman next. She was dreading it. She would never catch him in a vulnerable position like this again.

"Such a beautiful sight."

Jade pointed her sword at his heart. "I said shut...it," she gritted. This was difficult for her. Any compliment or praise from him enraged her.

Bossman gestured his hands as if he was surrendering. He couldn't raise them high as he was still tied to the chair.

Jade slowly walked closer to him and cut his ropes. Bossman rubbed his wrists as they were bleeding from him, trying to escape.

"I thought I was going to have to convince you," Razor said as he stood.

"I see the advantage of having him around for a while," Jade never took her eyes off Bossman. "You're gonna help me get him back to Helena," she demanded. "And then I'm gonna finish what *you* started."

Bossman smiled as he rose from his chair and bowed. "Whatever you say."

Jade hesitantly relinquished his weapons to him. "These better not be pointed at us during this trip."

"Trust me, Jade," Bossman sighed. "I need you both more than you need me."

"Yeah, well, that's the problem," Jade turned and walked toward Razor. "I don't trust you."

"You have any idea how to get out of here," Razor asked.

"No, unfortunately, I didn't get that far."

"I believe I know how," Bossman offered. Razor and Jade looked over at him, and he shrugged. "I wasn't passed out when they carried us into this place."

"Lead the way then," Razor stepped aside so Bossman could leave out the room first.

"Are you sure that's a good idea?"

"We don't have time for second-guessing, Jade," Razor said. There was exhaustion in his voice. Jade knew that he wasn't up for arguing. So, she stepped aside too.

Bossman quickly put on his gear and headed for the door. Razor was right behind him while Jade brought up the rear. Bossman paused before opening the door.

"Be ready to fight your way out of this place," he instructed.

Jade and Razor nodded. Bossman walked out of the room, and they followed. Like before, it was quiet out. A little too quiet for Jade. It was suspicious. Someone should've come across those bodies by now. Did Liam and the Radicals really have that much faith in Junior? It was odd how Liam relinquished so much responsibility to Junior, whom he barely knew. Or did Junior perceive himself to be more significant than he was? Jade guessed the latter. She refused to think that Liam was that much of a pushover.

The path out was confusing. Jade was shocked and reluctantly impressed that Bossman remembered it all. They'd be lost already if it had been up to her. There were way too many twists and turns for her to memorize. Jade did good by finding the weapons room and returning to where Razor and Bossman were kept.

After a few minutes of wandering, they finally heard voices. Jade figured that they had to be close to the exit. That seemed like it'd be a heavily guarded area. Bossman paused at the end of the corridor. You could only go left, and that's where the voices were coming from. It seemed like there were many people there. From what she could tell, the pathway probably led to a room, and it sounded like a big one.

Bossman turned to them. "I'm going to check it out," he didn't wait for a response. He quickly went to get a better view. He was silent and deliberate with his steps.

Razor moved further down to get a better view, and Jade followed. Bossman was peeking from behind the corner. After a few seconds, he signaled for them to join him. Razor and Jade crept to him.

"There's fuckin' DC officers here," Bossman whispered as they joined him.

"Chase couldn't have sent officers all this way," Razor said. "The bigwigs would never allow it. Plus, they have no jurisdiction here."

Bossman shook his head. "This makes no sense."

Jade was confused by the conversation. Who cares who was where? The pressing issue was their escape.

"Let's just get this over with," she said, annoyed. "We can analyze this at another time."

"I can't get a good number on how many are there," Bossman said, peeking at the area again.

"It doesn't matter. We're gonna have to take them on," Jade persisted.

Bossman smiled and shrugged. "Let's wait for the right moment then."

Jade sheathed her sword and took out her knives. She moved quicker with them, and speed was needed for their escape. Jade looked over at Razor. He pulled out his machete and nodded at her. Bossman pulled out a couple of knives himself. He looked back at them.

"All right, looks like we're ready," he stepped into the area. Razor and Jade followed.

Bossman already had two people bleeding out on the ground when Jade entered the area. She couldn't get a good count of them, but there were many of them rushing her way. Razor was cutting them down, while Bossman did what he did best—giving them horrible deaths.

Jade slashed her way through people. She could spot the exit ahead. They were about halfway there. It wasn't until she was stabbing a DC officer in the chest that she realized all of their assailants were DC officers. She assumed there'd be a few, but certainly not everyone in the room. Now she understood Razor and Bossman's concern. This was unusual. They were expecting to fight Radical members.

What was going on?

Something wasn't right here, but Jade remained focused. They needed to get out of here, and they were so close. Bossman was at the door, killing a couple of officers simultaneously. Razor was right behind him, and Jade was fighting off a straggler. She hoped Liam would be here, but he was nowhere in sight. As she finished off the last officer, Jade didn't even spot him when she glanced at the dead bodies scattered on the floor.

This was odd.

Bossman kicked open the door and ran out. Razor was right behind him. Jade took a few seconds to snag a few weapons off the dead officers and then ran out of the building. Bossman and Razor were waiting for her at the end of the alleyway. Razor looked distraught as she got closer.

Something was terribly wrong.

Bossman actually looked sympathetic toward Razor. He looked at Jade once she got closer. "It looks like you'll be stuck with me longer than you thought."

Jade followed his gaze, and she finally understood. Right in their eyesight, clear as day, a sign read: *Welcome to Ithaca, New York.*

~39~

Razor

This *can't be happening. This can't be happening. There's no possible way that this can be happening.* That's all Razor could think about as he stared at the sign. *Welcome to Ithaca, New York.* How could this be happening to him? Where did he go wrong? There was no need for that question. Razor knew precisely where he went wrong, leaving out of HQ without more backup. A recon mission. How stupid could he be? If he wasn't so distracted by Helena's pregnancy, he could've seen it for what it was—a trap.

They were stupid. And now they were so far away from where they needed to be. Razor was sure that Chase was on his way. How many days had they been there? How much time had passed? Stupid. Just stupid. For a moment, as he overheard Jade making her escape in the next room, Razor had a glamour of hope. And when Jade didn't need convincing about keeping Nick alive, he thought they would get out of all this with no problem. Boy, was he wrong. It felt like problem after problem was happening to him.

And to think, he was bringing a child into this chaotic world. What was wrong with him?

Razor leaned against the wall at the end of the alleyway. His breathing was suddenly becoming shallow. *How could this be happening?* He was so far away from Helena, and right now, he needed to be by her side. Razor struggled for his next breath. He clutched his chest as he hunched over.

This can't be happening.

This can't be happening.

How could he fail her like this? Helena would be worried, and not having him or Jade by her side would devastate her. Air just seemed to stop coming to Razor. He slid to the ground and slumped over.

"Just take deep, slow breaths," Jade instructed as she kneeled beside him. "Match my breathing."

Razor listened to her slow, rhythmic breaths, and he immediately followed. He closed his eyes and tried to block out his negative thoughts.

"Don't worry," she said. "We're gonna get to her. I'm gonna make sure of it."

Razor nodded as his breathing slowly went back to normal. Nick watched him from across the alleyway. Razor couldn't decipher his look. He recalled their conversation when Jade was out of the room.

"Finally got your wife pregnant, huh?" Nick asked. He was trying to be amusing, but Razor could hear the concern in his tone.

"That's what she told me."

"You're going to be more vicious, my friend."

Razor didn't say anything. He feared that would be the case. But how could he not be that way with his offspring? He was creating a family. Razor didn't intend to, but a small part of him was excited about it. And would do anything to protect it.

Now, Razor was on the corner of an alleyway in New York, having a nervous breakdown. Nick glanced around and then looked back at Razor.

"I had a similar reaction when I found out my girlfriend was expecting Aiden."

Jade looked over at Nick with narrowed eyes. He didn't seem to notice.

"That was the scariest moment of my life."

"I'm sure that's very different from this," Jade rolled her eyes and looked back at Razor.

Nick shrugged. "The world has always been dangerous and chaotic. And at the time, I was only a teen," Nick walked over to them and kneeled in front of Razor. "I failed to keep my son alive in the world before, but you, my friend, will be just fine. You've kept Helena well and alive in this world. You made her a fighter. I do not doubt that your child will thrive in this world, and you will make it so."

Jade looked over at Nick in disbelief, and so did Razor. After a few seconds, Jade rose to her feet and held out her hand to him. Razor took it, and she helped him to his feet. Nick stood too.

"Now, let's get back to Helena," she encouraged. "And we'll kill anyone who gets in our way."

"Sounds like a party," Nick smiled.

Razor smiled too. "Sounds like a plan," the three of them set off, heading back to Canada.

Back to Helena and his unborn child.

~40~

Helena

Downtown Toronto

Something's *wrong. Something's terribly wrong.* That's the first thing that ran through Helena's mind as Zara came rushing into command central alone. Where was Razor? Where was Jade? Helena walked closer to get a better view. Zara was franticly talking to Cole and Brice. As she got closer, Helena could see how bloody Zara was. Helena's heart dropped to her stomach. What the hell happened?

This was not how it was supposed to go. They were doing a recon mission. How could it have gone wrong? Then Helena noticed that the two captives were missing too. Was this their doing? It had to be.

Helena tried to slow her breathing as she recalled her last conversation with Razor. They were preparing to leave with the Radical captives, but Razor pulled her aside. He wanted to finish their conversation before the invasion happened.

"I can't leave here without knowing what's going on with you," he pleaded.

Helena didn't want to tell him something this important right before he was about to go on the road, but her gut told her to do it. Helena sighed deeply.

"I'm pregnant."

Fear and disbelief covered Razor's face. And then, after a few seconds, it looked like he was about to faint.

"Are...are you sure?" he finally asked.

"I'm pretty positive," she joked. Razor wasn't budging. Helena sighed. "I took the test three times."

"But...but those tests were probably expired, right," Razor scrambled.

"They were blood tests. Plus, I've missed my period, and that right there is a telltale sign."

Razor paced back and forth, shaking his head. "This can't be happening," he mumbled.

Helena stepped in front of him and wrapped her arms around his waist. This calmed him a bit.

"I know this isn't ideal," she sighed. "But we can get through this, and I have faith that we will. And besides, I think we'll make great parents."

Razor kissed her forehead and nestled his face into her hair. "I still miss the mint green color," he mumbled.

Helena laughed. "I *really* can't dye my hair now."

Razor pulled back so that he could look at her face. He didn't seem so worried at the moment. "I love you, Helena."

"I love you more," she stepped back a little. "Now hurry up and get this done so we can celebrate the news properly."

"You're unbelievable," Razor sighed as he shook his head. He wouldn't give her a laugh, much less a smile.

Helena shrugged. "I can't get pregnant twice."

After a few seconds passed, Razor chuckled. "I guess you're right about that," he kissed her softly. "We'll celebrate the news properly when I get back."

Helena smiled. After all these years, Razor still gave her whatever she wanted.

Now it was looking like that wasn't going to happen. At least, not anytime soon. Instinctively, Helena's hand went to her stomach. Her husband and her sister weren't there. And she didn't know what was going on. Finally, Zara looked over at her. There was pity in her eyes. Cole must've told her about Helena's pregnancy. No one knew besides Cole, Keeper, and Tatianna. Zara made her way to her.

"It was a trap," Zara stated. "A large group of Radical members ambushed us as we approached the spot. There was no way we were getting out alive."

Helena's heart began to race. There was an ambush. The enemy swarmed Razor and Jade.

"Razor and Jade demanded that I retreat here to get reinforcements," Zara went on. "I know where they are, and we will get them back."

There was nothing Helena could say. She was trying to wrap her head around the situation—around Zara's words. She was about to bring a child into this world, and Helena needed Razor and Jade now more than ever. She was terrified about this new change. She was going to be a mother. *Helena.* A mother in this world that she's so afraid of. How could she do this? She needed Razor and Jade to give her strength.

Helena rushed upstairs to her room and gathered all her weapons and supplies. She was going on this mission. No one was going to talk her out of it. Helena was going to get her family back, and she was going to slaughter anyone who got in her path.

A knock came on her door as she was finishing packing up. It was Keeper and Tatianna. They glanced at her gathered supplies and smiled.

"I made this as soon as ya got the news," Keeper held something up. It looked like some kind of corset but much sturdier. "It's to protect ya stomach when ya fighting."

Helena smiled as tears ran down her face. "Thank you so much, Keeper."

Tatianna helped her put it on. It was tight, but not too tight. Helena could still breathe and move around comfortably. It didn't hinder her moves at all. Helena ran her hand across her stomach. The little bean felt safe and secure. Helena smiled wider and cried harder at that. Tatianna placed her hand on Helena's shoulder.

"We're with you every step of the way," her friend reassured her.

Keeper nodded.

Helena wiped away her tears and recollected herself. She gathered up her supplies and placed her weapons in their appropriate areas. Finally, she was ready. She sighed.

"Let's go get my husband and sister."

Tatianna and Keeper nodded in agreement. They all headed for the door...

...and then the building shook.

The End

ACKNOWLEDGMENTS

Wow, here we are, back in Jade's world and at the end of book three. At one point, I thought I would never be here, but I'm so glad I decided to have faith in myself and carry on. Only one more book in the Surviving Red series to go!

I hope you all enjoy this journey and the world I've created. It's been a joy writing them.

As always, I would like to thank you, the reader, for taking time out to explore this world that I have created. I would love to hear your thoughts on this series.

I want to thank everyone who helped me assemble this book, including the cover artist, beta readers, proofreaders, editors, my husband Fred, family, friends, and more. Your support has meant so much to me.

Last but *never* least, I would like to thank God for guiding me on this writing journey. I thank you for pushing me whenever I began to get complacent.

Until the next time,

Jana' Chantel

ABOUT THE AUTHOR

Jana` Chantel is a writer from Detroit, MI. She holds a BA in Creative Writing from Grand Valley State University. Her work includes: *Into My Mind*, a collection of personal essays, and her debut dystopian series, *Surviving Red*, and *Razor & Helena: A Surviving Red Prequel.* She has written and filmed a sci-fi TV pilot with her husband entitled *Fault: Gamma*, which won the 2017 New York Film and TV Festival for Best TV Series Concept for a TV pilot. When she isn't writing, you can find Jana` working on a creative project with her husband at their company, About Right Media Group. *Fighting Red* is the third book in the Surviving Red series.

www.janachantel.com

Facebook.com/authorjanachantel

Tik Tok & Instagram: janachantel_theauthor